01-15

Collar Robber

Books by Hillary Bell Locke

The Cynthia Jakubek Mysteries
But Remember Their Names

The Jay Davidovich Mysteries
Jail Coach

Featuring Jay Davidovich and Cynthia Jakubek
Collar Robber

Collar Robber

A crime story featuring
Jay Davidovich and Cynthia Jakubek

Hillary Bell Locke

Poisoned Pen Press

Poisoned Pen Press
6962 E. First Ave., Ste. 103
Scottsdale, AZ 85251
www.poisonedpenpress.com
info@poisonedpenpress.com

Printed in the United States of America

Disclaimer

Collar Robber is a work of fiction. The characters depicted do not exist, and the events described did not take place. I made this stuff up. Invented it out of whole cloth. Just pulled it out of my imagination. I am aware that there is no such institution as the Pittsburgh Museum of Twentieth-Century Art. I made that up too. No matter who you are, trust me on this: You're not in here.

"The use of force is not an alternative to negotiation; it is a form of negotiation."
            —Richard Michaelson in *Washington Deceased*

For Major Eric Sigmon, M.D.: husband, dad, officer, doctor

The Last Thursday in March

Chapter One

JAY DAVIDOVICH

"No society in history has ever experienced a shortage of whores." I thought Dany Nesselrode was talking about the dead guy. He wasn't. By the time I figured it out the body count had risen—and one of the bodies belonged to someone I'd miss.

I got involved on the last Thursday in March.

◇◇◇

"All dressed up and no place to go?"

C. Talbot Rand, house counsel for the Pittsburgh Museum of Twentieth-Century Art, aimed this crack at Willy Szulz's lawyer, Cynthia Jakubek. Szulz wanted to sell a piece of paper to my employer so that it wouldn't have to write a very big check to Rand's employer someday soon. A check big enough for me to have spent one hundred twenty-seven airplane minutes scrolling on my iPad through a briefing packet that Proxy Shifcos had zapped to me through cyberspace. That's how I knew the names and roles.

"Don't be snide, Tally," Jakubek replied in a half-teasing lilt. "Willy isn't even fifteen minutes late yet. In the perspective of eternity, that's scarcely an eyeblink." If the serene confidence radiating from her olive-brown face was a bluff, she had a knack for that useful art.

"'Eternity' is a bit nebulous for us free-thinkers." Rand pointedly glanced from under bushy, charcoal gray eyebrows at a silver watch he pulled from a loden green vest pocket. "Patience is a virtue, but I report to a busy lady."

"I'll try him again." Jakubek unholstered a Droid and stabbed its screen a couple of times with her index finger.

Rand's condescending professor act put me off, but to tell the truth I was getting a little antsy myself. Not much of a party without the guest of honor. *Please tell me that I didn't put a computer hacking investigation on ice and fly fourteen-hundred miles on six hours' notice for coitus interruptus.*

"What's the deal, tiger?" Jakubek demanded into her Droid. "You're about three minutes away from a value-billing write-up." Over the next seven seconds serene confidence morphed into serious-as-a-heart-attack concern as she lowered the phone and swung her eyes toward Proxy and me. "He's been driving around downtown for twenty minutes because he thinks he's being followed."

I started pulling myself up from my seat even before I got Proxy's subtle nudge. At six-four and two-twenty, I have ten inches and more than a hundred pounds on her, and God hadn't created her WASP-Madonna face and inquisitive brown eyes to stop punches. The division of labor was obvious.

"What's our hotel?"

"Omni William Penn. On a street called William Penn Place, according to my itinerary. Intersects with Fifth Avenue."

Catching that one on the fly, Jakubek pulled the phone back up.

"Drive to the Omni William Penn, leave your car with the valet, and wait for us in the lobby....No, don't tell him you're checking in. Just give him a big tip."

Three minutes later I was striding beside Jakubek along Liberty Avenue in downtown Pittsburgh, about to turn the corner onto Fifth. Maybe Szulz was just a self-involved drama magnet, but that piece of paper he was hawking might save Transoxana Insurance Company fifty million dollars—which is why Proxy's maroon leather attaché case held codes and passwords she could use to wire-transfer up to one hundred twenty-five thousand dollars to buy it. People get killed every week in America for three orders of magnitude less than that, so I couldn't just blow off the being-followed stuff.

"So your buddy is something-something Risk Management and you're Loss Prevention-something—did I get that right?"

Jakubek managed this question without panting even though I was setting the kind of pace you'd expect from someone who'd just flown in from Albuquerque, New Mexico, in March without time to grab a Pittsburgh-worthy coat.

"My business card reads Loss Prevention Specialist. Ms. Shifcos is Senior Director—Risk Management—U.S. At thirty. If there's a pool on divisional VP by thirty-five, I'm going all-in on 'Yes.'"

"In other words, she's the suit and you're the muscle."

"That's one way to put it." I shrugged off the little locker-room towel snap. "Proxy says that in perfect loss prevention no one raises his voice—but on an eight-figure risk, perfection doesn't happen very often.

"Law calls muscle 'litigators,' although in our case it's meta-phorical. If everything went right when the C. Talbot Rands of the world negotiated their deals, trial lawyers would starve to death. Fortunately, they go wrong often enough to cover our bar-bills."

The intrigued glance I shot at her caught gently laughing eyes looking up at me. Or maybe mocking eyes, but I'm gonna go with gently laughing. She's not the dish Proxy is, but Jakubek looked just fine and she knew it. I figured she hadn't quite hit thirty yet, but she'd left any ingénue stuff way behind. Black hair pulled straight back with a clean part instead of Proxy's sassy helmet cut, a hint of an attitude in those eyes that reminded me of my wife, Rachel, and nothing wrong with her shape, either. I'd figured all that out in the reception area. Not that Jakubek had done anything flirtatious. Didn't have to. She's the kind of woman who produces head-snaps from straight males just by walking into a room.

"Not sure how I feel about sharing a category with trial lawyers," I told her. "Even metaphorically."

"Ex-cop, I'm guessing."

"Close enough. Two combat tours with an MP battalion."

"I bet you call all lawyers 'shysters.'"

"Only male lawyers. Women lawyers I call 'shysterettes.'"

Instead of a scowling eye-roll at that little payback for "muscle," Jakubek gave me a good-sport chuckle and a playful sock on the bicep.

I told myself right then to watch out.

Chapter Two

JAY DAVIDOVICH

As Jakubek and I walked I kept my eyes open, sweeping the street and sidewalks for a tail. Even for a pro, following someone solo is hard to do without standing out. Of course that doesn't mean that everyone who stands out is a tail. By the time we were one block-plus from the hotel I had three possibilities but no certainties.

A slender African-American woman in her mid-twenties walked up and down the sidewalk on the south side of Fifth, smoking a cigarette. She passed up three chances to huddle in doorways out of the cold. Just east of the corner of Fifth and William Penn Place, a white guy in a gray Corolla with dirty snow residue on its fenders looked here and there kind of randomly in what struck me as an affectedly casual way. He wore a down vest instead of a jacket or overcoat. A twenty-something with Mediterranean coloring stood on the northeast corner of the same intersection. He sported a ragged gray hoodie and dark pants that didn't look quite like jeans.

As we approached the corner the guy in the hoodie stepped toward a man in a fedora and a khaki London Fog who'd just left the hotel and begun walking toward Fifth. The hoodie panhandled the guy in a whiny, wheedling tone as he extended his left hand. London Fog blew right past him, careful not to make eye contact.

A familiar tension roiled my gut. I never want to walk down sidewalks dotted with invisible people, like Mr. London Fog just had. On the other hand, I don't like being a sucker, kidding myself about my two bucks going for food instead of subsidizing slow-motion suicide. I haven't figured that one out yet.

"I sometimes give panhandlers something if I think they're vets," I told Jakubek, "but I'm not getting a vet-vibe from this guy."

"I'm getting a guy-whose-shoes-cost more-than-my-coat vibe from him." When the hoodie stepped toward us Jakubek stopped in her tracks and looked him right in the eye. "St. Benedict's Open Door Café, just this side of PPG Place on Fourth. Free meals every day."

The panhandler stepped back, shaking his head with a disappointed frown. I took a look at his shoes: winterized Air Jordan Six-Rings, gleaming black. Not a penny under a hundred-and-a-half online, and probably twenty-five percent more in a brick-and-mortar shop. The shysterette apparently kept her eyes open too.

I had no idea what Szulz looked like, but I spotted him the minute we walked into the Omni's lobby. He wore a parka over a non-descript charcoal suit and pinned a battered yellow-and-black backpack between his calves. Forty-seven, according to Proxy's briefing packet. Two European languages: Czech and German. Curly hair thinning and going from dark brown to gray framed a roundish, animated white face. Pushing six feet but not quite there, and a good fifteen pounds overweight.

The instant he spotted Jakubek he sprang to his feet, pulling a Steelers watch cap from the parka's right pocket with one hand while he grabbed the backpack with the other. The hem of his suit coat came down a good two inches below the bottom of the parka.

"Okay, let's roll." He spoke with a peppery, machine-gun cadence. "Sorry about the cops-and-robbers stuff, but swear to God I had a dark Jap car tailing me all the way from the bridge."

Jakubek didn't turn around as the seller blew past us. After three strides toward the door he wheeled and showed us a puzzled, impatient face.

"C'mon, let's go!"

"Willy, this is Jay Davidovich, Loss Prevention Specialist with Transoxana Insurance Company. Mr. Davidovich, this is Willy Szulz, who's here to save your company fifty million dollars."

"Pleased to meecha." Szulz offered me his right hand as he slipped his left arm through one of the backpack straps. "Now—"

"In other words, Willy," Jakubek said in an unruffled voice, "you're in the presence of the enemy. Don't act like you're in a hurry, and don't say anything you wouldn't want to hear again in front of a jury."

"Bingo, C.J." Szulz had the grace to grin. "That's why you get the big bucks."

Now we headed for the door.

Chapter Three

CYNTHIA JAKUBEK

We made it back to the Museum with no more drama. The receptionist promptly showed us into an anachronism. The Olivia Stannard Room featured a long, blond table that was all lines and angles with form-follows-function chairs around it, like you might see in a *Perry Mason* rerun. An oil portrait of President Eisenhower graced the north wall, and a painting depicting the Japanese surrender aboard the *USS Missouri* took up at least sixty square feet of the intersecting west wall. Heavy glass ashtrays sat on the table, with a cylinder of cigarettes in the center.

"No kidding?" Willy said. "We can smoke in here?"

"I'm guessing no." I noted a flicker of relief cross Shifcos' face as I answered my client.

"But…?" Willy pointed at the cigarettes.

Fortunately for me, Tally strolled into the room at that moment through a discreet door under Ike's grinning face. Picking up the gist of Willy's protest, he saved me the trouble of explaining.

"Grace Stannard Dalhousie donated six-hundred-thousand dollars to the Museum in 1963, in memory of her mother, Olivia. One of the stipulations in the deed of gift was that this room would be kept in exactly the condition it was in on October 10, 1958, when Mrs. Stannard succumbed to a heart attack immediately after presiding over her last board meeting."

"Oh," Willy said.

"Ms. Huggens will be joining us presently." Tally moved to a chair immediately to the right of the table's head. With his perfectly cut ash-gray blazer and navy blue slacks contrasting nicely with the green vest, he looked like he had been born to occupy chairs like that in rooms like this. "Please help yourselves to coffee or water, and feel free to find a seat."

I went to the sideboard for coffee, and I took my time about it. I figured that Jennifer Stannard Huggens would let us cool our heels for at least ten minutes to punish us for my client's tardiness. I didn't particularly blame her, but I wanted to keep Willy under control in the interim. He'd let loose with some standard-issue Willytude on the way over, when we found red lights facing us for over five seconds from both directions at Fifth and Wood. "So *no one* gets to move! Great! It's like living in a Third World country!" His Jersey hustler routine could get old fast, and I didn't want him to blow up the negotiations before they started.

"Any for you, Tally?" I gestured toward him with the orange-topped carafe.

"No, thanks." He smiled pleasantly and did the pocket-watch thing again. If it said the same thing my Citizen wristwatch did, he saw that we were now just past three-ten, on the verge of starting our meeting forty-five minutes late.

Tally and I had intersected on another matter I was handling, which he'd gratuitously alluded to with his "free-thinker" crack. So far I had him down for a bronze medal in the asshole Olympics. This afternoon, though, I was counting on him. Huggens was the third managing director he'd worked under in his not-quite-fifteen years as inside counsel for the Museum. The first director had had a reputation as an old-school, old-money, model of rectitude. The second had wanted to jack up the endowment without a lot of chat about technicalities along the way. Huggens was a by-the-book pragmatist who dreamed of someday reading in the *New York Times* that Pitt MCM had put together a world-class collection.

Tally had gotten along smoothly with all three. He'd tacked nimbly to the prevailing winds, deftly shaping his advice and his formal opinions to get his client of the moment wherever she wanted to go. And in all three cases he'd generally gotten her there without abrading the delicate susceptibilities of heirs, trustees—or courts. That made my job simple: make Tally think Jennifer Stannard Huggens wanted to spend Transoxana's money to save a painting for the Museum.

I choked back vestigial blue-collar resentment as Huggens entered with a gracious smile and a firm handshake for each of us. Not her fault she'd been born blond and rich. She'd worked full time at real jobs in the twelve years since completing her second degree—not as hard as I had, but not many people outside Chinese sweatshops do. I could tell she charmed Willy right out of his socks. For a second I was afraid he was just going to hand her the goods right then and there.

Once we finally took our seats, Tally spent thirty seconds on the usual thanks-for-coming-and-welcome-to-the-Museum palaver. Then he looked at me.

"It's your party, Ms. Jakubek. What's your pleasure?"

I began by passing around a redacted photocopy of a handwritten German bill of sale dated 23 March 1938. It documented Dietrich Heinzen's purchase of a painting titled *Maiden in Apron* from Scholeim Himmelfarb for eight thousand marks. Or at least it would have documented that purchase if I hadn't blacked some stuff out. I had an English translation attached to it, with blanks instead of blackouts. I'd stapled the two-page packets into blue construction-paper backings like lawyers used for Very Important Documents fifty years ago. I hoped that would make them seem more like something worth the kind of money my client wanted.

"Why have you blacked out the names of the seller and buyer and the painting sold?" Huggens asked.

"Because I don't want to tempt Transoxana to try to track down a duplicate original of this bill of sale instead of buying the one Mr. Szulz is offering."

"So the painting isn't the one the Museum owns, Klimt's *Eros Rising?*"

"No."

"Then what good would this document be to us?"

Tally came in right on cue.

"Comparable sale would be my guess."

"Explain. Please." Huggens added the "please" as an after-thought, but give her credit: she got it in.

"On the tenth of October, 1937, Gustav Wehring sold *Eros Rising* to a Swiss industrialist for seven thousand marks. Not chump-change, but it might strike many as a derisory sum for a painting purchased by a generous American benefactor for three million dollars in 1973, appraised at more than twenty million when he donated it to the Museum in 1996, and valued at fifty million today."

"Comes the dawn." Huggens gave Tally the kind of smile that high school teachers offer students who combine clever with earnest. "Wehring's heirs are claiming that he sold *Eros Rising* for far less than its real worth in 1937 because he was forced to by the Nazis, making that sale illegitimate. But if a comparable painting sold around the same time for something like the same price and without any hint of coercion, that would show that the original sale of *Eros Rising* was a legitimate, arm's-length transaction at a fair price."

"Exactly."

Huggens turned her plum-colored eyes toward me.

"And you're saying your client could prove that happened?"

"No." I wanted to be real clear on this next part. "I'm saying Mr. Szulz can sell you documentation of a roughly contemporaneous sale, in the same price range, of a painting that has gotten appraisals in the same ballpark as appraisals of *Eros Rising* at around the same time. What that proves will be up to you."

"Or up to a court." Huggens' smile now had *Gotcha!* written all over it.

"Not exactly," Shifcos said, shifting her gaze to Huggens. "The statutes of limitation have run on all possible legal theories that could be used to challenge the sales. You have a bulletproof defense to any legal action seeking to recover *Eros Rising*—unless you choose to waive that defense voluntarily."

"What about the Washington Convention?" Huggens' eyes darted back and forth between Shifcos and me, as if we were in the middle of a long rally in a tennis match. "Doesn't that treaty waive the statute of limitations and other technical defenses? And hasn't the United States signed it?"

"The United States has signed the Washington Convention, but the Pitt MCM hasn't," Shifcos said. "The Convention binds most European museums because they're essentially government institutions. The Pittsburgh Museum of Twentieth-Century Art is a private entity and therefore not bound by the treaty."

"Ms. Huggens is aware of that," Tally said, lying with angelic sincerity. "But ethical private American museums have informally agreed to abide by the Washington Convention's waiver of technical defenses as a moral obligation in cases where they feel that a claim for a particular work of art is valid on the merits."

Shifcos gave Tally and Huggens a cocked eyebrow, which I roughly translated as: *Transoxana Insurance Company isn't in the moral obligation business. You blow off a killer defense, we don't write a check. Save your souls on your own dime.* This struck me as a good time to jump back into the conversation.

"I agree with Mr. Rand. Especially the 'on the merits' part. If the Museum decides that the claim for *Eros Rising* is meritorious, it may feel morally compelled to waive technical defenses. But if the Museum itself reaches the opposite conclusion, there'd be no reason for any waiver and therefore no basis for a judge even to look at the bill of sale Mr. Szulz is offering—much less decide what it proves or doesn't prove. You're the sole judge of that. All you'll ever have to say in court is, 'Statute of limitations, we win.'"

Willy beamed. "Is this a great country or what?"

Chapter Four

CYNTHIA JAKUBEK

Tally looked at my client like he was a glass of Ripple at a lobster dinner. Then he smiled at me.

"Fair enough. Even if we're judge and jury, though, we're not just going to go through the motions. We'll take a good faith look at the heirs' claim—and we can't verify anything with a redacted photocopy and an interesting story."

"You won't have to. For two hundred thousand dollars Mr. Szulz will provide you with an authenticated duplicate original of the 1938 bill of sale for a comparable painting. You can verify it to your heart's content."

That answer earned me my second *Gotcha!* grin from Huggens.

"And how much do we pay Mr. Szulz if we decide that your documentation isn't enough to validate that 1938 sale?"

Yeah, like THAT'S going to happen. "Good faith look" my ass. All you want is enough paper to cover your fanny and we both know it. Saying that out loud would have been rude, so I said something else.

"In that case, of course, you will feel morally obligated to turn *Eros Rising* over to the heirs who are demanding it. If you surrender the painting within three months, Mr. Szulz will return seventy-five percent of your payment; within six months, fifty percent; within nine months, twenty-five percent. If you keep the painting for at least two hundred seventy-one days after we give you the original bill of sale, then Mr. Szulz keeps all the money."

"Two hundred thousand is a lot of money," Tally said.

"Less than one-half of one percent of fifty million."

"Sorry." Shifcos shook her head. "Two hundred is too high. I think it's out of line, and in any case I don't have authority for a payment that large."

Last, best, and final offer. Take it or leave it. I wanted to say that more than I've wanted anything in a long time—more than I'd wanted a cigarette after dinner the first day I quit smoking, nine years earlier. But I choked the words back and shrugged at Shifcos.

"I understand. As a goodwill gesture, Mr. Szulz will wait twenty-four hours before transferring the document in question to any other buyer." I paused to look at Tally and then back at Shifco. "No charge for that accommodation."

"Ms. Jakubek," Tally asked, "are you representing to us that there is another prospective buyer in the picture?"

Opening my briefcase, I took out three copies of a four-page contract and passed them around. I hadn't bothered with blue backings for these.

"This is an agreement spelling out the terms I just offered. As you'll see, it disclaims all representations and warranties except for the authenticity of the bill of sale." Then I caught Tally's eye and held it. "But if you didn't think there was another buyer in the picture, you wouldn't have insisted on having this meeting on such short notice."

Tally, Shifcos, and Huggens eye-fenced for about six seconds before Huggens spoke.

"Would you mind stepping outside for a few minutes? We'd like to caucus."

Chapter Five

Cynthia Jakubek

"Why didn't you use that 'take-it-or-leave-it' line with them? I love when you do that."

"Tally might have thought his manhood was on the line if I'd said that. It takes a very self-confident man not to let his insecurities and his mom issues and all that crap get in the way when a woman hands him an ultimatum—especially if he's sitting between two other women."

"But you would have been giving our ultimatum to one of the chicks, not Tally."

"Tally is our real target." Didn't appreciate "chicks," but I had thick skin and bigger fish to fry. "They're caucusing so Shifcos can ask Huggens how much the Museum will chip in. Tally is the key to that discussion."

"Got it." Willy rubbed his hands together. "We want him thinking from behind his eyebrows instead of his zipper."

"Bingo."

"You gotta gimme a pass on 'chicks,'" Willy said then, a bit sheepishly. "It kinda just slipped out. You know, Willy being Willy."

"Speaking of which, try to keep the Willyisms on ice once we're back within earshot of the big guy."

"I hear ya. I noticed he wasn't coming on to you while we walked back over here, so I figure he's gotta be gay, right? I'll watch my mouth."

"Or maybe he just loves whoever has the wedding ring matching the one he's wearing. But what concerns me is the other ring, on the little finger of his right hand. Silver signet ring with a Torah-scroll-and-candle design."

"Blond hair, blue eyes, the build of a small forward—and you think he's Jewish?"

"I don't think he got that ring for being the best altar boy at St. Stanislaus. Might be a good idea to skip light-hearted remarks about stormtroopers taking five-finger discounts on fine art."

"You got it." He nodded vigorously. "No wisecracks until we've got Transoxana's signature on the dotted line."

I sensed movement behind us and turned back toward the inside of the reception area. A substantial woman in her mid-fifties moved ponderously toward us.

"Not sure what her problem is," Willy muttered, "but I think we can rule out anorexia."

I sighed. *No wisecracks.* Right.

"Ms. Huggens asked me to tell you that they're ready for you in the conference room," she said seven seconds later when she reached us.

I thanked her and herded Willy back toward the hallway that led to the Oliva Stannard et cetera. I wanted to put distance between us and the woman before Willy dropped another impulsive *mot.*

"Think we've got a deal?" he asked.

"Nope. If we had a deal, Tally would have come out for us."

I was right. As soon as we were seated, Shifcos squared up and looked directly across the table at me. She had her forearms on the table and her hands folded lightly in front of her. No tension. Her face with its peaches-and-cream complexion seemed open and empathetic. What I read in her eyes wasn't hard-nosed bitchiness or cold ruthlessness but something scarier: confident certainty. She *knew* that well south of two hundred thousand dollars would mean more to my client than fifty million meant to her company. Even more important, she *knew* that the Museum would put more on the table than it had while Willy and I were passing time in the reception area.

"We need a week. Possibly less, but a week to be safe."

Shit. With someone maybe following Willy around, delay struck me as a bad idea. But we couldn't look like we were afraid to give them a chance to check out Willy's story. At the same time, it might be interesting to know how much they wanted it.

"Twenty-four hours was free. Weeks are going for ten thousand each these days."

"Five thousand." Shifcos shook her head, the way an assistant principal might when telling you she's sorry but she has to give you detention. "We appreciate your position, but five is the best we can do. And if we do make a deal, the five thousand counts against our final payment."

"Well we *are* going to make a deal so it's a zero-cost concession for you anyway. Let's just split the difference."

Again with the head-shake. Again with the certainty.

"Five thousand. Last, best, and final offer. Take it or leave it."

"We'll take it," Willy said.

Willy can be a pain in the butt, but he is a self-confident pain in the butt.

Chapter Six

JAY DAVIDOVICH

"I have some things to discuss with Mr. Rand." Proxy said this to me as everyone was standing up and she was stowing her mobile phone in her attaché case. "Why don't you go to the hotel and get started on our trip report? I'll give you a call around six to talk about dinner plans."

I took this as Proxyspeak for *see if you can figure out whether Szulz is really being followed.* Especially since she unobtrusively slipped the rental car fob into the left pocket of my windbreaker. That's why I left at the same time as Jakubek and Szulz. Figuring Jakubek had spotted the fob-pass, I decided to put it on the table as soon as our tight little group hit the sidewalk.

"If I can remember where we parked the Buick Avis rented to us, I'll be happy to give you a ride back to the Omni."

"I wouldn't have a GM car, personally," Szulz said. "After the way Comrade Obama shafted the bond-holders when he was 'saving' General Motors, I'd feel like I was trafficking in stolen goods."

"Thanks, but it's only a few blocks." Jakubek said. "If we don't see you again, it's been real."

If you don't see me again it'll be because I'm doing my job right.

I found the dark blue Ford Escape right where Proxy had parked it, just down a side-street called Stanwick that intersects on the diagonal with Liberty Avenue near the Museum's main entrance. I'd made the "Buick" crack so that I'd be the farthest thing from Szulz's mind if he happened to notice a Ford SUV making the same turns he was when he drove from the Omni to his next destination. I was betting they wouldn't take me up on my ride offer. If they had I would've come up with something to explain the Buick thing away, but I'm not sure what—so it's a good thing they didn't.

When it comes to following someone, I prefer heading to tailing. People associate being followed with having someone behind them, so the smoothest way to bring it off is to start from the front. You slip to the back if you have to along the way, then get in front again when you can.

The Escape's GPS wanted to route me along Liberty, but that's where Jakubek and Szulz were strolling toward Fifth at the moment, so I took a quick right on Fourth instead. That made the GPS scold but its illuminated map still worked fine. I managed a left on Smithfield after two blocks east on Fourth, and rode that to something called Oliver Avenue, between Fifth and Sixth. A right on Oliver and our hotel was almost staring me in the face.

Time to wait. I'd noticed by this time that downtown Pittsburgh is very hilly. No, let me rephrase that: hill-wise, Pittsburgh makes San Francisco look like Des Moines. That meant I'd have to wait closer to the intersection of Oliver and William Penn Place than I would have liked. The pale March sun would be in their eyes if Jakubek or Szulz happened to glance in my direction, though, so I figured I was probably okay.

I finally spotted them trooping by on the opposite side of William Penn Place maybe seven minutes later. I sat tight until they actually reached the hotel entrance. Then I eased into a right turn and found an almost-legal parking space that let me get a decent view of the hotel's front door in my side-view mirror. I was betting that Szulz would drive back in the direction of the Museum, which was the most direct route to his condo if the address in Proxy's cyber-packet and the Escape's sulky GPS were right. If he turned north instead of south I'd need to do some fancy wheel-work, but I decided to go with the odds.

By the time I had the parking brake on, Jakubek was already making her way on foot toward Sixth Avenue. I got a little gut-flutter because I couldn't see Szulz for a second, but then I spotted him in shadows north of the entrance, handing his claim check to a valet. Less than five minutes later a garnet-red Mercury Sable that had to be twelve years old pulled up front. A guy in a gray-with-red-trim hotel uniform got out of the car. Szulz slipped him something and climbed in.

He swung the Sable toward the southbound lane. Maybe thirty feet ahead of him I pulled into the outside driving lane, framed him in my rearview mirror, and got ready to turn onto Fifth ahead of him. Smooth as silk.

Then the gray Corolla I'd spotted on my earlier excursion to the hotel pulled out behind Szulz and got on his tail. Smooth as sandpaper.

Son of a bitch. Maybe Szulz really was being followed.

Szulz turned onto Fifth behind me, as I'd expected. I guessed that he'd take Smithfield rather than Wood south from Fifth, but he crossed me up. After turning left on Smithfield I picked up a quick flash of him continuing west on Fifth instead of making the same turn I had.

The only difference that made was that when I started following Szulz again it was from behind him instead of ahead. I'm not clairvoyant or anything, but if he was going home he had to be headed for the Fort/Pitt Bridge. A drive-time left turn at the major intersection of Liberty Avenue and Fifth figured to be a bitch, so the money play had to be to take a side-street south to Fort/Pitt Boulevard, head west, and then basically merge onto the bridge when he reached Liberty.

That's what Szulz did and that's what I did—and that's what the Corolla did. Driving west on Fort/Pitt Boulevard, I'd made it almost to Stanwick when Szulz tire-squealed onto Fort/Pitt from Wood, not quite a block behind me. I could have pulled out to stay in front of him but the Corolla must have spooked him because he was making tracks now. I decided to let him and the Corolla power past me and then slide elegantly and inconspicuously into their wake. I managed it. Before you knew it all three of us were making our way southwest over the gray, choppy Monongahela River.

Strictly speaking, I already had what I wanted. I knew that someone really was following Szulz. I had the Corolla's license number, I could tell that it was a Pennsylvania registration and wasn't a rental, and I had a halfway decent description of the driver. Plus, it looked to me like the driver was either a rank amateur or he wanted to make damn good and sure Szulz knew he was being followed. I found both alternatives intriguing. No real reason I couldn't just look for the first chance after the bridge to do a U-turn and retrace my steps.

Except what if Willy Szulz ended up dead or with a concussion and someone had noticed a Ford Escape rented by Proxy and driven by me following him? Or what if Szulz and the Corolla driver were co-stars in a little community theater production ginned up to make us think there really was someone else interested in Szulz's bill of sale, implying that our price should go up? I decided I might as well stay on the tail until Szulz got to his condo, and see what the Corolla did then.

The Corolla mooted that question about thirty seconds after we reached the other side of the bridge. No sooner had we put the river behind us than the Corolla's driver grabbed his mobile phone for a five-second conversation. The instant he put the phone down he swerved into the inside lane, looking to me like a guy very anxious to head back the way he had come. I stayed with him for the half-mile he needed to reach a gap in the parkway separating the southbound and northbound lanes, and followed the Corolla through it to head back toward the bridge. Two drivers sat on their horns, and I couldn't blame them a bit.

The Corolla slowed down, as if daring me to confirm that I was following by slowing down myself. No thanks. Headed northeast in heavy traffic, with Szulz moving at a decent clip in the opposite direction, there were only two places the Corolla could go. One was the William Penn Omni, and the other one wasn't. I only cared about the first. I swept past the Corolla like it was standing still and set course for the hotel.

I made a lot better time than the Corolla did, maybe because the driver was trying to hang back out of my sight. I'd already jumped out of the rental and traded the fob and two singles to the valet for a claim check when I spotted the Corolla waiting to make a left from Fifth onto William Penn Place.

And because I was looking intently in that direction, I also spotted something else: the guy who'd panhandled Jakubek and me not quite two hours before. Instead of a ragged hoodie, he now wore a North Face three-in-one jacket—but he still had those shiny Air Jordan Six-Rings on his feet. More important, he was carrying a maroon leather attaché case that looked a lot like Proxy's. He was hustling toward the corner, which is what I'd be doing if I wanted a pick-up from the Corolla.

I went tearing after him just as the Corolla turned the corner. When he glanced over his shoulder I could tell he wasn't happy to see me. I had closed to within about ten feet by the time the Corolla completed the turn. Three more seconds and I'd have him. No way the Corolla could get there by then, and the ex-hoodie wasn't going to outrun me unless those Air Jordans had jetpacks

He did the only thing he could have done to keep me from tackling him. He stopped, turned, and faced me with angry indignation scrawled across his face. I pulled up just in time to avoid a collision.

"What you doing?" I picked up a faint Middle Eastern accent that I hadn't noticed when he was begging. "Why you trying to mug me? Leave me alone!"

I probably should have just carried my charge through and knocked him over without any conversation. That really would have looked like a mugging, though, and if there were any cops in the neighborhood I could have wound up in handcuffs while Junior here took Proxy's case for a ride. So I stopped nimbly (for me), maybe three feet from him.

"I'm looking for my colleague's attaché case, which suddenly went missing not long ago. If you're taking it to lost-and-found, you're going in the wrong direction."

By now the Corolla had screeched to a stop beside us. Its front passenger door swung open.

"You're crazy! This is mine!"

I'd already pulled out my mobile phone. Now I punched the speed-dial for Proxy's number. Two seconds later the first three bars of *A Little Night Music* sounded from inside the attaché case. Proxy's ringtone.

The guy only looked non-plussed for half a second or so, because that's all the time I needed to park a decent left jab in the neighborhood of his right temple. Without letting go of the case in his right hand, he grunted as he planted a solid left on my sternum. An inch lower and it might have done some real damage, but it landed where it landed and all it did was hurt.

Out of the corner of my eye I glimpsed the Corolla's driver clambering across the front seats and levering himself out of the passenger side. I put my right elbow right between his eyes with some authority behind it. This discouraged him, at least for the moment. Unfortunately, the distraction gave the other guy a chance to start scampering around the back of the car. I slid across the trunk lid in a head-first horizontal dive, with designs on grabbing his pricey jacket somewhere. He managed to elude me by swiveling away from the car, but the evasion cost him a precious second or two. Landing hard on the street, I popped up from the pavement with skinned knees and plenty of time to reach the driver-side door before he could.

All at once, from maybe three feet away, he brought the attaché case up with his right hand, more or less horizontally over his left shoulder. He swung it at me sideways. It caught me right in the puss. The top edge smashed the bridge of my nose, and the lower edge split my upper lip. By sheer reflex I got a grip on the case with both hands as it creamed me. My fanny smacked the pavement hard, but the case came with me. The momentum of my tumble tore the handle out his grasp.

I was blinded for just an instant. My vision cleared in time for me to see him hesitating between the open car door and the top of the chassis, wondering if he could grab the case back. My blood was up and I kind of hoped he'd try.

He didn't. He had the sense to duck into the car and concede the attaché case to me. *You keep the case and let us get away. Last, best, and final offer.* I took it.

Chapter Seven

Jay Davidovich

Maybe I could have stopped him if I'd dropped the case, but I had two more important things to worry about. The attaché case was only the second. I climbed gingerly to my feet with it firmly in hand as the car roared away.

The afternoon's events fell into a clear pattern in my throbbing head. The two dudes I'd just scrimmaged with had no way of knowing that Proxy would check in while Szulz was headed home with the Corolla on his tail. When she got to the hotel the phony panhandler had grabbed her attaché case after urgently summoning the Corolla to scurry back and pick him up. Proxy hadn't been in the vicinity when I'd spotted him, which meant he hadn't just pulled a snatch-and-grab. He must have done something to incapacitate her. That made finding her Job-one.

Blood streaming from my nose and oozing from my lip, I hustled toward the Omni's main entrance. The parking valet seemed to be bracing himself behind his little portable counter to the right of the front door as he put down a phone.

"I need to talk to hotel security, fast!"

"I think you can count on it, buddy."

He nodded toward the door, where a black guy almost as tall as I am and with similar musculature was coming out in a hurry. His left hand held a two-way radio, and his right was parked underneath his gray sport coat.

"Sir, may I see some—?"

"Jay Davidovich, Transoxana Insurance." I slapped a business card and my old military ID on the counter and held up the attaché case. "That weasel slapping me around on the street just now stole this from my colleague, Proxy Shifcos. Must've jumped her while she was going into her room after checking in. We need to find her pronto. If he conked her head, we don't have any time to waste."

He glanced at my ID and then, mouth slightly open, turned dark brown eyes with gold rims around the irises toward me.

"You said her name is what, now?"

I bit back frustrated epithets and fought the urge to yell at him. "Shifcos, Proxeine Violet." I spelled *Shifcos* for him. "Probably checked in within the last half-hour.'"

Raising the radio to his lips, he nodded slightly to me while he spoke into it. He had to go back and forth twice with whoever was on the other end, but he finally got something that apparently verified Proxy's check-in. Lowering the radio, he turned his steady gaze on the valet parker.

"Call Mr. Blue in Guest Relations and give him a status report."

"Roger that," the valet said, as if he'd just joined Seal Team Six.

"All right." The security guy's head turned back toward me. "Let's go."

He opened the door for me because no way was he letting me get behind him. I followed his discreetly whispered directions to the middle bank of elevators by a route that wouldn't show my bloody face to too many conventioneers and visiting software salesmen. He took it from there, getting us onto a car and pushing the button for the eighth floor. Once we got there he picked up the pace. We were downright sprinting by the time we reached Room 821.

No one home was the first thing I thought after the security guy used his master-key and pushed the door open. Just to the right of the door I saw Proxy's electric-blue roller suitcase knocked over on its side with its handle still fully extended—but no Proxy. Then I heard an urgent and indignant "UHMPF! UMPH!" from between the twin beds.

I got there in two good strides, tossing the attaché case on the bed as I went so that she'd know I'd recovered it. I saw Proxy, gagged with a white gym sock knotted crudely behind her head and hog-tied with thin electrical cord. "Hog-tied" as in trussed like a stoat on the first stage of his way to a *goyim* breakfast. Lying on her stomach, she had her hands and arms pulled behind her back and the lower half of her legs up and pulled as far toward her waist as they'd go. The electrical cord tied her wrists and ankles together and to each other. The guy who'd tied her up wasn't any sailor, that's for sure. The knots he'd managed were ugly blobs without a trace of rope-craft to them.

As Proxy twisted her head over her shoulder at my approach, I read blind fury in her eyes. She'd been humiliated, degraded, and (worst of all in her eyes) deprived of control over her situation. The way she looked at things, my coming across her like this was way worse than surprising her stark naked. She figured to be one pissed-off lady.

"Knife!" I barked at the security guy.

He produced a folding Buck knife at least four inches long and slapped it into my palm. I pulled the blade out and felt it lock into place, but before I went to work on the restraints I began loosening the gag between Proxy's teeth as gently as I could. I really wanted to hear the first words out of her mouth. Proxy doesn't do spontaneous cussing. She might let loose with an occasional, carefully calculated "bullshit" during a meeting when it will get maximum attention, but I've never heard her use off-color language in an angry outburst. If it was ever going to happen, I thought, today would be the day.

"Steady, soldier," I told her soothingly as I unknotted the sock and began tugging it from between her teeth. "Police are already on their way." I figured that the security guard's "Mr. Blue" instruction to the parking valet was code for, "Call the cops." I pulled the sock out without taking any of her dental work along with it and braced myself for her reaction to being

mugged and left tied up like a bondage freak. Her face contorted
in barely controlled wrath and the words came.

"Davidovich! You're hurt!"

Chapter Eight

JAY DAVIDOVICH

"My name is Proxeine Violet Shifcos, I'm at the Omni Hotel in Pittsburgh, and about half an hour ago I got mugged in my own room."

Holding a blue coldpack against the top-back of her head, Proxy said this to the hotel's staff nurse. Along with the coldpack, the nurse had just given her an Advil and the standard verbal concussion test: tell me who you are, where you are, and what's happening. I'd gotten that oral exam a couple of times during high school basketball games. The next step is to tell you to count backwards from a hundred by threes. When the trainer had tried that one on me, one of my teammates had said, "Oh come on! He couldn't do *that* before the game started!" The nurse here didn't bother with the backward-counting stuff.

"Nasty bump," she told Proxy instead. "I recommend going to the hospital for an EEG and observation."

"Noted—but I'd rather have a comp upgrade."

Proxy accompanied that remark with a mini-smile. The security guard picked up the crack but not the smile.

"Working on it," he said solemnly. "Cops are headed up, by the way."

A brief frown creased Proxy's face. She wanted a copy of a police report on the incident, because heaven forbid any manila folder in her file on Pitt MCM Potential Claim should stay empty. At the same time, chatting up a cop right now had to be way down her priority list. I handed her the piece of hotel stationery where I'd written down descriptions of the Corolla and the two guys I'd scrapped with, along with the car's license number.

"He'll talk to you before he talks to me," I said. "Maybe you can get him to call in the license number right away."

"Check." All business again—good sign. "Meanwhile, call what'shername, the lawyer, and tell her what happened."

It was pushing seven by now, so I figured I'd end up leaving a two-minute voice-message. Wrong. Still beavering away diligently at her desk, the shysterette answered on the first ring.

"Jakubek."

"Jay Davidovich from Transoxana."

"You have a counteroffer for me?"

"No. Transoxana counteroffers don't come from muscle. Your client was right: someone in a Corolla *was* following him, just like he said."

"Not a complete surprise. He called me not long ago and said he'd for sure spotted the guy tailing him again on his way home tonight."

"He nailed it. Now I'll up the ante. That panhandler you and I ran into this afternoon tried to steal my colleague's attaché case."

"Holy shit." Alarm and interest now colored Jakubek's voice. "Was there any dope about Willy in that case?"

"Doesn't matter. The thief stumbled over some muscle and left the attaché case behind while making his getaway—which he did in the Corolla that had been following your client."

I was kind of expecting a "thank you" right about then. I got one, but Jakubek didn't exactly linger over it.

"Thanks. You got my attention with that 'stumbled over some muscle' line. Are we talking physical violence here?"

"Yep."

"Weapons?"

"Only if the attaché case counts."

"Hmm." I imagined Jakubek drumming her pen on her desk blotter during the six seconds or so that followed this syllable. "Okay. This really helps. But it sheds some new light on that one-week delay, doesn't it?"

"You saying you want to back out of that?"

"Nope. A deal's a deal. You bought a week and you've got a week. The sooner the better, though—from both our standpoints."

"I expect Proxy will see it the same way."

"Good. Thanks again. Anything else?"

Not that I could think of. We exchanged goodbyes and hung up.

The cop was still talking to Proxy, so I busied myself with getting her some bottled water over ice. She thanked me with a flash of perfect teeth without missing a syllable in her cop-chat. By the time I'd checked my Droid, the cop and Proxy were wrapping up. He made me part of the wrap-up.

"How sure are you about that license number?"

"Hundred percent."

"The plate is assigned to a 2012 VW."

"So it's stolen."

"Stolen," he said, nodding gravely, "or you were wrong."

"Stolen." My turn to nod. "Any chance of spotting the Corolla just based on the description of the car?"

"Long shot. Probably in a chop-shop by now."

"So we're dealing with real pros," I said.

"Well," Proxy said after sipping some water, "you've dealt with pros before. And at least you won the first round."

"And I'm kind of looking forward to the second one."

"I don't want a second round," she said. "I'm going to push the folks in Hartford for a quick response to Szulz's offer. 'Quick' as in 'yesterday.'"

"I'd say that's a unanimous view."

The cop stood up and replaced his pen in a little side-slit beside the left front pocket on his blue uniform shirt.

"I'll let you know if we come up with anything," he said.

"Right." Proxy gave him her patented earnest gaze. "Can you leave me a copy of your report?"

He did. Exit cop. That left Proxy and me alone. I wanted to tell her it was okay to tremble with rage or fear and not be sure which it was; okay to cry just to wash the nervous tension out of her system; okay to puke; okay to have me fetch some brandy; okay to bark at me just because there weren't any other candidates around. I'd been in combat and I'd seen damn good soldiers—soldiers better than I claimed to be—do all those things. As she gazed up at me and smilingly got ready to speak, I could tell she read me like an Excel spreadsheet.

"How soon can I get back to my unit, doc?"

The First Monday in April

Chapter Nine

Cynthia Jakubek

"One veggie wrap, please."

"You got it. Chips or drink?"

"Nope, I'm good."

I pulled toasted dough wrapped with origami-esque elegance around grilled rabbit food from the shiny aluminum counter of the Woodshed Meal Wagon parked outside the McCallister Building in downtown Pittsburgh. I gave a five to my client, Sean McGeoghan, got a one and change in return, and dumped the coins into a plastic cup serving as tip-jar. I have a little zinger about how, at three-fifty a pop, these must be the finest veggie-wraps in the world, but Sean had heard that one so I skipped it.

This was early afternoon on the Monday after the three-way negotiation with Transoxana and Pitt MCM. I hadn't heard from Shifcos yet, and I'd halfway expected to by now. I *had* heard from Rand, but he'd been calling about another matter—which was why I was now investing in slightly overpriced fast food.

Sean pronounces McGeoghan "McGuffin." Don't ask me why. My genes are Slavic. My ancestors were as far from Celts as you can get and still be on the same continent. Sean takes the McGuffin pronunciation pretty seriously. He gets a little testy the third or fourth time someone tries to turn his name into MICK-GO-*HEE*-GAN or MICK-*GO*-AGAIN.

"If I step out for a talk with you does that mean the cost of the sandwich goes on my bill?" Sean flashed me a grin under twinkling blue eyes. Maybe I should have used the zinger after all.

"No, I'll take it as a business expense. That way if I have a good year Uncle Sam will pick up thirty-seven-and-a-half percent of it."

"I'm on my way, then. Helping people pay lower taxes is the reason God put me on Earth."

I chanced a nibble on the veggie-wrap while Sean was getting his coat, bidding farewell to Tommy Andreopolous, the guy who actually owns the Woodshed, and extricating himself from the lunch-wagon. I'd call the wrap good but not great. Tomatoes, lettuce, and so forth aren't really the Woodshed's point. Specialty of the house is roast beef on warm rolls, grilled over a real wood-chip fire. Hence the lunch-wagon's clever name. Veggie-wraps are a grudging sop to my end of the downtown gender-demographic, so that couples hooking up over the noon hour can get lunch-on-the-run at the same place. Sean didn't get to an eight-figure net worth by being dumb. Adding meat-free entrées to the Woodshed's menu was his idea.

Sporting a black cashmere overcoat and Greek fisherman's cap, Sean pulled on sleek black leather gloves as he came around the wagon's near end to join me on the sidewalk. Sean's is the middle name in Werther-McGeoghan-Warburg Group. WMW puts small cliques of investors together for ventures that Sean thinks have a lot of upside potential but could never get past the loan committee at your average bank. The Woodshed is a good example: you can't outsource curbside meal service to China; the real-wood-chip-cooking thing is a marketing hook; and if you could franchise the concept across the South and Midwest, in three years you'd need lawn and garden bags to haul your money to the bank. That's Sean's vision, anyway, and he's right a lot more often than he's wrong. One of the reasons is that before he invests penny-one he dives in and does hands-on stuff in the business until he feels like he really knows it. That's why he was helping out behind the counter today.

Sean plays bigger than he looks, as basketball coaches sometimes say about small forwards. He's an inch or so under six feet,
and packs less than a hundred seventy pounds on a compact
frame. Somehow, though, he takes up more space than that.
I've never seen him strut, but he doesn't just walk, either. He
strides or paces or does something damn close to marching. He
treats conversation almost as a contact sport—I think that tying
his hands would strike him mute. Even when he stands in still
silence his eyes sweep the area around him in a measured, curious
way. Under a generous mane of gray and white hair bespeaking
his fifty-plus years, his face cycles through puckish, intrigued,
skeptical, welcoming, and jovial expressions, all over a smile
that gives away absolutely nothing. Radiating positive energy, he
generally seems to be the center of any group that includes him.

The prominent Wall Street law firm of Calder & Bull, which
spent three years paying me more money than anyone my age who
can't dribble has any business getting, accused me of stealing Sean
when I left to set up a solo practice here in Pittsburgh. Calder &
Bull got things exactly wrong. Sean stole me from C&B—and it
was C&B's own damn fault. But that's another story.

"Did you get a chance to talk with Abbey while I was trying
to shake euros out of Germans across the pond?"

"I spent most of Sunday before last with her. A very together
lady. Congratulations."

"Thank you. Did you get anywhere on our little canon law
adventure?"

Sean's light-hearted tone didn't fool me. I knew that in his
mind, our "little canon law adventure" ranked well ahead of the
potential investment group for the Woodshed and whatever he
had going in Europe.

In calling the forty-seven-year-old package of brains, energy,
and common sense named Abigail Northanger "together," I
wasn't just stroking an important client; I meant it. On the
Sunday I'd referred to I'd watched her absorb a solemn explanation of Purgatory at a class for future Catholic converts in the

morning and then heard her laugh her head off at a *Fifty Shades of Grey* parody during a matinee that afternoon.

Sean wanted to marry Abbey. He wanted to marry her in the Roman Catholic Church, in front of a priest who would bless their rings and formally witness their sacramental union during a proper wedding Mass with all the bells and smells the Church provides. And he wanted to marry her before sexual intimacy between them. A lot of people I know would have called that quaint or even morbidly repressed; it struck me as kind of sweet.

Unfortunately, twenty-six years earlier an Elvis impersonator had pronounced Tally Rand and Abigail Northanger man and wife in the 24/7 Chapel O' Love on Fashion Center Boulevard just off the Strip in Las Vegas. A Nevada judge had dissolved their union less than a year later, but the Church gives zero weight to a secular jurist's opinion on the bonds of matrimony. That meant that Abbey needed to get this so-called "marriage" formally annulled before she and Sean could tie the knot.

"I made some progress," I told Sean in answer to his question, "but Tally Rand has been your basic brick wall—at least up until this morning."

"First things first. Does Abbey have grounds for annulment?"

"For sure. She told me she was sky-high on primo grass when she and Tally exchanged vows. *Ergo* lack of capacity for informed consent, *ergo* invalid marriage in the eyes of the Church."

I gave this answer pretty confidently for an attorney who knows literally nothing about canon law. Trust me, you won't find a class on *that* at Harvard Law School. Fortunately, one of my brothers is a priest, and he knew at least one thing about canon law: the telephone number for the archdiocesan chancery. The helpful young woman I tracked down there was happy to share.

"Tally denies that Abbey was baked at the wedding?" Sean asked.

"Tally is keeping his cards close to his vest. His official position is that the marriage was a genuine union of committed love *et cetera*, and as a proud non-believer he doesn't intend to play along with what he calls 'the hypocritical charade of Catholic divorce.'"

"A 'union of love' that didn't last much longer than a politician's campaign promise and ended in a quickie divorce?" Sean seemed genuinely indignant as he put his gesticulating right hand gently on my elbow. "That's unmitigated…nonsense."

"I agree." I smiled at Sean's hasty substitution of "nonsense" for the more colorful term we'd both had in mind. Old-school gentlemen don't use words like "bullshit" in front of ladies.

"So whoever makes the decision will believe Abbey instead of him, right?"

"I expect so. Not really the point, though."

"What is the point, then?"

"With Tally's cooperation, the annulment process will take six months, maybe eight. If he chooses to contest it, the annulment could take six *years* to get through, complete with appeals to Rome, whether his position has merit or not."

"Ouch," Sean said. "Ouch ouch ouch ouch ouch ouch ouch."

"Yeah." I finished the veggie-wrap and slowed my pace long enough to stow deli paper in a proper receptacle.

"Any chance of a making a crack in that brick wall?"

"Until this morning I would have said no." I stopped, which made Sean stop, and I caught both of his eyes in my gaze so that he'd know my next words were important. "But at nine sharp Tally called me and said he wanted to talk to you personally about an unrelated matter."

"Namely?"

"He didn't say."

Sean looked to his right and his left, which is one of his ways of thinking, then started walking again. I fell into pace beside him.

"How do you feel about the direct contact idea?" he asked.

"I don't have any problem with it. You eat guys like him for breakfast. You don't need a lawyer running interference for you. Besides, I'm dealing with Tally on an unrelated case. If I demand that he go through me on anything relating to you, he might think he could get me to take my eye off the ball by playing one case off against the other"

"Probably right about both of those."

"Nine to one, though, this is a shakedown."

"It won't be the first one I've ever dealt with if it is."

"I know," I said. "But if he does put extortion on the table, we might be able to turn it around and use it against him."

"Bite him in the fanny with his own blessed teeth!" Sean flashed me a mega-watt beam. "I love that idea! I'll call you as soon as I've talked to him."

We both stopped now, because we were about to head in opposite directions. The twenty-thousand-a-year retainer that Sean pays me helps cover my rent, but in Pittsburgh solo start-up law practices have offices in a very different part of downtown than successful investment groups.

"How's the Woodshed project coming along?" I asked.

"Not sure." Sean shook his head, in a rare display of a mood short of unbridled optimism about a potential deal. "The woodchip-fire hook is cute but my gut says we need something beyond that—something with a little more pizzazz."

"If I think of something I'll let you know."

"I'll take anything I can get." He doffed his cap and swept it over his head in elegant farewell. Just like that, the optimist was back.

Sean didn't let any grass grow under his feet. Less than ninety minutes after I emailed him Tally's contact information, Sean called me.

"Nailed it on the shakedown," he said. "He wants me to give him a four hundred thousand-dollar interest in a pending investment package of his choice as compensation for 'strategic consulting' services he'll supposedly perform. In exchange he'll cooperate on the annulment."

"Did he really make it as explicit as that? He could get himself disbarred."

"No, he put the *quid pro quo* between the lines and talked about making a presentation about his services so that I could decide if they'd be useful. European contacts, experience in major transactions, German language skills—that kinda stuff."

"As if you'd have to throw six figures at a graduate of New Mexico Law School to get that."

"That's where he went?" Sean asked. "New Mexico?"

"That's what his online profile says. The chatter about European smarts might be halfway legitimate, though. He did some undergraduate stuff at a place in central Europe that I can't pronounce."

"My gut says to string him along for awhile. I'd write a big check to get Abbey and me our stained-glass wedding without thinking twice about it—but I hate being treated like a wimp who'll roll over just because he tells me to."

"Your gut is as good as gold. Maybe if he stews in his own juice for a couple of days he'll come back to me with something we can use against him."

"We have a plan. I can use heading back overseas as an excuse to put him off for a bit. White lie in pursuit of a greater good."

"All right," I said. "I'll let you know as soon as I hear something."

All that left, aside from the kinds of cats-and-dogs work that keeps the lights on during a new law office's early going, was waiting to hear from Shifcos. With serious bad guys in the picture and my client in the cross-hairs, we were way past posturing. Every instinct I had told me Shifcos was going to call.

At four-thirty she did. But she didn't say what I wanted to hear.

"We need another week."

"Ten thousand." I said that out loud, after saying "shit" under my breath.

"Same proviso? Full credit against the final price?"

"Same proviso."

"We've got a deal. I'll send you a confirming email before I leave the office."

We hung up. *Then* I said "shit" out loud. Then I called Willy.

Chapter Ten

Jay Davidovich

"So," Rachel said on Monday night as we enjoyed dinner at one of Virginia's finer Olive Gardens. "Whose lipstick was it that I found on the shirt you brought back from Pittsburgh?"

"Not lipstick, blood. Mine."

"You got beaten up by a *girl*?"

"Guy."

"You're sleeping with guys now?"

"I was fighting with this one. I've never hit anyone I slept with. Even you."

"Oooh. Tou-fuckin'-ché, tough guy."

"Damn right."

Her hair told me something was up. Rachel had wrapped her luscious blond mane in tight, meticulous braids that circled her scalp. Must've taken her an hour. That generally meant something along the lines of *Attention to orders, soldier.* So I was hanging on every word out of her mouth and every muscle tic that might qualify as body language.

Some chick-law apparently makes it illegal for women to actually *say* what the hell the deal is. At least if it's important. To them. You have to get at it by some combination of intuition and ESP. If you can't figure it out, that means you're clueless and insensitive. Because you're male they already knew that, of course, but this is additional evidence.

What I'd gotten so far was that my coming back from Pittsburgh with a bruised face bothered her. Can't blame her for that, but Rache had seen me with a lot worse than a swollen nose and a couple of owwies without getting all sideways about it.

"So when do you head back to Albuquerque?" she asked, pivoting nimbly away from her riff on imaginary adultery.

"Day after tomorrow."

"This is the computer-hacking thing at the church?"

"Seminary."

"And you're supposed to prove it isn't covered by their insurance policy?"

"It's covered. I'm supposed to figure out how to keep it from happening somewhere else. The seminary was the second church-related target for this off-shore hacker. The bean-counters are now officially tired of writing checks."

"So the hacker is pilfering confidential data or stealing identities or something?"

"Not as far as we can tell." I shook my head. "It looks like it's just cyber-vandalism. Destroying records."

"Clergy-abuse victim. Revenge."

"You sound pretty sure for someone who hasn't seen the file."

"Take it to the bank. Write that in your report, and you won't have to bother with the trip. You can stay home for a while. "

"Interesting angle, but we can't find any claimed victims or abusers who fit the timeline and have any connection to the area."

"I thought the pedophile-priest thing was happening all the time, pretty much everywhere."

"Apparently not."

"Nuts," Rachel said. "That would have simplified things a lot."

Now she raised her left hand to her mouth with the first two fingers slightly apart. She then lifted her cupped right hand to maybe four inches in front and leaned her head toward it with her left hand still in place. After that she brought the right hand back down to her side, pulled the left hand to her side at roughly breast level, rocked her head back, and blew toward the ceiling.

"Rache?"

"Yo, muscles."

"Can I ask you something?"

"Shoot."

"What the hell are you doing?"

"Air smoking."

"Like air guitar except without a cigarette instead of without a guitar?"

"Pretty much." She pantomimed another drag and flicked let's-pretend ash onto the ground.

"Interesting."

"Someone has this theory that it helps overcome the urge to smoke if you go through the gestures and body movements, because they're comforting in themselves."

Rachel smokes *maybe* a pack of cigarettes a year. Not exactly hard core. But I figured that, whatever head-game she was playing with me, letting logic crash the party would probably spoil it.

"How's it working?" I asked.

"As far as I can tell, the theory is total bullshit."

"Oh."

My mobile phone chirped. I ignored it.

"You'd better get that," Rachel said on the second ring. "Might be your boss."

I shrugged and checked the number. Proxy. Proxy is *not* my boss. Proxy is the one who tells my boss that she wants me instead of some other loss-prevention specialist for a particular job. That makes her a *lot* more important than my boss. I answered.

"Do you have a current passport?"

"Yes," was about all I contributed to our conversation, which ended roughly seventy seconds later. I re-holstered the phone and looked at Rachel.

"Well, I'm not going to Albuquerque the day after tomorrow."

"Great!"

"I'm going to Vienna."

"The one in Austria or the one in Pennsylvania?"

"Must be the one in Austria. I don't think you can fly to Pennsylvania from Dulles International."

"Mm," Rachel said, nodding. "By the way, I'm pregnant."

The First Wednesday in April

Chapter Eleven

Jay Davidovich

I'm not sure the chocolate-brown Mercedes Benz qualified as a limo, but the part behind the front seat easily accommodated Franz Meininger, Proxy, and me, with Meininger on a jump seat facing us. While we sped—and I mean *sped*—from Vienna International Airport toward the Hotel am Stephansplatz, Meininger spent seventy-five seconds welcoming us to Vienna and thanking us for coming. Then he got down to business.

"We are playing this on spec. No documentation. No way to verify the pitch. Two reasons I asked that you come. One: Dany Nesselrode has proven credible on a couple of big matters in the past. Two: he wants to deal directly with line-personnel responsible for the matter—not glorified messenger-boys like me."

"What's Nesselrode's resumé?" Proxy got ready to make notes on the iPad in her lap as she asked the question. "Short form."

"Thirty-eight. Three languages, including English. Degree from the LSE."

"London School of Economics." Proxy muttered this for my benefit.

"Six years with the Cultural Preservation Foundation—one of the many international NGOs that make their home in Vienna."

He paused in case Proxy wanted to tell me that "NGO" meant "non-governmental organization." She didn't. Either I already knew, or I didn't need to.

I liked Meininger. He'd gone to the trouble to find out that Proxy favored Evian bottled water and had brought some along for us. He hadn't asked if it would be okay if he smoked because he knew that Proxy would have said sure and she wouldn't have meant it. The deep blue of the stones in his cuff-links precisely matched the diagonal stripes in his silk tie and complimented the paler blue of his shirt. I liked all that. Liked his breezy use of American suit-speak that somehow seemed more elegant when spoken with a German accent. Liked not seeing any condescension in his alert brown eyes when he looked at me.

"Is the Cultural Preservation Foundation a cover for something else?" Proxy asked.

"Don't know. A lot of NGOs in Vienna are, but no hard data on CPF." He pulled two pages from an envelope-style briefcase that he'd parked on the floor beside him and handed them to Proxy. "This is the rundown we have so far."

"Thanks."

Proxy began speed-reading the pages. Meininger looked over at me.

"Do you travel overseas much on business, Jay?"

"Not since I left the Army."

That got me a quick take and a wry smile. Proxy glanced up from the second page.

"So CPF's funding comes mostly from New York and Israel."

"Yes." Meininger nodded again. "Dany is a diaspora Jew. Never lived in Israel, but he'll play the Holocaust card in negotiations without blinking."

Proxy has a pretty good poker face, but no one could have missed her *whoa!* expression at that lapse into political incorrectitude. I didn't know what protocol Transoxana's employee manual prescribed for reactions to Ethnically Insensitive Remarks, but I suspected Proxy had it down cold. I figured a chat about Diversity and Inclusiveness wouldn't move the ball much, so I jumped in.

"I know what you mean. This guy I know, Jewish fella, when he was maybe thirteen years old, tells his mom it was too bad the

Germans surrendered in World War II before we got a chance
to drop the big one on them. Some crack he'd heard from one
of his buddies. After he laid this on his mom, he thought for
the third time in his life that she was going to hit him—and the
first two times he'd been right."

"Yes," Meininger said with a knowing grin. "And by now I'll
bet this boy is a congressman from Connecticut and sitting on
the Foreign Affairs Committee."

"Actually, he's a loss-prevention specialist with Transoxana."

Meininger spent a couple of seconds putting the pieces
together as *oh shit* slipped over his face and red flushed his pale
Teutonic ears. He licked his lips a couple of times and leaned
forward earnestly.

"I'm terribly sorry. I certainly hope that I didn't offend you."

"No sweat. Don't give it another thought."

I said that because *you didn't "offend" me, you pissed me off*
would sidetrack us—something I *really* wanted to avoid. I'd spent
nine hours flying four-and-a-half thousand miles to accomplish
something, and I wasn't going to accomplish a damn thing if
our Vienna company liaison spent the rest of our stay looking
for bureaucratic cover.

Looking relieved, Meininger glanced at his watch.

"We are meeting Nesselrode in not quite two hours. So you'll
have a little time at the hotel to freshen up before I bring him by."

Proxy's ears pricked up at that.

"We're meeting him at the hotel instead of Transoxana's
offices?"

"Yes. He wants to do it that way."

This better be good. Proxy didn't say that, but her shrug did.

"I'd tell you more if I knew more." Meininger glanced from
Proxy to me and back. "But whatever it is, he said he wants you
to hear it from his lips."

Chapter Twelve

Jay Davidovich

"What if the painting is fake? A forgery?"

That's what we'd come to hear from Dany Nesselrode's own lips. We heard it nestled in a cozy booth in the hotel's Kaisereine Café—a marvel of intricately carved walnut and subdued lighting that managed to suggest a midnight tryst even at one-thirty in the afternoon.

Nesselrode had hair the color of India ink, reminding me of the blue-tinged black you see on gun barrels. I made him at five-ten, maybe one-sixty-five. He didn't have an ounce of fat that I could see so he must have watched his diet like a hawk, but enlarged veins around his nose and under his eyes suggested other indulgences. He was smoking a fat cigar and Proxy was taking it like a big girl, maybe because it smelled like a *really* good cigar. Just breathing the air gave me a flashback to beer call and after-action parties in Iraq.

"If it's a forgery," Proxy said, "then a number of highly credentialed experts have been badly fooled over a period of decades."

"Art experts get fooled all the time." Nesselrode waved the cigar dismissively. "Few will say it out loud, but most people who know what they're talking about estimate an error rate of ten to twenty percent—and that's on seven-to-nine-figure art, where the very best experts are being paid top dollar. And don't get me started on the 'experts' who get bribed to come up with the right answer. If doctors were wrong as often as art experts, half of us would be dead."

"Dany has an admirably high level of self-esteem." Meininger said this in between bites of a glazed cherry torte the size of a discus. "Even when he's in error, he's not in doubt."

Proxy kept her eyes on Nesselrode.

"If someone proves the Museum's painting is fake, the Museum still has a loss, and Transoxana still has a claim to deal with."

"What loss? The Museum will have the painting it has always had. It paid nothing for the thing, so even if it's worthless the Museum is out of pocket zero. It doesn't have the painting it *thought* it had, but who cares? I'm assuming Transoxana doesn't insure blissful fantasies."

"Besides," Meininger said, "the Museum will *have to* deny the forgery assertion. And if Dany is right, it will find an expert to back it up. It couldn't make a claim against Transoxana without undermining its own position."

I noticed just a hint of impatience in the *clack* that sounded when Proxy set her tumbler of bubbly water with a lime twist back on the table.

"So what's the theory?" she asked. "That the heirs will threaten to expose the painting as a forgery unless the Museum gives it back to them? That would mean they'd gone to a lot of trouble to try to get a *fake* painting back."

"Perhaps the heirs have a slightly more sophisticated ploy in mind."

"Namely?"

"'That's a nice reputation you have there—what a shame if something happened to it.'"Nesselrode smiled wickedly.

"So the Museum is going to give away the crown jewel of its collection in order to keep extortionists from making what the extortionists themselves presumably believe is a *false* claim that the painting is worthless?" This would be Proxy getting intense. "Not gonna happen. The Museum will dispute the claim and hire some culture-whore to support its position. It would rather have a questioned masterpiece than an empty space on its main gallery wall."

"She's right, Dany," Meininger told him. "You must have cards you haven't shown us yet."

"I do."

"This would be an excellent time to turn them over." Meininger made that suggestion before Proxy could—which was a shame, because her version would probably have been more colorful.

"I am thinking about an amicable resolution. Win-win." Nesselrode paused, milking the suspense while he took a moment to pollute his lungs. "Five-part deal. One: the Museum recognizes that the heirs are making their claim in good faith and blah-blah-blah. Two: the heirs stipulate that the Museum's position that the painting was legitimately acquired in an arm's-length transaction is defensible. Three: the heirs 'donate' their claim to the Museum because art should be seen by the people and all that crap—and make that the basis for an obscene tax deduction, which the Museum will back up. Four: the Museum throws the heirs a bone—names a gallery after gramps and nana or something. Five: In further recognition of the heirs' magnanimity, the Museum lends the painting for, say, three years to, say, the *Osterreichische Galerie Belvedere* here in gramps' native country where, don't forget, Klimt actually painted the damn thing, in exchange for a loaned work of comparable renown from the *Galerie*."

And six, I thought, *Willy Szulz gets screwed and C. Talbot Rand gets a pat on the back and maybe a little bonus at the end of the year.*

Proxy nodded, not in agreement but in recognition of the sheer neatness of the idea. Meininger's eyes glistened with interest as he turned them toward her. I would have bet you anything that I knew what both of them were thinking, because I was thinking the same thing: *If it works it solves the problem at zero cost to Transoxana—and even if it doesn't, it motivates the Museum to chip in a LOT more toward the price of that piece of paper Szulz is peddling.*

"This has possibilities." Proxy settled back in her seat, relaxing a little. "But we need to get a handle on the evidence for the forgery allegation. What documentation do you have for it?"

"The best kind: the real painting."

If that line impressed Proxy, she didn't show it.

"Where is it?"

"I don't know." Nesselrode shrugged at this technicality. "But I can take you to someone who does."

"Let's go."

Proxy started to scoot toward me as a hint that we should both get out of the booth. Nesselrode checked the time on his mobile phone.

"Not now. I have to do a little trailblazing first."

"Then when?"

"Vienna is lovely late at night. Ten o'clcock?"

We were only a few hours off of a plane after a nine-hour-plus red-eye. Even so, Proxy took just five seconds to run through every logistical option that might make Nesselrode's clinically insane proposal feasible. She came up with one.

"One of us will see you then." She finished climbing out of the booth behind me. "Franz, I wonder if it would be convenient for you to take Mr. Nesselrode wherever he needs to go next, and then perhaps give me a call?"

"Certainly." The glint in Meininger's eyes told me he'd gotten the message: wherever you take him and whatever you notice there should come up in the phone call.

Next thing I knew, Proxy and I were standing at the front desk, with Proxy saying stuff in German and the desk clerk replying in English. I'd seen this movie before, when we'd reached the hotel a little over two hours ago, so I knew what to expect. They'd checked us in then but they'd had the usual hotel excuses for not letting us into our rooms right away. That figured to be the subject of Proxy's discussion now. Proxy would continue speaking German until either the clerk started answering in German or Proxy got what she wanted, or both. Since this could go on for awhile, I decided to pass the time by thinking about why Meininger's "Holocaust card" remark had pissed me off.

If I had Nesselrode pegged right he was a slick hustler typecast for Oppenheim the Goldsmith. I sure wouldn't put it past him to use the Holocaust to try to guilt-trip *goyim* in negotiations—especially if the *goyim* in question spoke German. In tipping us off to that, Meininger was just doing his job, although I suppose he could have phrased it a little more tactfully.

As a rule, I don't walk around with a Jewish chip on my shoulder. When I'd shown up at my high school gym to try out for the freshman basketball team, the coach had said, "Son, you do understand that med schools don't offer athletic scholarships, right?" Hadn't fazed me. Double-stereotype from an authority figure, and I'd taken it as standard issue jock-josh, not some kind of high-caliber ethnic slur. But I'd had to work to keep from jumping down Meininger's throat.

I guess I'm an okay Jew. Not "good," necessarily. Rache and I try to eat kosher, although we probably miss a nuance here and there. Temple on high holy days, plus two or three other times during the year—and we write a decent check. Go to *bar* and *bat mitzvahs* for friends' children. Don't observe Christmas. If the kid in Rachel's tummy is a boy, he'll be circumcised.

On the other hand, the average baby-boomer who watched sitcoms during the fifties and sixties probably knows more Yiddish than I do. I never really connected with the American-Jewish cultural thing. Mom and Dad hit Connecticut from the Ukraine when they were twelve and thirteen. When they got old enough to make babies, they focused a lot more on the "American" part of things than the Jewish part. They'd signed my birth certificate "Davidson." I'd changed it back to Davidovich myself.

So here was Jay Davidovich—full name Judas Maccabeus Davidovich—helping a multi-national insurance company keep a masterpiece that had maybe been extorted from an honest Austrian Jew out of the hands of his heirs. I hadn't given it a second thought until Meininger's crack. Now, suddenly, I wasn't so sure how I felt about the whole thing.

Proxy turned and handed me a key-card envelope. Knowing German is *exactly* the kind of thing Proxy would do. Not Spanish, which she could use every day on either coast in the U.S. Not French, which would stamp her in the U.S. as a cultural high-flier with an elite education. German. And give her credit: she'd gotten us into our rooms a full hour before they were supposed to be ready.

"I hate to screw up your biological clock even worse than it already is after a trans-Atlantic flight, but can you handle the Nesselrode thing with seven hours of sleep?"

"Two hits of Red Bull and I could handle it on five."

"Good. Go up and crash so you can meet him at ten tonight. I'll go to Transoxana's Vienna office and see if Meininger and I can figure out how to find another copy of the comparable sale documentation Szulz is peddling."

"Got it." I hoisted the duffel bag that's as close as I get to luggage if I can help it. "While Willy Szulz sits innocently in Pittsburgh, we're moving on two separate fronts in Vienna to cut him out of the action."

"Yep," Proxy said, in a rare lapse from Standard English. "Good thing he's there and not here."

Chapter Thirteen

CYNTHIA JAKUBEK

"So I'm getting up from my desk to go to lunch and the phone rings. Zack's number on the caller ID. Guy I was seeing at the time. Zack calling means I can spend the noon hour either eating salad or having sex. I picked salad. In the elevator I realized it wasn't really a close question. I met Sean on my way back from lunch that day. Ten months ago. Fate. Or providence. I'll go with either one."

Abbey Northanger speaks in paragraphs. Entertaining paragraphs, but big blocks of words all the same that draw a little extra verve from her animated face and the gently curling auburn hair above it. She either has violet eyes or the best set of contact lenses I've ever seen in my life. She makes her living as a professional event planner. Judging from the Versace and Armani stuff that tastefully drapes her in public, she must be pretty good at it. We were meeting in my office around ten o'clock in the morning—early evening, of course, in Vienna, where Shifos was, even though I didn't know it at the time.

"So Zach versus Sean was no contest?"

"Form held, as they say in the NCAA. I'm not putting you off with this frisky-fossil stuff, am I?"

"Calling people your age ancient is for kids who still need fake IDs."

"Zach was pretty typical of what I call my B-S period—'Before Sean.'" Abbey let an almost wistful smile slip across her face and disappear. "I don't mean just sowing some wild oats. I mean giving Quakers and Ralston a run for their money."

"I hope the priest you get for your first confession isn't fresh out of the seminary." I smilingly imagined a fledgling cleric listening to Abbey describe her demolition of the sixth and ninth commandments. "His head might explode."

"Oh, I'm sure they've got some crusty old ex-military chaplain who's heard it all with jam on top lined up for me. Anyway, enough foreplay. Down to business. Sean said that you and I should talk."

"Right. You up to speed on Tally Rand's little stunt?"

"Yep. Pure Tally. Anyone who says grass doesn't impair judgment needs to tell me how someone with my brains got hooked by that weasel in the first place. He'd come back from his junior year abroad or whatever it was with some *éclat* that came across as pretty smooth out West, and he had a knack for standing up to cowboy wannabes who resented it. More muscular than he looks, and had a good right jab. Still, I should have smelled the shit even if it *was* in a silk stocking."

My ears pricked up at *Pure Tally*. Not my favorite lawyer for sure, but up to now I hadn't stumbled over any hints about him bumping up against the criminal code.

"You mean he's pulled this kind of thing before?"

"Depends on how broadly you cast the net. About ten years ago when I was going after an event-planning gig at the Museum, he hinted that my chances might improve if I gave him a tumble just for old time's sake. After I got the gig—without sleeping with him, by the way—he suggested that I give the audio-visual subcontract to a company that I'd never heard of and that isn't in business anymore. I smell kickback on that one. If he pulled that kind of small-time grift with me he must have tried it with others."

Interesting. Early on I'd pulled the Museum's annual report from the Pennsylvania Secretary of State's online files. The

Museum had paid Tally one hundred five thousand last year—
down five percent from the year before because of across-the-
board salary cuts. A nice piece of change for sure, but striplings
only a few years out of law school were pulling down twice that
much at firms like Calder & Bull—me, for example, before I
abandoned Wall Street for solo practice in Pittsburgh.

"If he's a little bent," I said, "that could actually help us with
what Sean wants us to talk about."

"You mean the give-him-enough-rope thing?"

I'm pretty good at poker faces but my eyebrows edged up a
sixteenth of an inch at that one.

"He's already discussed it with you?"

"I've practically convinced him it was my idea in the first
place." Big grin—Abbey is *not* good at poker faces. "The concept
rocks, but I'll need some help with the details. I have a middle
name, and it ain't finesse."

"Okay. Details." I sat up straight, rested my forearms on my
desk blotter, and folded my hands. "One, no private eye stuff.
Surreptitious tape recordings, hidden cameras—forget about it."

"Nuts. I'd already started researching voice-activated digital
recorders on the web."

"Two—and a *lot* more important—no hints. We can't seduce
Tally; he has to make the indecent proposal on his own initiative. He has to get the idea that you're the back door to Sean.
We hope that he'll be less guarded with you than he has been
with Sean so far—that he'll say something more explicit about
how if you get him into Sean's next venture for free then you're
already halfway down the aisle."

"Right." Abbey's eyes flashed with enthusiasm that bordered
on scary. "He does that, and then we ask him how much he
enjoys practicing law."

"We'll have to find an ethical way to frame that question.
But that's my department."

And when push came to shove on that one, the question for
me wouldn't be whether I'd do it but how. When I'd started at
Calder & Bull, I'd decided that I'd give Wall Street four years,

then make a go/stay decision. Around the end of year-three, a number of things said STAY. Most of them were money. True, I was working on cases with very high stakes but, when you get right down to it, reviewing documents on a computer screen and putting together witness files that people two or three years senior to me would use to prepare executives for depositions— well, that's just as tedious if you have nine figures on the table as it is if you have five. I wasn't helping clients, I was helping partners. I'd helped a client once when I was in the pre-C&B wilderness, and I missed it.

Even so, I'm betting that, without Sean, I would have ended up staying past my four-year cut-off just out of inertia. Sean brought enough big-ticket stuff to the firm that they'd handle the plebian part of his business too, just to keep him happy. At least two layers of lawyers separated me from him, but I'd been allowed to meet him a couple of times, ostensibly because I'd grown up in Pittsburgh, where he lived. Mostly it was a way of patting me on the head and telling me what a good girl I was. We'd hit it off.

Then C&B made the mistake bailing out of representation on an indie film that Sean was trying to get financed. The firm had bailed because a senior partner was afraid that an activist group would lower C&B's favorability rating if it associated itself even obliquely with a film that the group wouldn't like—and it for sure wouldn't have liked this one.

"Gutless." That was what Sean called it when he took me to lunch afterward. He'd spoken the word in a cold, disgusted tone and with a sad shake of his head.

"Not exactly a profile in courage," I'd said tactfully (for me).

"Let's get down to the short strokes." He'd actually blushed a little as he'd realized that the expression was a tad off-color. "How often do you think about blowing off the big-firm racket and opening up your own shop back in Pittsburgh?"

"Three times a week."

"Have you run the numbers?"

"In a half-assed kind of way." I did *not* blush at that unladylike adjective. "I could sublet office space from a lawyer I worked with while I was on hold with C&B. I could live cheap in my dad's house 'til I got on my feet. I have something like a hundred-thousand saved. That should be enough to buy a photocopier and a computer and see me through until I find out whether I can really build a practice or not."

"No." He'd shaken his head firmly. "Don't support your practice or yourself with your own savings. Put that money in a bank that will give you a line of credit for your practice. *Always* use other people's money."

"Good advice."

"And don't buy any office equipment. Lease. If something appreciates over time, buy it. If it depreciates, lease it."

"I'm convinced."

"Look, you're smart as hell, and somewhere along the way you got slapped around a little by life—which is good. You're not experienced enough for me to pay you to negotiate with regulators or restructure financings. But you've got guts. If you decide to make that jump, I can throw twenty thousand a year in business at you. Not scintillating stuff. Evictions, collections, enforcing noncompetes. But it'll help pay the rent."

So now, here I was. In my thirteenth month of solo practice, doing it on nerve and bluff. And if you ignore the *de facto* rent subsidy from dad and my stepmom, actually breaking even. But Sean and Willy between them accounted for about a third of my billings, which is way too much for two clients. For the foreseeable future, Sean had to keep thinking that I had guts.

My desk phone rang. I didn't recognize the number, so I ignored it. Abbey didn't.

"That's the number of the Vodaphone Sean uses as his mobile when he's overseas."

Sure enough. In a couple of seconds I had him on speaker.

"How's the jet-lag, big guy?" Abbey asked.

"Running on pure adrenaline, and praying that the eurocrats aren't planning on one of their famous late-night suppers with schnapps in between courses of raw sausage. How are things going over there?"

"I can't say the cat's in the bag and the bag's in the river, but we're getting there." Abbey winked at me.

"Really? What's happened?"

"Well, technically, nothing. Yet. But Cindy has just taken me through Entrapment for Dummies. When Tally calls I'll be ready."

"*If* he calls."

"Oh, he'll call, all right. Tally has never seen an angle he could resist playing."

"That reminds me," Sean said. "Cindy, there's something I have to tell you so you can yell at me."

"Namely?"

"Willy Szulz and I ran into each other at the Monongahela Athletic Club yesterday morning. He mentioned that we had the same lawyer, and just like that I conformed to an ethnic stereotype. Ran off at the mouth. Told him more than I should have about our canon law matter."

"Well, consider yourself scolded. Willy gets about seven good ideas a day. Generally at least one of them is dangerous. The trick is figuring out which one it is. I'll call him and say something about the virtues of discretion."

"I'm sure you'll come across as your usual persuasive self. I'll touch base tomorrow if I get a chance."

So, exit Sean and, a few minutes later, exit Abbey. Time to call Willy. It didn't strike me as urgent or anything, but no sense putting it off, either.

"Hey, Willy here," his recorded voice said. "I'll be away from the office for a few days, with limited access to voice-mail and email. Really wanna talk to you, though, so leave a number and I'll get back to you fast as I can."

Limited access to voice-mail and email. Hmm. I got a little tingle from that one. Not a real belly-drop, just a hint of a shiver. Willy's a big boy, but he gets a kick out of skating close to the line. He was now mixed up in two legal messes intersecting at C. Talbot Rand—and I wasn't sure where the line was on either of them.

Chapter Fourteen

Jay Davidovich

Seven o'clock sharp in Vienna and I got out of bed. Hungry. Simple as that. Nine o'clock would find me even hungrier and with less time, so I figured I might as well bite the bullet. Cold water splash on the face, comb through my hair, good to go. On my way out of the room I dug up a web page that Rachel had printed for me about Frank's American Bar & Restaurant in Vienna. What I was hungry for wouldn't pass for schnitzel with noodles.

I told a clerk at the front desk where I'd be in case Herr Nesselrode came calling before I returned. I didn't see any way I'd be late getting back, but just in case. He nodded and smiled. After I gave him five euros of Transoxana's money, he nodded again and smiled again and fetched a Valkyrie type who could speak English. Another five euros, a decisive nod from Her Aryan Highness, and I figured there'd be floggings all 'round if the staff managed to miss Nesselrode.

Here's my key travelogue take-away from downtown Vienna at night: bikes. Coming out of the hotel to look for a taxi, I saw gently weaving white lights coming toward me like midget cyclopses, moving too slowly and rhythmically for car headlights. And I saw small, flickering red and green lights that made me think of drunken fairies describing clumsy up-and-down ovals as they moved away from me. I had to stare at the scene like a moron for four or five seconds before I got it: bikes. The white lights were headlamps and the colored ones were leg-lights, wrapped around riders' calves. Full dark for going on two hours now, and still way more bicycles than cars filling the street.

The taxi took close to half-an-hour to get me to Frank's American et cetera. Longer than I'd expected. I guess it takes time to dodge all those bikes. If I managed to get lost wandering around this strange city, getting back to the hotel by ten could turn into an adventure. So I over-tipped the cabbie and asked him to pop back here at a quarter of nine to pick me up. Wasn't at all sure we'd communicated until he said, "Twenty-forty-five, Mac, got it," and grinned.

A little snag getting seated. Frank's apparently didn't specialize in parties of one. Finally got it done. Ordered my New York strip medium rare, my onion rings, my Miller Genuine Draft and, while I was dining, picked up snatches of tourist conversation. Mostly in American English, with an occasional Brit accent thrown in. A lot of sports chat, because the NCAA basketball tournament was still going on back home, but some local color stuff in the mix as well.

"Right *here*. Almost five hundred *years* before 9/11. Stopped the last Islamic invasion of Europe right at the walls of Vienna. No wonder Bush and Obama didn't impress them. When they discuss *jihadists* they know what they're talking about."

Okay. Pretty sure I didn't know that. Interesting.

"You kidding? My bracket busted in the first round."

Yours and mine both, brother.

"So Napoleon tells the general, he says, 'Look, if you're going to take Vienna, take Vienna.'"

Yeah, first time I heard that one it came from a second lieutenant.

"Four most beautiful words in the English language: 'Pitchers and catchers report.'"

Ah, old school. Gotta love it.

Anyway, I'm feeling just fine for a jet-lagged Yank wearing the only suit he owns. Steak not bad, MGD pretty good, onion

rings long gone; okay on time. Then I picked up another con-
versational tidbit, from over my right shoulder.

"I feel like the guy who invested all his money in brothels
'cause his broker said he should have a broad-based portfolio."

The voice rang a bell. Not just the voice but the genial smart-
ass tone of the crack itself, the edgy little chip-on-the-shoulder
subtext. *Yeah, this is the way we talk in Jersey. So what?*

I don't really do discreet very well, but I took a stab at it,
glancing cautiously in the direction of the voice. I saw a waiter's
back and the outside frame of a booth. Before I could take my
investigation further, a different voice ringing a different bell
came from my left.

"May I join you, Mr. Davidovich?"

Nesselrode. Quick, nervous glance at my watch as I mumbled
"Sure." Just past 8:15. *Hmmm.*

"I'm early." Nesselrode slipped into a chair kitty-corner to
mine on my left. "The trail-blazing went faster than I expected."

"So should we be making tracks?"

"Finish your steak." He glanced around and gestured discreetly toward a waiter. "Our friend will be engaged in the
Gürtel area until around twenty-one-thirty. Sorry, nine-thirty.
When things fell into place so quickly I got the brilliant idea of
meeting him at the place where he'll be engaged instead of at
his flat forty-five minutes later."

"What's the Gürtel area?"

"A place you wouldn't want your wife or your mother to
know you'd visited."

A waiter appeared.

"Hacker-Pschorr Weisse," Nesselrode told him.

As soon as the words were out of his mouth, the waiter pivoted toward me.

"Another draft, sir?"

"No, thanks. It'd be like taking your girlfriend to a super
models' convention."

I'm not sure the waiter got it, but he bowed and strode away.

"Did he actually click his heels?" I asked Nesselrode.

"No, that's just your imagination."

"So. Who's our friend?"

"I know him as Abba Ertel, but I'm betting his mother calls him something else. Sort of like Saul of Tarsus. When he was talking to Jews he was Saul. Put some *goys* in the audience and he suddenly morphed into Paul. Same idea."

The waiter came up with a frothy stein and set it in front of Nesselrode. The beer looked much darker than my MGD. I'd run into a fair number of beer snobs in the Army. Lifers who'd served a tour in Germany and acted ever since like they could barely choke down Miller or Bud and would puke if they accidentally swallowed some Coors. Nesselrode went to work on the beer and made what looked like a quarter of the stein disappear on the first gulp. I saw a chance to squeeze in a question.

"And Mr. Ertel has a line on the genuine painting?"

When Nesselrode put the stein back down as he got ready to answer my question I blinked. I thought I saw a watch with the hands at twelve on his wrist. Then I realized it wasn't a watch. It was a tattoo—a tattoo of a watch showing midnight. In the center of the black face, right where "Movado" would have appeared on a real watch, I read "Masada." *Whoa.* Masada. The Judean fortress where nearly a thousand Jews died rather than surrender to the Romans. They didn't die to the last man. They died to the last man, woman, and child. *Hoo-boy.* Might be more going on with Dany Nesselrode than I'd imagined so far.

"Mr. Ertel has an interesting story. Seems Gustav Wehring had a copy of *Eros Rising* painted when he realized he'd have to sell it to keep the Nazis from grabbing it. Wehring then hid the original and sold the copy as cover. Ertel has some papers that he says back this up."

"But not the real painting itself?"

"He claims he knows where it is and can get access to it."

I leaned back in my chair and stretched my legs out under the table. I was *really* feeling the steak—a good feeling—and I'd still be tasting the onion rings when I went to bed.

"So our job tonight is to find out whether Ertel's story is true."

"Not exactly," Nesselrode said. "Our job tonight is to figure out whether it's a hundred percent bullshit or only eighty percent. Because if it's only eighty percent, we might actually have a commercial proposition on our hands."

More of Nesselrode's beer went away. A lot more. I wondered if he got a quantity discount on the stuff. He checked the time on his mobile phone. Then he looked at me kind of sideways, from under hooded eyes, as if he didn't want to seem obvious about it.

"When I walked up you were looking over your shoulder at one of the booths against the wall. Were you looking for anything in particular?"

"Thought I heard a familiar voice. Seemed like an odd coincidence. Wanted to check it out, but I couldn't get a good look."

"Would you like some help?"

I was about to say why not when I heard the voice again.

"You don't take American Express? Jeez, it's like eating in a third-world country."

"Never mind. I'm pretty sure I've got it nailed."

Chapter Fifteen

Jay Davidovich

We didn't leave for another forty minutes, so I ended up drenching my bladder with another draft anyway. Nesselrode ordered a second Hacker-Pschorr to keep my stein from feeling lonely.

"For a second there," he said as the waiter deposited our beers and moved away, "I thought you were going to order a German beer, just to be polite."

"I once did something just to be polite. I'll never make that mistake again."

"Very sound." Nesselrode clinked his stein against mine. "Continentals don't expect *politesse* from Jews, Brits, or Americans. They stereotype Brits as meticulously correct and rude at the same time, and Americans as naively direct. Jews, they haven't figured out yet."

Back and forth like that for close to forty minutes. Taking each other's measure, talking about everything in the world except what we hoped to accomplish that night. An outfit that depends on money from New York and Israel has to produce results now and then that impress people in New York and Israel. He was trying to get something done with *Eros Rising* that would qualify, and I couldn't blame him for that. But a tingle along my spine told me he wanted something more than that, and so far I hadn't figured out what it might be. That didn't make him a con man, but it didn't exactly rule it out.

When he'd finished his third beer—I wasn't even trying to keep up with him—he set his stein down, met my eyes, and made sure I noticed it.

"So, am I a *gonif* or a *mensch*? Or are you still making up your mind?"

"A little of each—like most of us." I reached for my wallet to pay the tab the waiter had just dropped off. "'Us' meaning 'guys,' of course. Chicks can get complicated." I pulled out a Visa card. I had plenty of cash, but I figured it might come in handy later in the evening.

"Well, thanks for partial credit on *mensch*, anyway." Nesselrode still had his eyes locked on mine. "A step up from your first impression this afternoon, I hope."

"Pretty much. One reason I don't trust first impressions."

◇◇◇

We took the subway to a station called Westbahnhof. No bikes on the street we reached after our climb up the stairs from the station. Not many people either, except for a blonde in lederhosen and her twin sister, shivering in a white-leather mini-skirt. Stepping out of shadows the blonde asked us something in what I assumed at first was German. Three strides past her I figured out that she'd actually been taking a stab at "Wanna date?" in English—except with a *V* in place of the *W*. Three more strides and I'd pulled *Danke, nein* out of some cubbyhole in my memory. Too late, but it's the thought that counts.

In the middle of the next block Nesselrode stopped at a building with dim light visible behind dark curtains drawn over smallish, nine-pane windows on either side of the door. He pointed to a plaque-sized sign at eye-level.

"That says, 'This establishment welcomes native speakers of German.'"

"I'll keep my mouth shut."

"Good plan."

Shouldering the door open, he led me inside. A few tables with wooden chairs, and wooden benches built into the walls. Most empty. A couple of kids with "nineteen" written all over them sat on the bench in the near corner, making out in a homecoming-dance sort of way. A hawk-faced twenty-something glanced up from a laptop to give us a wary glare, then went back to committing poetry or Marxism—or hedge-fund managing, for all I knew. I picked up a smell of burning dust, like the one you get in your house in autumn when the furnace kicks back in after its summer vacation.

I followed Nesselrode to a bar running lengthwise from the back wall. Nesselrode said something that produced two bottles of schnapps. Handing one of them to me, he took the other to a table where he could keep his eye on both the door and a flight of rickety, naked stairs opposite the bar.

He checked his mobile phone. Frowned. Glanced up over my right shoulder with his eyebrows rising and his eyes widening, and shook his head. I looked in time to see a woman retreat back into shadows under the stairs. Nesselrode took a schnapps hit. Checked his mobile phone. Frowned. I looked at my watch. 9:31.

The front door opened. The chick in lederhosen came in, followed by a middle-aged, portly guy. He was working hard at not looking nervous, but not hard enough. They headed straight up the stairs. Less than a minute later the fraulein's golden braids reappeared above the bannister three steps below the second floor as she leaned over to address the bartender.

No idea what the two Teutonic syllables she barked at him meant, but they got the job done. Next thing I knew the barkeep was around the near end of the bar and hustling for the stairs. Not quite running, but not wasting any damn time either.

As the bartender clumped up the stairs I saw Nesselrode coiled tight, as if it took a lot of effort to contain himself. He managed it until we heard the first loud rap on a door that couldn't have been very far down the second-floor hallway. By the second rap Nesselrode was already rising from his chair. He put a strong right hand on my forearm.

"Stay here."

"Bullshit." I muscled my arm free and stood up.

"Suit yourself."

Nesselrode headed for the stairs, with me right behind him. Somewhere around the fourth stair the door pounding stopped and I heard keys rattling. Actual keys—kind of a quaint sound in a public place these days. At the top I ignored lederhosen-chick for the second time that night and joined Nesselrode at the doorway to a room maybe ten feet down the hall seconds after the bartender got the door open.

That's as far as we got, because the bartender had stopped cold, blocking the doorway. He was nothing like tall enough to keep me from looking into the room over his shoulder, though.

I saw a man sitting on a bed that a barracks-rat would have spit on. Back braced against the wall at the pillow-end of the bed. Trousers and underpants bunched down around his ankles. Fair-sized laptop PC resting on hairy thighs and hiding what was between them. Eyes bulging, mouth gaping, tongue peeking from the corner of his mouth, head lolling onto his right shoulder. The braided rope around his neck explained a lot.

I made the rope for well over two yards long, doubled and tied so that it had a loop at one end and two loose ends at the other. A neat, elegant knot secured the looped end in a choking circle around the man's lifeless neck. From the knot the doubled strand went slackly around the bedpost and back toward the body, with the two free ends lying close to the body's hip.

My eyes drifted toward his feet: gleaming black Nike Air Jordan Six-Rings. I recognized his face from the close look I'd gotten of it just before he clocked me with Proxy's attaché case. Nesselrode shook his head in weary disgust.

"No society in history has ever experienced a shortage of whores."

Chapter Sixteen

Jay Davidovich

Nesselrode twitched reflexively toward the stairs. I moved my head maybe an inch back and forth. Unnecessary. He stifled the impulse on his own. We'd done the same instant analysis and reached the same conclusion: *Stay or go? Stay.*

Fraulein Lederhosen was the first one to do anything constructive. Scooching in between Nesselrode and the bartender, she nudged her way into the room and headed unflinchingly for the body. She snapped something at the bartender on her way. I don't know, maybe "snapped" is too strong. Maybe everything in German sounds like an order to me. I'm guessing that she'd told him to call the police, because the bartender responded by digging a phone from under his apron. Punched one button on the phone, raised it to his ear. *Has the local heat on speed-dial. Figures.*

The hooker felt the body's neck and wrists. Didn't take her long. She looked back at the three of us.

"*Tod.*" Dead. Even I knew that one. No surprise, but she was right: someone had to check.

The bartender was jabbering away on the phone by now. The hooker stalked back out of the room and crossed the hallway to the john she'd brought in from the street. That drew my eyes to him for the first time since I'd seen the body: pasty face, wide eyes, rapid, shallow breaths, lips puckered in a little "o."

Shock? Don't think so. Then it came to me. *Sonofabitch! The guy is turned on!*

Reaching under the left lapels of the john's overcoat, suit coat, and vest, the blonde fished a pack of Dunhills and a lighter from his shirt pocket. She pulled a cigarette out of the pack with her lips, then offered the john one of his own smokes. He accepted with touching gratitude. Cigarette still dangling unlit from her lips, she punched the bartender on the bicep to get his attention. When he turned impatiently toward her, she held the pack out to him. He took one too. Then she offered one to Nesselrode and me. *About time to conform to an American stereotype.*

"*Nein, danke.*" I got that out without too much trouble. Nesselrode picked up the hint and said the same thing.

"Tell them we'll wait outside until the police come," I instructed Nesselrode as the blonde lit her cigarette and passed the lighter around.

I assume that's what Nesselrode said, because none of them batted an eye when we headed downstairs. We could probably have found a cozy corner of the bar area for the chat I wanted to have—the patrons downstairs had all prudently decamped—but we went all the way outside anyway and parked our backs against the windows to the right of the door. I flicked my eyes to look at Nesselrode without turning my head.

"The bartender knows your name, right?"

"Yes," Nesselrode said. "So do the police."

"I left word at the hotel about where you could find me, and I look so American I might as well have 'YANK' stamped across my face in Day-Glo. So it wouldn't take the cops long to figure out that I was the one here with you tonight even if you didn't tell them—which you'll pretty much have to do."

"Pretty much."

"So we both wait," I said. I could already hear an apologetic little siren only a few blocks away.

"Absolutely right. What is it that you insurance people call it when someone chokes himself to death while he's beating his meat to computer porn?"

"'Auto-erotic misadventure.'"

"Think they'll buy that?"

"Not a chance in hell."

"I have to agree." Nesselrode glanced to his right as the sound of the siren drew nearer. "So we'd better get our story straight."

"Simple. The truth. The absolute truth. No way we pass ourselves off as a couple of horny Rotarians who stumbled into this place looking for a little action. I came to Vienna to work with Transoxana Insurance Company's Austrian branch on investigation of a forged painting claim. You dug up the name of someone who might be able to help. We came here to meet him. Unfortunately, someone else met him first."

"Yes, that'll have to do. Let's go back inside."

We did. The other three, plus the woman who had briefly come out from under the staircase to try her luck with us, were gathered in a smoky group at the far end of the bar, as distant from the door as they could get. Nesselrode and I sat down at the table where we'd been killing time when all the excitement started. I could hear the low-key siren right outside the door now. Green and white light blinked through the windows.

"Absolute truth," I whispered to Nesselrode.

"Absolute truth."

It took less than fifteen minutes for one of the two cops who'd come to get to me. This one spoke English. After he'd copied down every scrap of information from my passport, he turned a page in his notebook and glanced up at me.

"Did you know the dead man?"

"Never saw him before in my life."

The First Thursday in April

Chapter Seventeen

CYNTHIA JAKUBEK

"One hundred forty-five k."

The number sat there on my computer screen over the initials PVS—the first email I'd opened after hitting my desk at 7:55 a.m. PVS meant Shifcos, but she'd sent it from büro1263@ troxwien.aus instead of the email address I remembered for her. So she'd used a company computer at Transoxana's Vienna office instead of her own laptop. That meant she was gallivanting around Austria, presumably looking for a cheaper version of the bill of sale Willy was peddling.

The thing had hit my computer a little after ten o'clock last night, so she must have sent it at the crack of dawn her time. I'd sized her up as a pretty good negotiator—good enough to know you don't want to seem too anxious to make a deal. Something must have happened yesterday to make getting her hands on Willy's piece of paper urgent enough to trump that axiom.

I was suddenly so hot to move on this thing I could barely keep my butt parked on my desk chair. Speed-dialing Willy got me voice-mail. I left a message.

"Almost a hundred-and-a-half on the table now. My gut says there's more where that came from. We need to talk in a big hurry."

I trudged through my other emails while I waited impatiently for a call-back. Nothing from Sean or Abbey or Tally. One email about "hot Russian babe want big American man." I turned to other work while I waited for Willy.

I'd gotten a handwritten letter yesterday from a client whose case I was handling on the taxpayers' tab. Appointed-counsel work in criminal cases generated twenty percent of my billings. The chap who'd written the letter was doing sixty-seven months for convincing people they could pay their taxes with "Citizen Warrants of Credit," which he provided over the net for a modest deposit in his PayPal account. Someone had to handle his appeal. I'd gotten the gig.

The letter had comments on the draft brief I'd sent him for review. He couldn't understand why I'd missed the key points. He was a Sovereign Citizen/Free-Born Man of the Soil, not subject to the jurisdiction of any court! He had never accepted the benefit and protection of U.S. law! Plus, the Internet was *NOT* the U.S. Mail, so no mail fraud! And he was strictly a Wi-Fi type, so no wire fraud either! Wi-Fi doesn't use wires! That's the *whole point* of Wi-Fi! This was all *OBVIOUS!* I would please insert these points into the brief *IMMEDIATELY!*

I spent sixteen minutes dictating a letter thanking him for his input and advising him that his contentions would not find their way into the brief that I'd file later in the week. Every penny I charged for that three-tenths of a billable hour (rounded up) came out of your pockets. I deeply appreciate it and, anyway, it's a small price to pay for freedom.

The letter might have spilled over into another tenth of an hour, but the phone rang. Willy's land-line. YESSS!

"Willy?"

"No, this is Amber. Amber Gris. We met when Willy had you over for dinner after that pissing match with the condo association."

Ah, yes. The first case Willy brought to me, nine months ago. I remembered Amber as a buxom redhead with a megawatt smile, an adoring gaze for Willy, and polite interest for everyone else.

"Right. I remember. What can I do for you, Amber?"

"Willy has a question for you. He's going to call you in, let's see, wait a minute…a little over an hour…ten o'clock our time, I guess. Unless it's eleven. No, I'm pretty sure ten. It's a time-zone thing. Anyway, he told me to give you a head's up about the question."

"Okay. What's the question?"

"He bought some cigars. And they're like *Cuban* cigars. But he didn't *buy* them in Cuba. He bought them, like, somewhere else. Legally. From a shop and everything, not on the street somewhere. So he wants to know is it, like, a prison thing if he brings them back into the country with him?"

"Got it. Do you know where he bought them?"

"Not for sure on that. Not Italy 'cause he's flying *to* Italy right now. That's why he can't call you himself yet. 'Cause he's, like, in the air. He just said this thing for me to call you about while we were on the phone about other stuff."

"Okay, Amber. Thanks. I'll be ready with an answer when Willy calls me."

Hmm. Yesterday, when something pretty dramatic had apparently adjusted Shifcos' attitude, Willy had been spreading Willyisms someplace within two or three hours' flying time of Rome. Lots of places qualify, but my guess was that Willy had been breathing the same Danube-scented air as Shifcos. Could be coincidence, I guess. Sure it could.

Willy had never technically been indicted. He had come uncomfortably close about four months ago. I'd had to work my ass off to keep that one from happening, doing work that IMHO the U.S. Attorney should have done for himself. If Willy had ever killed anyone he hadn't shared that with me, although he had mentioned unpleasant dealings with, as he'd put it, "a shylock who needed killin'. But that was almost thirty years ago." Right, so it hardly counts. So, bottom line, betting on Willy in the middle of a mess involving money wouldn't exactly qualify as a low-percentage play.

I spent ten quick minutes brushing up on the Trading with the Enemy Act. I did that just to be safe. I didn't think the upcoming call would have much to do with Commie tobacco.

Chapter Eighteen

Jay Davidovich

Rachel always scolds me about ethnic stereotypes but, excuse me, Germans make *really* good cops. German Germans, Swiss Germans, and Austrian Germans. By the fourth hour of my interrogation—excuse me, my *interview*—by Hauptman-Inspector Schumacher and a buddy of his whose name I didn't bother to remember, the Vienna constabulary had really moved the ball on the Ertel homicide. It had established that Ertel had walked alive and well into the happy room at that sleazy dive sometime between eight and eight-thirty last night. Even better, they had established through independent witnesses where Nesselrode and I were literally every minute of the time between then and when our merry little group found the body—including the time we were on the subway.

So it followed that neither Nesselrode nor I had killed the little weasel. Going to see him that night made us interesting people, but we weren't killers. Aiders and abettors, co-conspirators, material witnesses—maybe. Killers—no.

"Don't worry, we don't use water-boarding here." Schumacher used that knee-slapper to begin the interview that he insisted wasn't an interrogation.

I did *not* come back with a smart-ass crack or a little snappy banter. Didn't come back with anything at all. Just sat there in a ladder-back chair at a metal table in a small room that looked like the set designer for *Law and Order SVU* had decorated it. Hardest thing in the world to teach people about being questioned: if you're being *questioned*, wait for a question; if you wait long enough, sooner or later the interviewer/interrogator/asshole will ask a question.

Schumacher asked plenty and I answered them all with the unvarnished truth except for the ones where I lied through my teeth. The whole forgery claim/real painting claim/possible deal to finesse insurance exposure thing—I'd put that on the table without an ounce of spin.

"And you believed this story Herr Nesselrode told you?"

"Not without checking it out I didn't."

"And that's why you went to the cat house—to 'check it out'?"

"Yes."

"Are you an art expert?"

"No."

"Then how did you intend to 'check it out'?"

"One step at a time. First, meet the source. Second, see the supposed original. Third, report. Fourth, wait for instructions."

This went on for quite awhile, until about three in the afternoon, when someone in a uniform knocked on the door and handed Schumacher's buddy a piece of paper, which the buddy passed on to Schumacher. My guess? The message reported on my movements the night before, and matched up with what I'd already told him. When he got back to business with me he suddenly seemed a little bored, like a cardiologist does five minutes into a stress test if only normal numbers turn up. He started running down a list of names and asking me if I recognized any of them. That's generally the last thing you cover in a squeal room.

I answered "No" over a dozen times as he threw out names I'd never heard. I sensed from the finality in his tone that we were approaching the end of the list.

"Frau Alma von Leuthen."

"No."

"Father Herman Utica."

I glanced up sharply.

"What?"

"Father Herman Utica. Catholic priest. Do you know him?"

"Yes. He's the rector at a seminary in the United States. I talked with him on an unrelated case that I was working on before I was called into the *Eros Rising* matter."

"Where in the United States?"

"Albuquerque, New Mexico."

"Which is it, U.S. or Mexico?"

"U.S. New Mexico is a U.S. state. Part of the territory we got from Mexico in the 1840s as part of our Manifest Destiny policy."

"'Manifest Destiny?' What policy is that?"

"'We'll buy it if we can, and take it if we have to.'"

"And why do you say it is unrelated?"

"I don't know of any connection. That was a computer hacking case. Three decades of old data destroyed. It'll take over a year to reconstruct. Very expensive, and my employer will be paying the bills."

"Ah. Thank you." Schumacher made a fussy little note on an unlined leaf in the vinyl-bound notebook he'd been using during our chat.

"What does that have to do with Ertel?" I asked.

Stupid question, but give me credit for trying. For the first time since his opening salvo about water-boarding, Schumacher smiled at me. A condescending, bureaucratic smile. Then he stood up and held out his hand.

"Thank you very much, Mr. Davidovich. You have been very helpful." As we shook hands, he glanced over his shoulder at his colleague. "Return Mr. Davidovich's passport."

Chapter Nineteen

Cynthia Jakubek

"Hunnert-forty-five, huh? Whadda you figure the ceiling is?"

"I'm guessing one-sixty." I drew a small, three-dimensional sketch of a house in the margin of the legal pad on my desk. "She expects us to come back at one-seventy-five. She'll move to one-fifty. We'll both posture a bit, then she'll go to one-sixty like she's doing us this tremendous favor."

"Prob'ly right. See if you can get it done at one-sixty-five. That'll be one-fifty net of what we've already got in the bank."

"Will do. When are you back in the states?"

"Tonight, but jet-lagged and horny—tough combination. I'll probably be worth something sometime tomorrow morning. Now, what about the cigars?"

"Bottom line, it's against the law. Best case if they catch you, they confiscate the cigars. Next best, they confiscate the cigars plus fine you four times their value. Worst case, they threaten you with a criminal prosecution to try to squeeze some dope out of you on someone they really care about."

"Worst case would be bad. How about if I put the cohibas into a box of Upmanns from a duty-free shop?"

"I'm the wrong one to come to for advice on smuggling tobacco, Willy. I couldn't even smuggle cigarettes past my mom. By the way, did anything major go down in Vienna yesterday?

I'm wondering what spooked Transoxana into fast-tracking the negotiations all of a sudden."

"Probably just got sick of drilling dry holes looking for what I'm trying to sell 'em. Gotta go. Catch you stateside in a coupla days."

As I hung up I started parsing the sentence that preceded Willy's brushoff. I kept on parsing it while I whipped out my quick reply to Shifcos:

> Your counter-offer is a substantial and construc-
> tive step in our negotiations and we appreciate it.
> Instead of taking baby steps, my client has autho-
> rized me to go to $180,000 in the hope that we
> can get this done without wasting time. Let's get to
> YES.
>
> Regards,
> Jakubek

My analysis of Willy's answer reached its climax as I sent that missive into cyber-space. I'd asked whether something big had happened in Vienna, and Willy had told me a lot. That he had indeed been in Vienna. That he'd known Transoxana was up to something there. That what it was up to had something to do with Willy hustling an old bill of sale. What he hadn't told me was *No*.

Chapter Twenty
Jay Davidovich

"They returned my passport and then showed me the door."

I gave Proxy that report by phone about five seconds after reaching the sidewalk outside the Vienna *Politzei Unterprefaktur Zwei*. I figured she'd want the news in a hurry. I was right. She'd answered on the first note of her ringtone.

"So far, so good then," she said. "Anything about enjoying Vienna's attractions for a few more days in case they'd like some more help with their inquiries?"

"Just the opposite." I looked up and down the street for a cab without seeing one. "More like, 'Here's your hat, the door's right there.'"

"Maybe we should take the hint. I'm back at the hotel, but there's still time for me to get someone working on a flight sometime tonight."

"Before they change their mind, you mean."

"That's what I mean."

"Negative, if I have a vote." I was beginning to think I'd walk all the way back to the hotel before I spotted a cab or stumbled over a subway station. "A name came up at the tail end of our chat. It ties this circus into the computer-hacking thing I was looking into in New Mexico."

"I don't want to sound flippant," Proxy said, as if that would have set some kind of precedent, "but so what?"

"I'm the common denominator. Seems to call for some follow-up."

"How do you plan to follow that up in Vienna?"

"By tracking down Nesselrode." Still not a cab in sight.

"Easily done. He's sitting right here, and he's as anxious to talk to you as you are to him."

"You're kidding."

"I'm not kidding."

"She's not kidding." Nesselrode's voice. "How fast can you get back to the hotel?"

"Hell if I know. Apparently every cabbie in Vienna is on vacation."

"Kittens, drunks, and Americans," Nesselrode muttered. "God looks out for you—and you make it a full-time job for him. Listen. At the end of the block across the street from the police station you should see a café kind of place, little basement thing. See it?"

"Let's see…Esterhazy something?"

"Yes."

"Got it."

"I'll meet you there in twenty minutes." He was off the phone before I could say okay.

He made it with two minutes to spare. He looked like hell: hair hastily finger-combed, day-old growth of beard, bloodshot eyes, and a suit that looked like he'd slept in it, except not long enough. I probably didn't look much better, but at least I'd gotten a couple of hours of shuteye before my appointment with the cops. I let him sit down with a mug of nutmeg-scented coffee before I opened up on him.

"I'm working on my bachelor's degree in Abba Ertel. Educate me."

"A hood." Nesselrode shrugged. "Palestinian. Made his chops running errands for Hamas but he liked money even more than he hated Jews so he started doing freelance computer penetration against soft targets."

"He apparently branched out from there."

"They usually do."

"Who was his partner?" I shot that question out without warning, hoping to surprise him.

"What makes you think he had a partner?"

"Wild guess."

"You're right, he must have." Nesselrode took a big gulp of what I figured to be throat-scalding coffee. "It's not like he spent six years at the Sorbonne studying twentieth-century European art, is it? Had to be just an intermediary."

"But you don't know who he was working with or for?"

"No."

"Nuts."

My turn to sip coffee. *Damn this stuff is good.*

"So," Nesselrode said, "where does Transoxana go from here?"

"That's Proxy's department, but I'm betting that the whole painting swap finesse is dead now that it has a corpse's fingerprints on it. Company policy is to look for an exit when the body-count hits one."

"Sort of like your President Obama and Afghanistan."

"I'd say we did our bit in Afghanistan." I flared a little at his crack and didn't bother to hide it.

"Sorry, shouldn't have said that." He turned his profile to me, then swung back around, slapped his palms on the table, and looked me in the eye. "Who do you think killed him?"

"Don't know. Not you and not me. I smelled cigarette smoke in the room, so we can probably rule Proxy out. Not Osama bin Laden because my President Obama greased him a few years ago. After that I'd say it's wide open."

"A falling-out among thieves, possibly." Nesselrode muttered this as if he were just thinking out loud. "Or maybe he hacked the wrong target and it caught up with him."

Yeah. Or maybe he annoyed a stateside hustler with his eyes on a nice payday and learned about the New Jersey version of alternative dispute resolution.

"Let's go." Nesselrode stood up abruptly. "I'll drive you back to the hotel. Pay the bill."

By the time I'd crammed myself into the cream-colored VW he'd parked a block away from the café, Nesselrode had already taken a hit from a brandy flask stashed there. The way he drove on our way to the hotel would make the average New York cab-driver look like a pussy with a PhD in Driver Education.

"Hitler won." He said this to the windshield, one mile and two more brandy hits into our trip. "He didn't kill all the Jews. But he destroyed European Jewry. The most dynamic engine of culture and civilization that ever existed. The Renaissance and the Enlightenment were Rotary Club cocktail parties compared to the Jews in *Mittel Europa*. And that bastard wiped them out. Either killed them, or drove them to America or to Israel—neither of which, and I mean no offense, many people would mention in the same breath as culture."

"No offense taken. Except for HBO I only have basic cable, so my idea of culture is *Duck Dynasty*."

"You know what?" Red-faced, Nesselrode turned his head and half his body to glare at me as he repeated the slightly slurred words. "You know what? Fuck you."

"If that's an apology, it's accepted. If it's a proposition, the answer is no."

He started laughing. A little manic, a lot scary. He tossed the bottle to me. I caught it barely in time to keep brandy from slopping all over my lap. I let things sit right there until he started to pull to a jolting, tire-squealing stop in front of the hotel.

"I just remembered something," I said as I clambered out of the car. "A briefing I got said you'd never lived in Israel. I may suggest that they double-check that."

He leaned way over and strained his neck to look up at me with saucer-wide, red-rimmed eyes. His diction suddenly got crisp and clear.

"Dany Nesselrode has never lived in Israel."

Chapter Twenty-one

CYNTHIA JAKUBEK

We got the deal done at two in the afternoon my time, which meant that Shifcos was clocking some major overtime. We'd fenced a bit, mostly for pride's sake I think. Just before noon she'd written, "I need you to come off $170k," so I knew we had it made. All we were arguing about now was bragging rights.

I phoned Willy's number and left a message wishing him safe travels. For the next twenty-two minutes I piddled around with my brief on the hopeless appeal for my Free-Man-Born-of-the-Soil Sovereign Citizen client. While doing that I fantasized about beads of sweat popping out on Shifcos' well-sculpted WASP brow. Then I replied to her email:

> I've phoned my client. I can go to $168,500 for a
> deal today. I can't talk to him again until tomorrow
> at the earliest.
>
> Regards,
> Jakubek

Every statement in those three sentences was literally true. That took some work. I got Shifcos' reply three minutes later:

> Done at $168.5k gross, $153.5k net of $15k
> already paid. Other terms of your draft accepted.

Pls confirm, complete, and email duplicate original
w/electronic signature. Pick-up 10:00 a.m. local
time Monday. Your office or Pitt MCM? Pls advise.
Send wire transfer instructions for your trust
account. Payment to be completed within thirty
minutes after verification document is in hand.
   PVS

I responded that we'd deliver the document at my office and
gave her my trust account wiring instructions. Then I sat back
in my chair to bask for a minute or so in a warm, tingly feeling.
Negotiations are like those baseball games for eight-year-olds
where no one keeps score. You know whether you've accomplished your objective, but you don't know whether you've left
money on the table. In pure competitive terms, you don't know
whether you've won.

Except when you do. I'd won. I'd kicked her butt.

The First Friday in April

Chapter Twenty-two

CYNTHIA JAKUBEK

I was still in full bask at seven-thirty the next morning when Amber called. Not the sunny, ditzy Amber I was used to but a guarded, pouty Amber whose petulantly disappointed tone asked why people just couldn't be *nice*. Her words had an ominous thickness to them. First thing I wondered was whether Willy had gotten home cranky and slapped her around. I really hoped not, because I liked Willy and I didn't want to stop liking him.

"Okay," she said, "this is like a *strange* question. But Willy told me to ask you."

"Shoot."

"He said you'd told him a few months ago that he was legal owning a certain thing. He wants to know if you're for sure about that."

And he thinks his line might be tapped. And he might be right. I knew exactly what she was talking about.

"The answer is yes. I'm for sure about that."

"Good. Thanks." Click.

Okay.

The Second Monday in April

The Second Monday in April

Chapter Twenty-three

CYNTHIA JAKUBEK

The fifteen-hundred bucks a month I pay to the Law Offices of Luis Gonzales to sublease nine hundred square feet of space includes a receptionist/rent-a-cop at a raised, square desk in the sixth-floor lobby outside the much more impressive quarters where Luis G and the seventeen people who work for him do their stuff. At nine-fifty-eight on Monday the receptionist buzzed me to say that "some gentlemen" were there to see me.

I strode out expecting Davidovich and Rand. Half right. I saw Davidovich and Barry Akin, a Pittsburgh cop I'd last encountered the week before on the stand in municipal court. Davidovich looked like he'd just gotten back from deer camp, sporting what I took to be a high-end zippered hunting vest from the yuppie edition of an Eddie Bauer catalogue. Akin, in a blue blazer over an open-necked dress shirt, came a little closer to urban office-building standards.

In his left hand Davidovich toted a brushed-steel attaché case with recessed locks that must have weighed a ton and looked like it could shrug off a point-blank shot from anything short of a .357 magnum. Under the left armpit of his blazer, Akin was packing heat without being shy about it. So whatever happened in Vienna had made someone classify this morning's pick-up as hazardous duty. That probably explained why Rand hadn't joined the party. Frankly, I saw his point.

"Hey, Barry, how's it going?" I shook hands with both of them.
"Holding aces and eights with my back to the door, what else?"
"Well, we're about two thousand miles from Deadwood so you should be okay." Cops don't like lawyers, as a rule, but you can make it onto their not-a-total-asshole list if you understand cracks about the hand Wild Bill Hickock was holding when he got shot in the back during the last poker game he ever played.

I led them toward the heavy glass door to my office. What you see through the door isn't desks or chairs but waist-high area dividers made out of blond wood, with broad-leaved green plants on top of them. Cheap privacy until I can afford a bigger office with my own receptionist. I glanced over my left shoulder at Akin.

"You can ignore the statutory notice."

Six-by-eight inches, the framed sign at eye-level next to my office door is to let people know where I stand on the keep-and-bear-arms thing:

NO FIREARMS PERMITTED ON THESE PREMISES
DEFENSE DES FUSILS ET MITRAILETTES
ARMAS DE FUEGO PROHIBIDO
SCHUSSWAFFEN VERBOTEN

I'm not a gun wimp, but twenty-first century Pittsburgh isn't the Wild West—and there are plenty of other lawyers around for clients who think it is.

I led them to my desk and gestured toward the two guest chairs. My safe is just a bottom file drawer with a combination lock, so it didn't take me long to pull out Willy's very expensive piece of paper and the authenticating declaration. I set it on my blotter with the bottom toward Davidovich so that he could see the faded, elaborate signatures and the embossed notary seal. Then I put the receipt I'd drafted next to it. Davidovich leaned toward the bill of sale for a few seconds.

"Can I get three copies of that?"

"For what Transoxana is paying for this thing you can get thirty." I picked it up and turned toward the printer/copier parked beside my desk.

"On onion-skin."

"Seriously?"

"Those are my instructions." Davidovich shrugged as he unholstered his mobile phone.

"Can do." My turn to shrug.

It took me two minutes to come up with onion-skin paper for the copier. By the time I had the duplicates made Davidovich was slipping his phone back into the plastic holder on his belt. He nodded at me.

"The wire should be on the way."

"I'll get some coffee while we wait for confirmation of the payment."

Interesting current of tension in our little group while we sipped Hill's Brothers from china mugs. (I don't do Starbucks and I don't do paper cups.) If this deal didn't fall apart in the next few minutes, I'd send Willy a bill at the end of the month and he'd pay it. That payment would guarantee that, sometime next month, I'd be able to pull the largest draw I would have allowed myself so far during my solo practice adventure. I had three thousand in mind. If I managed to pay myself three thousand a month for the next year, I'd be making about fifteen percent of what Calder & Bull would have paid me. Of course, I planned on making a lot more down the road. But that wasn't really the point. The point was that nothing I'd do for a quarter-million a year at C&B would generate anything remotely like the rush surging through me right this second.

About seven minutes into our chat, my computer pinged to tell me I had mail. I glanced at my inbox screen. Mellon Bank thought there was something I should know. One mouse-click gave me the news: Confirming deposit of $153,349.50 into the trust account of Cynthia Jakubek, Attorney at Law, net of the bank's tenth of a point for the trouble. Banks, like bookies, always get their piece.

"Okay. Transoxana just bought itself a piece of paper. Congratulations."

"Thanks."

Davidovich leaned forward, signed the receipt acknowledging that he'd gotten the document on today's date, and handed it to me. Then, balancing the attaché case on his knees, he snapped it open and took out two large brown envelopes, one with a white adhesive tag marked ORIGINAL and the other with a tag marked COPIES. He put the original of the bill of sale in the first envelope and the copies in the second. I guess insurance guys like to do it by the book. Closed the attaché case and snapped it shut, with substantial-sounding locks clicking into place.

"One more thing," Davidovich said. "Men's room. 'Cause that was really good coffee."

From my bottom drawer I fished out a key on a ring attached to a long, Lucite rectangle.

"To your left out the door, little corridor about fifteen feet down."

"Got it. Oh, you don't validate parking tickets do you?"

I almost laughed out loud. He'd just dropped a hundred-and-a-half-and-change on me and he was sweating a six-dollar parking fee.

"Sorry. Only for clients."

I figured I had at least five minutes before he and Akin waltzed back with the key, so I called Willy and left the good news on his voice-mail. The likable little hustler had pulled off another one.

Chapter Twenty-four

JAY DAVIDOVICH

Ten feet or so down the sidewalk, Akin and I climbed into an illegally parked white Ford Crown Victoria with police department license plates. No ticket, of course—not that either Akin or I would have paid it if there had been.

"So," he said as he pulled into the street, "we deliver the document and you go kill some ducks, right?"

"Travel vest," I said, picking up the josh about my North Slope insulated outerwear. "Has a separate pouch for anything you might have in your pockets, plus your belt and mobile phone. Stuff whatever you're carrying into it as you approach airport security, drop it into a bin with your shoes, and you're ready for the scanner in five seconds flat. Once you're through, slip back into your loafers, pick up the vest, and before you know it you're halfway to the bar, passing two sales reps and a lawyer still digging car keys out of plastic bowls on the way."

"Travel vest." Akin slapped the heel of his right hand on the steering wheel and shook his head. "Shoulda thought of that. Coulda made a million bucks."

"Maybe next time."

"By the way, what was that bullshit about validating your parking ticket?" Akin's eyes moved constantly, in a steady survey of everything around us. Cops' eyes do that a lot, except on TV.

"Jakubek is going to call her client to tell him how things went. If he happens to fish for dope about how we're getting to the Pitt MCM and she happens to drop a hint or two, I'd rather have him looking for us at the exit from the parking ramp than here."

"She's actually not bad for a lawyer—especially a lawyer in a skirt. You think she's bent?"

"No, I don't." *What I think is that her client was in Vienna when a guy with a different agenda got dead.* "But stuff happens."

Our drive would cover less than a mile. I almost felt sheepish about not walking, but loss-prevention specialists don't get paid to tempt fate. The State Department's Embassy Security Directorate has produced studies showing that you're actually more vulnerable to an ambush if you're in a car than if you're on foot. Well, I've been ambushed on foot and I've been ambushed in a car, and I'd rather be in a car.

We made it to the Museum without incident. Akin parked his Crown Vic directly under a sign saying NO PARKING HERE TO CORNER. At least it wasn't a handicap spot. We saw Rand waiting for us at the reception desk as we walked in the front door. All smiles and not quite as blasé as at our first meeting. Kind of peppy, in fact, with a little bounce to his step.

"We'll do the handoff in Ms. Huggens' office," he said as he led us toward a dimly lighted corridor on the opposite side of the reception area from the one that led to the conference room. "You'll want her to sign the receipt, and it will go faster there than assembling in the conference room and calling her down."

I shrugged. I didn't care if we did it in the employee lounge, as long as we got it done.

The corridor led to an inconspicuous elevator clearly not designed for use by busloads of school kids on field trips. Small, but sleek and freshly spruced up, with a tasteful STAFF ONLY PLEASE sign just above the call buttons. After we all got in, Rand flashed a card at a black screen and touched 4 on the digital keypad that appeared.

We'd made about a floor-and-a-half when the lights went out.

Metal-shearing screech punctuating the sudden darkness. Abrupt CLANG! that made my ears ring. I pitched toward the door as Newton's Second Law of Motion did its thing. Judging from the grunts and expletives around me in the inky blackness, the other two had the same kind of experience. A blinding light from just above the ceiling immediately hit us with what felt like physical force. I threw my left forearm across my stinging eyes to shield them from the fiercely painful beam.

I sensed rather than saw Akin reaching under his blazer toward his left armpit. "DON'T!" was just about to spurt from my throat when I heard a sound sort of like an air-wrench makes when a grease-monkey uses it to unfasten lug nuts. A high-pitched *WHINE-pfft* kind of thing. Akin let out a short, strangled scream and slammed backward to the floor, arms and legs flailing spastically.

Tasered. Shit. This was damned serious.

I dropped to one knee to check him out. A voice from behind the light stopped me cold.

"Freeze! Or you'll get one too."

I froze.

"Give the case and the keys to gramps so he can hand it up here." Whoever gave these orders had done something to distort his voice.

"Okay." It took every particle of will I could muster to keep my voice calm.

"DO IT! DO IT RIGHT FUCKING NOW! DON'T FUCK WITH ME!"

"I'm doing it. I'm sliding the case across the floor to Rand." Unhurried, no-drama voice. The guy could see me doing exactly what I said I was doing, but a soothing narrative can supposedly calm down someone in a confrontation. "The keys to the case are in my right trouser pocket. I'm going to reach into that pocket with my right hand."

"JUST DO IT!"

"I'm doing it. I'm taking the keys out. I'm going to transfer them to my left hand, and then give them to Rand." You carefully explain everything you do in a situation like this. At all costs you want to avoid surprising the guy.

I passed the keys, first to my left hand and then to Rand. I did it slowly and none too smoothly, expecting any second to get jolted with a Taser-slug worth of juice that would lay me on the floor next to Akin and play hell with my central nervous system in the process.

"Okay, gramps," the voice said, "now stick one of the keys in the lock."

Rand managed that. I wouldn't have blamed him if he'd fumbled a bit, but he got a key in on the first try.

"Now stand up and push the far end into the black space around the light."

Rand made it to his feet. A little shaky, and who wouldn't be? His hands slipped awkwardly around the case as he braced it against his chest and then finally got it moving toward the opening. I held my breath. The far end of the case disappeared. Then someone out of sight grabbed it and pulled it free of Rand's grip. A couple of seconds later I heard the locks snap.

I couldn't stop the thought going through my head as I imagined the guy checking the case's contents. *One second to reach Akin's gun. Two seconds to pull it from its holster. One second to raise it and start firing through that opening. Unless Akin had the safety on—which he probably would because he's a cop and cops obey the rules on gun-stuff. So add half-a-second to find the safety and click it off.*

I heard paper tearing. The bad guy was opening one of the envelopes. Probably a two-handed job. Couldn't be doing that and paying a lot of attention to us at the same time.

Without moving my head, I shifted my eyes down and to my right at the bulge under Akin's blazer. Five seconds. Suppose I did some nifty little shoulder roll thing. Could the guy glimpse my movement, grab the Taser, aim at me, and puncture my hide with a couple of mega-watt prongs in less than five seconds?

Yeah, he sure as hell could. I sighed. Dumb question. Dumb, *dumb* question. Academic to boot. You have to go with your gut, and thinking about something like that is your gut saying no. The light snapped off. Blackness surrounded us again. Hissing sound, thud on the floor, gas smell. *Please be tear gas and not something worse.* The ceiling panel slapped back into place.

Cursing under my breath, I fought the urge to squeeze my eyes shut. The sergeant who trained my National Guard unit had insisted that if you could keep your eyes open during the first five seconds of exposure to tear gas, a film would form over the pupils, protecting them from the gas. Guess a West Pointer came up with that one. Hadn't worked in training, but what did I have to lose?

Jumping straight up I punched as hard as I could at my best guess about where the loose ceiling panel was. Busted my knuckles doing it, but the son of a bitch moved. Not out of the way, just up half an inch at one edge and then back into place—but it moved. So the presumably escaping bad guy had something on top of it but he hadn't re-secured it.

I heard ragged, scary coughs and realized that a third of them were coming from me. I wouldn't call my next idea inspired, exactly, but it sure beat what came in second, which was nothing. Backed off to the far corner of the elevator car as the gas cloud floated thickly toward the ceiling. One springing diagonal stride forward on my left foot, then a leap, kicking my right foot out and up while throwing my head and shoulders back, like I was trying to do a bicycle kick in a soccer match. Smashed the ceiling panel with the ball of my right foot. Hoped the *crack!* I heard was the panel and not one of the bones in my foot, because from the searing pain running through my instep and up my shin it sure could have been.

I felt something substantial hit my leg as my shoulders crashed into the floor. The sudden updraft sucking gas out of the car meant the something was a chunk of the ceiling panel. A clanging alarm bell started insistently ringing. A muffled voice over a speaker somewhere in the elevator asked what our emergency was. Rand started coughing a response. I decided to leave that to him. At the moment, hurting in at least three places and getting ready to retch my guts up struck me as a full-time job.

I lay there on the floor, grateful for the pure air that started to circulate as the draft pulled tear gas up the elevator shaft. Still in the dark. At least eighty percent blind even if we'd had light to see anything by. Throbbing pain in my knuckles, shoulders, and foot. At least one serious casualty in the form of off-duty police officer Barry Akin. Missing one brushed steel attaché case. But at least we had help on the way, so lying there on the floor struck me as a Grade A strategy.

Did I think about hoisting myself up into the elevator shaft to go after the escaping bad guy? I did not. In the first place, he had at least a forty-five-second head start, so he'd have to be the Stephen Hawking of thugs not to be well away by now. In the second place, I had him right where I wanted him. Or thought I did.

Chapter Twenty-five

JAY DAVIDOVICH

From the time the alarm sounded, it took the fire department and Museum security between them thirty-seven blessed minutes to get us out of that elevator and onto the second floor. Akin first, obviously, and off to the hospital for observation. Rand next, pale and shaken, but not bad for a late-forties/early-fifties guy who'd just left his breakfast on the floor of a disabled elevator.

I came last. The first thing I saw on the floor outside the elevator shaft was the attaché case, open and empty except for the concealed tracking device that was now about as useful as Robert's Rules of Order in a knife fight. Best laid plans *et cetera*. Shit. I turned toward the first person in uniform that I saw.

"Where did you find the case?"

"In the shaft. That's what the perp used to block the ceiling panel."

"I guess it won't be much help tracking him down, then."

"We got the confetti. That should be enough."

I gave her a blank stare. (I'm pretty sure the officer was a she. Call it sixty-forty.) I made a *zoom* motion over my head with my right hand.

"When someone fires a Taser, it shoots out hundreds of tiny slips of paper with the particular gun's serial number on them. We can track the gun to the buyer. He'll say it was stolen and he didn't bother to report it, we'll point out that that's bullshit, and pretty soon he'll be singing like a drunk at a karaoke bar."

"Wow. Learn something new every day." I checked my watch: 11:02. "I know you'll want a statement, but I need to see the Museum's executive director sometime soon. We were headed for her office when this guy started playing Taser-tag with us. Do you want to do the statement before or after?"

"After. After you've been to the hospital. We need to get you looked at."

"Skip it. Just scrapes and bruises. The EMT's first aid was plenty."

"Suit yourself. It looks like Detective-Sergeant Lamarr is just finishing up with the older gentleman. I'm guessing you're next."

"Thanks."

A couple of minutes later Rand nodded at a plainclothesman and started to walk in my direction. Looked like he had some of his old piss and vinegar back. The detective gestured toward me. Just before passing Rand I caught his eyes.

"Maybe you could explain to Ms. Huggens about our being unavoidably delayed and suggest that we meet at eleven forty-five."

Rand stopped and turned an interesting expression toward me. Puzzled, which I'd call fair enough. But also a touch of *who the hell do you think you are?*

"Ms. Huggens is now chairing a meeting of the Acquisition/Deaccession Committee that began at eleven o'clock. It's likely to run well into the afternoon."

"Perhaps she could take a little recess at the first restroom break."

I didn't mention the cooperation clause in Transoxana's policy. C. Talbot Rand, Esquire, could probably have recited the thing from memory. If some judge someday said that Pitt MCM had forfeited coverage of a fifty-million dollar loss by copping an unconstructive attitude, no one was going to pin that on Tally Rand.

"I'll see what I can do."

Willy Szulz's name came up in my chat with Detective-Sergeant Lamarr, which told me that Rand had mentioned him. I gave Lamarr the whole story and I gave it to him straight. When a cop has been shot, you don't play coy with the officers investigating the incident. Let me amend that. I gave him the whole story except for my suspicion that Szulz had visited Vienna recently. Lamarr didn't ask about that part, and I didn't tell.

I had to cool my heels for awhile after Lamarr had finished with me Eventually, though, Rand came back for me and led me to his office. His office, not Huggens', but Huggens was waiting there for us. Not much Charming Hostess in her expression, and as soon as she said, "Good morning, Mr. Davidovich," I knew right where I stood. She said it with the kind of for-the-record politeness that chicks use when they're pissed off at you for no reason that a guy would understand. As far as she was concerned, I was supposed to deliver critical documentation to help save the Museum's prize holding, and I'd shown up empty-handed.

"Good morning." I smiled blandly at her.

"On behalf of the Museum, I apologize for your unpleasant experience this morning. I can assure you that we will conduct a full investigation of our own, as well as cooperating with the police."

Unpleasant experience? Seriously? Rachel saying, "Not tonight, Hot Pants, I've already had my bath" is an "unpleasant experience." I'd put this morning's adventure on a different level, somehow.

"In loss-prevention, that's sometimes the way the game is played. Please don't think another thing about it."

"Thank you. Is there anything further we have to discuss?"

"Well, there's the document that Transoxana bought for you."

I slipped off my travel vest, unzipped a long pocket inside the back of the thing, and pulled out the bill of sale and authenticating affidavit that Jakubek had turned over to me. In the men's room before leaving her building, I had taken the thing out of the attaché case, folded it once lengthwise, and stashed it in that pocket, along with one of the copies I'd had Jakubek make.

Then I'd attached one of the other onion-skin copies to a phony authentication that I'd tricked up using Rachel's notary sealer to make an embossed stamp on the signature I'd forged. I'd tacked on a red wax thingie from her corporation minute book kit, just to enhance the illusion that some self-important European *notaire* had spent all morning fussing with it. It wouldn't have stood up for more than three minutes to a careful examination. Your average snatch-and-grab, though, involves something closer to three seconds than three minutes.

"So the thief got a fake?" Huggens had the grace to seem dumbfounded and ambivalently pleased at the same time.

"Yep. Oldest trick in the book." I took out a receipt attached to the last copy Jakubek had made for me. "Please date and sign on the line at the bottom. No need for a notary. Mr. Rand will be happy to witness your signature, and I'm sure that no one would question his word."

"So you've managed to throw this thing in our laps after all, and the clock is now ticking."

"That's one way to put it." I handed her a pen.

She favored me with a game smile as she accepted the pen and bent over Rand's desk to execute the receipt.

"Well played, Mr. Davidovich."

I couldn't help wondering whether she'd said the same thing to the cox of the St. Paul's boat crew after his shell came in ahead of Groton's when she was seventeen. Except I'll bet his name didn't have a "vich" in it.

Chapter Twenty-six

CYNTHIA JAKUBEK

"Lemme get this straight." On your basic redness scale, Willy's face had gone past fire-engine and was careening toward candy-apple. "If I *hadn't* reported the theft, that would prove the gun wasn't really stolen and I was the perp. But because Amber *did* report the theft three days *before* the paper grab, *that* proves the gun wasn't really stolen and the report was just part of my clever plan."

"Dial it back a couple of clicks, buddy." I said this to Willy, but mostly for the benefit of Detective-Lieutenant Rod Plichta. It was seven hours since I'd turned the bill of sale over to Davidovich, and I suddenly found myself in the middle of an unplanned house call at Willy's condo. I'd gotten there fifteen minutes after the police had, and that took some doing.

"'Dial it back?' Did you see that split lip the burglar gave Amber when she surprised him? Amber, show them your face again."

"Save it, Szulz." I could read on Plichta's mahogany face that he'd seen phony indignant histrionics before, from guys who were just as guilty as hell. "Your Taser shot a cop, the burglary is way too convenient, and for all we know you could have busted the girl's face yourself. You're in shit up to your eyebrows."

I got two good handfuls of Willy's coat and shirt and held on for all I was worth. One thing Willy didn't need right now was a rap for assaulting an officer. He was just about to shake me off when Amber jumped in, God bless her.

"No. Willy has *never* hit me. Except, you know, little love-slaps in fun, during five-play."

"WHAT?"

Plichta's bleat suggested genuine astonishment. I couldn't blame him. Amber blushed like a tween who'd let a cussword slip out in front of mom.

"Willy says that what we do is *way* more than foreplay." She bobbed her head earnestly. "So he calls it five-play."

Plichta spun on the ball of his foot and took a couple of steps away from us, muttering something about how he could have been a bouncer at a casino but *nooo*, he had to pick police work.

"Okay." I let go of Willy and spoke to the back of Plichta's head. "You've tossed the place like a rock band in the middle of a groupie-strike. You haven't found a Taser. You haven't found anything else listed on your search warrant. Mr. Szulz has answered your questions. You have my card. If you think of anything else you'd like to ask him, give me a call and we'll set up an interview."

Plichta turned angry features in my direction. Now he was pissed off at me instead of Willy—which was the idea.

"We have enough to arrest him right now!"

"An arrest stops the conversation. He wants to help, but he won't say word-one in custody."

Plichta tapped his notebook three times on the tips of his right fingers. He nodded slightly and even managed a tight little smile.

"Maybe I'll take you up on that interview offer. Or maybe the next time I see your client the only conversation we'll have is me reading him his rights."

It took him and his colleagues five more minutes to clear out. They left a world-class mess and a volcanically fuming Willy Szulz behind them.

"Amber," I said, "what are the chances of getting some water over ice?"

"You got it." She sashayed toward the condo's kitchenette.

I sat down on a black leather footstool in front of a black leather recliner. Willy took the hint and dropped into the chair. He'd pulled out a handkerchief and now started mopping his face, muttering, "Goddamn fascists. It's like living in a third-world country." I just sat there, taking calm breaths, until he'd gotten it out of his system. Then I leaned forward and waited for him to look at me.

"Okay, Willy, listen up. I'm not one of those new-age lawyers. I don't lose sleep fretting over whether my clients might not technically qualify as plaster-cast saints. I'm old-school. I don't care who you are, what you did, or what you think. If you can pay my fee I'll take your case. But I need you to play straight with me."

Willy relaxed a little. Looked me straight in the eye. Gave me a hipster smile that said *Don't hustle a hustler.*

"I didn't do it."

"Good enough for me. Now tell me the rest. The whole story."

He didn't, of course. Clients never tell you the whole story even if they're trying to, and Willy wasn't. But he put a pretty good percentage of it on the table. I nodded from time to time. Didn't take any notes, just let his words flow into the Univac that God blessed me with for a memory.

"So anyway," he said, winding down, "I'm just through customs at Kennedy—no Commie cigars, by the way, thanks for that one—when I pick up a voice-mail from Amber about this burglar giving her a clop across the chops while he's making me for my Taser. I told her just to make absolutely sure with you that I was legal to have that thing, and if I was then she should report the burglary pronto."

"Did he take anything else?"

"Just some crap electronics to make it look good."

"Okay." I paused, took a deep breath. "This looks easy, then. Who knew you had a Taser except you, Amber, and me?"

He blushed. I swear on *Black's Law Dictionary* that he blushed. "A few people. I let my tongue flap about it."

"A few people such as…?"

"Well, the only one that matters is a guy whose name I don't know. He and his partner were the towel-hats who might have bought the bill of sale if you hadn't cut the deal you did with the Museum and the insurance company."

"How did your Taser come up in the conversation with them?"

"When I told him he was a day late and a dollar short and was prob'ly gonna be outbid, he starts making like the baddest ass in the camel-jockey hall of fame. So I said, 'Hit me with your best shot, A-Hab. I've got a Taser and in your honor I'll put bacon grease on the prongs.'"

"This conversation didn't by any wild chance take place in Vienna recently, did it?"

"Nah. It was just before I left for there."

I took a look around the condo. Nothing fancy or over the top except for a big-screen TV that looked like it wanted to be an IMAX when it grew up. Nice view of the Monongahela, but otherwise just your basic living quarters.

"You have a security system, right?"

"Sure. Pretty good one. But turning it on makes Amber nervous, so when I'm away she just relies on the deadbolt."

Maybe. Or maybe she'd seen you with this guy often enough that she let him in when he fed her some line about leaving something here for you. Maybe there were some things you didn't choose to share with your lawyer, Willy.

"Okay. You want to tell me what happened in Vienna?"

Willy's face sagged a little sheepishly. He fished out a pack of Marbs, remembered for once not to offer me one, and lit one for himself.

"Sorry, I shoulda told you about that. I would've, but I was on a mobile phone the last time we talked an' you know how it is—someone might be listening."

"Should've told me about what?"

"A-Hab's partner got caught short of breath with his pants down. Once in a lifetime experience for him. At least that's the way I heard it."

"Is this guy's name really Ahab, or are you just trying to get the PC police on you on top of everything else?"

"I dunno what his name is. I call all towel-hats A-Hab after this song from the sixties: 'A-Hab, the A-Rab/the sheik of the burning sands.'"

"Well, that explains that."

Willy grinned at me through a rich cloud of blue-gray smoke.

"I didn't do the guy in Vienna."

"Good. I'll add that to my list of crimes you haven't committed. Just in case it comes up, though, do you have anyone who can tell the police where you were the last night you were in Vienna?"

"Matter of fact I do. Karl von Leuthen. I was talking to him in his apartment around the time A-Hab's partner apparently bought the farm."

"How do you know the approximate time of death?"

"'Cause when von Leuthen told the Vienna cops what time we were together, they lost interest in me. At least that's his story. The message he left hinted that he might have some memory problems down the road."

"Shakedown?"

"Yep. And a shakedown like that only makes sense if he's a genuine alibi."

I spent about three seconds processing that. Damned if it didn't make sense, in a sleazy, underbelly-of-humanity kind of way. The next question was obvious:

"What did you want to see Karl von Leuthen about?"

"Nothin'. I wanted to see his mother, Alma. But she wasn't home."

"You wanted to see her about documentation for famous paintings?"

"Nope. I wanted to see her about something you and I can't talk about yet."

Chapter Twenty-seven

CYNTHIA JAKUBEK

Back in my office at six-thirty I read the list of proactive steps for Willy's case that I'd spent fifteen minutes jotting on a legal pad:

ALMA VON LEUTHEN?

TRANSOXANA/SHIFCOS/DAVIDOVICH?

Not much to show for three-tenths of a billable hour (rounded up).

Further effort, though, would have to wait. The time I'd spent holding Willy's hand during execution of the search warrant was ninety minutes that I'd planned on using to put the finishing touches on my Sovereign Citizen *et cetera* brief. I couldn't let anymore grass grow under my feet on that one, so my vision of stir-frying vegetables in my wok at home had pretty much evaporated. I needed food I could eat at my desk.

Downtown Pittsburgh offered a decent array of healthy options. And my scale this morning had insisted that I was two-point-eight pounds over my target weight. Screw it. I called for a pizza anyway.

I had the finish line for my brief in sight when the guard at the delivery entrance in the building's basement finally called to let me know that someone there had a pizza with my name on it. Clock-check: fifty-four minutes since my call. About time. Telling myself to deep-six the grumpiness, I headed for the elevator.

The man with his back to me standing at the guard desk seemed a little overdressed for a pizza delivery guy. Before I could draw any useful conclusions, he turned toward me—and I did a double-take right out of a seventies sit-com. Phillip Schuyler, assistant United States attorney for the Western District of Pennsylvania, offered me a sheepish grin and a medium, thin-crust cheese pizza.

"Mischievous impulse," he said. "I happened to see the delivery truck pull up as I was headed back to my place. I confirmed that it was for you and talked the driver into letting me take it the rest of the way."

I'd recovered a little by the end of his speech, but I was still a liter or so short of aplomb.

"You went to all that trouble just to talk to me? I mean, you could have phoned."

"The last time we talked you said that it wouldn't be fair to me for us to start seeing each other because you were in the first few months of starting your practice, you wouldn't have time for anything but your work and your clients for a while, and you'd end up treating me like crap, which I didn't deserve."

"That does sound familiar."

"Well, you were probably right." Tenderness and a charming timidity warmed his voice. "But I've had several months to think it over. I'm a big boy. I've been around the block. Walking into this with my eyes wide open, I'm willing to take the thorns with the rose."

I didn't need ten months to think that one over.

"Let's go up to my office. The guard is blushing."

Next thing I knew we were sitting on the carpet in front of my desk with the open pizza box between us. I practically had to get a court order to get him to take a slice of pizza for himself. His next words came around a gentlemanly nibble.

"So, how's the solo practice adventure going?"

"First nine months I lost money and lived on borrowed funds. Worked my rear end off, but mostly on client-development stuff that I couldn't bill. Next three months I basically broke even and took a little draw. Lot of work on spec or at a discount or for capped fees. I started my second fiscal year this month, and I'm actually going to make some money."

"Here's to success." He raised a plastic bottle of water that I'd scrounged.

"A relative term."

"You got that right. Why did you do it? Leave a top Wall Street firm paying you more than federal judges get, trade the bright lights of Manhattan for provincial Pittsburgh, give up work on billion-dollar securities cases for the kind of bread-and-butter stuff you can do here? I know Calder and Bull is a sweatshop, but you're probably working even more hours here than you did there. Why?"

"Hard to explain. Now or never kind of thing. Had a client offer me enough business to cover my rent because he liked me, and Calder and Bull had pissed him off. I wanted to help clients instead of just doing assignments for partners. Bottom line, I guess, I wanted to star in my own movie, even if it's a barebones indie flick, instead of work as an extra in a big-budget epic."

"'I'd rather be the first man here than the second man in Rome.'"

"Julius Caesar, right?"

"Yep."

"Who ended up catching a shiv from his fifteen closest friends."

"But you can't say he didn't get the point."

Settling back a little on my fanny, I dabbed cheese from the left corner of my mouth, where it had dribbled while I was laughing at Phil's line. I felt a happy, comfortable warmth flowing through me. How many months had passed since I'd just had fun like this? Not professional satisfaction, not winning a negotiation or a motion. Pure fun.

Too many.

I got a kick out of being pursued, having a good-looking guy with wispy, straw-colored hair and perpetually curious Alice-blue eyes compare me to a rose. A guy who could bat around allusions from ancient history. In New York, recreational sex is easier than smoking but real intimacy is as rare as a feminist rapper. And once I'd opened my own shop in Pittsburgh—forget it. By now I was as hungry as hell, and not for pizza. Our lips began moving toward each other.

The phone rang. Burred, actually, in a politely insistent way. Phil looked toward it.

"Should you get that?"

"Not a chance."

He didn't need any more than that. Shoving the pizza box across the rug, he reached me in one heroic knee scoot. Supporting my back with his right arm, he gave me a kiss like I hadn't had since the last presidential election. I kissed him right back. Clutched his shoulder and back with the arm I'd used to keep Willy from the cop. Let him know I meant it. We kissed through four rings and past the voice-mail beep.

He could have had me right then and there, rug burns and all. Off the pill for well over a year, no condom, I didn't care. I could tell he knew it. But he didn't take me. He pulled back from the kiss, breath coming in brief pants, eyes alive with fierce desire.

"I don't want to cheap this out. The first time we make love, I want us to do it right. I want you to feel as wonderful about it as I will."

What *I* wanted was to slap him and tell him not to do me any favors. He was probably right and I hated that. I didn't slap him.

"You're a gentleman," I whispered instead. "I'll take the thorns with the rose."

He smiled—and it's a good thing for him that he did.

Ten minutes later, after another deep kiss and an exchange of fanny pats, I closed my office door behind him, returned to my desk, and retrieved the voice-mail message.

"Hi, this is Abbey Northanger. Tally bit."

The Second Tuesday in April

The Second Tuesday in April

Chapter Twenty-eight

Jay Davidovich

"Look at that." I'd finished scanning the headlines so I clicked off my iPad. "Putin hasn't massed troops on Ukraine's border for two whole days now."

"It's great having a foreign policy expert in the family." Rachel murmured this without looking up from her own iPad. "But if they make you secretary of state and we have to move to Washington, I'll need a new dress."

"I only know three things about foreign policy: Israel has a right to exist, don't go to war by mistake, and Russians are assholes."

"Jews should know better than to traffic in ethnic stereotypes."

"Maybe—but don't pick a fight in an Irish bar."

"What's with the blood-is-thicker-than-water stuff all of a sudden?"

"Not sure, to tell you the truth."

Actually, I knew exactly where it was coming from. It was coming from Dany Nesselrode. Keeping a magnificent painting out of the hands of the Jewish family it rightfully belonged to (maybe) was a cultural tragedy, gnawing at his guts. For me it was business as usual, interfering with my enjoyment of the NCAA Basketball Tournament. That's why he'd cussed me out. That bothered me. So I chalked it up to displacement, or whatever the shrinks are calling it these days.

I put my left hand on Rachel's belly. I knew I didn't have much chance of feeling anything yet, but it just seemed right, somehow. Sitting here in the OB/GYN's waiting room like some regular guy who worked in an office and didn't encounter thugs and Tasers on the job. What would that be like, having a real office job? Ten-fifteen, time to grab some more coffee! Ooh, quarterly budget report due in three days—pressure-city, baby! No whiffs of electrically burned human flesh. No wondering whether I'd get iced before the tyke in Rachel's womb had his first Little League game or her first Suzuki recital.

A woman in nurse duds appeared at an internal doorway on the other side of the waiting room. She called Rachel's name. Planting an affectionate peck on my forehead as she rose, Rache strode off in response to the summons.

Just in time, because my mobile phone started to vibrate. Pittsburgh number. Shysterette? Yep. I stepped out into the elevator lobby to take the call.

"What's up?"

"You guys can't close your *Eros Rising* file until the Museum decides for sure that it won't return the thing, right?"

"Not my call, but that makes sense. Why?"

"I have a name you might want to check out. Alma Von Leuthen. She could have something to do with the excitement in Vienna just before we closed the deal."

I couldn't see playing dumb. After all, unless I missed my bet, her client had been there. I decided to ask a pertinent question instead.

"What can you tell me about Alma whoever?"

"Not much. Spent most of her life in Vienna. Probably late fifties, early sixties by now. Not clear where she is at the moment, except probably not Vienna."

"And what do you think she might contribute?"

"Maybe nothing. But if some kind of wheels-within-wheels thing is going on with that painting, the way her name came up makes me think she probably has her fingerprints on it somewhere."

"And just how *did* her name come up?"

"Can't tell you."

I mulled that over. *Some kind of wheels-within-wheels thing?* Yeah, that thought had crossed my mind, for sure. The snatch attempt on the elevator meant that Ertel's surviving chum, or Nesselrode, or Szulz, or somebody else wasn't going to give up just because we signed some papers. Plus, Nesselrode was Transoxana's collaborator and Szulz was shysterette's client, so we both still had skin in the game. Shysterette not telling me where she'd gotten this Alma character's name probably meant she'd gotten it from Szulz—and Szulz was a walking red flag.

"I'm guessing that you're calling me with this," I said, once my mull had run its course, "because you and Szulz don't have the wallet to do a proper work-up on Miss Alma, so you'd like Transoxana to do it for you."

"Pretty much."

"What's in it for us?"

"Oh, I don't know. Maybe after your adventure in the elevator there are some things you'd like to learn from people who value my good opinion."

Boy, that was subtle. No way around it, I liked the shysterette. Couldn't help it. Just did.

"Can you guarantee delivery on that?"

"Don't know yet. By the time you have the work-up done, though, I will."

"Okay, I'll run this up to the next level."

"All I ask. You have my number."

I called Proxy with the pitch.

"I'll have to give that some thought," she said.

Translation: *Only if it's on someone else's budget.* So twelve to five the answer was no. I shrugged.

Chapter Twenty-nine

CYNTHIA JAKUBEK

"He said he got the idea from you, Cindy." Abbey said this to Sean and me in Sean's personal office, which is only a little smaller than the floor space for my entire suite. "A hundred thousand up front and guaranteed, with the remainder vesting on the day Sean and I are married."

"Well, at least we know what he is." Sean favored us with an impish, tight-lipped smile. "Now we're just negotiating."

"No doubt about it." Abbey nodded. "He's a whore."

"He's not just a whore," I said. "He's a whore in a hurry."

That got me Sean's full attention.

"Why do you say that?"

"He's scarily close to proposing an explicit *quid pro quo*. He could be putting his license at risk—not to mention his job. He wouldn't be doing that this early unless he suddenly decided that time wasn't his friend anymore."

"Isn't that what we wanted?" Sean said. "Hasn't he fallen into our trap?"

"He's either fallen into our trap—or he's called our bluff." Looking from Sean to Abbey and back, I could tell that they both knew exactly what I meant.

"You're right." Sean's tone suggested more reluctance than I like to hear when I'm right. "So what are our options—other than just, uh—"

"Bending over and enjoying it," Abbey suggested, completing her prim lover's thought. "Yes, other than that one, because I don't like it very much."

"Option two," I said, "is I come on like Sister Mary Hardnose with a ruler. Send him a nastygram about how I have a duty to file a complaint with the bar unless he tells me that, on reflection, he realizes how inappropriate his proposal was. Best case, he responds with a *pro forma* denial but feels that he has to back the denial up by cooperating truthfully with the annulment process."

"What's worst case?" Sean's question.

"Worst case, he says that Abbey fabricated the whole thing, dares me to go to the bar with a complaint, and backs it up by turning his back on the annulment procedure for good."

"High risk/high reward." Sean's expression took on a sudden calmness as I imagined him absorbed in mental mini-max exercise. "How about Option 3?"

"We bluff right back."

"Love the sizzle." Abbey grinned. "What's the steak?"

"Give him an appointment to make his presentation about how he's worth four hundred thousand dollars. Suggest sometime late next week and see if he pushes hard to do it earlier. If he does, agree. Have him submit his CV. Hear him out, with a couple of colleagues who aren't tone-deaf."

"Get to the bluff part." That was Sean in no-nonsense mode, but I could tell from the gleam in his eyes that I had him hooked.

"Make some encouraging noises after he's finished. Tell him you'll get back to him promptly. Then, as things are breaking up, take him aside privately. Tell him you liked what you heard, but there's someone offering the same services for fifty thousand instead of four hundred. Suggest that he think things over and get back to you. You—not Abbey."

"Yes!" Sean's eyes lit up like a batter's when he spots a hanging curve. "Odds are he panics, comes back to Abbey with an explicit proposal, and we'll have him right by the, uh—"

"Throat," Abbey said sweetly.

The Second Wednesday in April

Chapter Thirty

Jay Davidovich

"Who just joined?" Proxy's question, right after a mellow tone sounded on the conference call line.

"Andy Schuetz." Andy and I get along fine. He joined Transoxana after mandatory retirement from the FBI. Still has some friends at the Bureau, and knows guys in Brooklyn who'd like to get off with community service if the subject ever comes up. Gets his calls returned, so it doesn't take him long to put together a dossier.

"Is that everybody?" I asked, ready to click off ESPN.com on the computer on my kitchen table.

"It'll have to do." I visualized Proxy glancing at the clock in the lower right corner of her computer screen at her office. "I have another meeting in twenty minutes."

"Okay. Alma von Leuthen." Andy cleared his throat. "Sixty-two years old. Austrian family that goes back to before the Thirty Years War. Had the 'von' from birth, but by the time she came on stage it didn't have much money attached to it anymore. Fine arts degree from Salzburg University. Married twice, widowed once, divorced once. Husbands were a concert pianist and a banker, in that order. Bounced around Europe a bit, but Vienna has always been home."

"She apparently started bouncing around again recently, according to Willy Szulz's lawyer," I said.

"Specifically, on the day this Ertel dude passed away." I distinctly heard pages in Andy's old-school spiral steno notebook riffling over the line. "Caught a flight for Geneva around three o'clock that afternoon."

"Suggestive," Proxy said.

"Suggests she didn't kill the guy." Andy sounded like a cop on a roll.

"But maybe knew about it before it happened." I threw that in just for luck.

"Because why?"

"Because otherwise it's a damned funny coincidence."

"I think you're ahead of the data curve, Jay," Proxy said. "But it's a provocative thought."

"So where is she now?" I asked.

"Don't know, except not Vienna and not Geneva. And wherever it is, I'm betting she didn't get there on a passport issued to Alma von Leuthen, because it's not showing up, and it should be."

Dong!

"Who just joined?" You had to have a delicately tuned ear to pick up Proxy's impatience at the late entry.

"Dan Quindel. Sorry I'm late."

"You get a pass since your department is footing the bill for Andy's work." Every piece of internal work at Transoxana gets charged to somebody's budget, and Proxy gets a real thrill when it's not hers.

"What have I missed?"

"I'm emailing you a recap right now," Proxy said. "We're just getting to the good part—I hope."

"Guess I have the floor again." Andy cleared his throat. "Frau von Leuthen has a bit of a rep. Known in certain circles as a notch-cutter."

"Meaning what? She's a slut?" That came from Quindel, so I relaxed while the inevitable Quindel/Andy "mine is bigger than yours" thing ran its course.

Andy: "More like a power groupie. A Pamela Harriman. Back in the early days of the space program, when the original seven astronauts were training at Cape Canaveral, this bevy of hotties would run around at cocktail parties, saying 'three' or 'four' or something to tell how many of the guys each one had gotten into the sack with. Same idea here, except without the advertising."

Quindel: "I didn't know they had astronauts in Vienna."

Andy: "In von Leuthen's league it was more like royalty, prime ministers, ambassadors, generals, some of the senior UN types that Vienna is crawling with, and the occasional cultural superstar when things got slow. Sometimes actual affairs and sometimes one-night stands. She never nailed anyone who helped elect a pope, but not because she didn't try."

Quindel: "Too bad they didn't have G-Eight summits when she was in her prime."

Andy: "At least one guy from last year's G-Eight summit would say she's *still* in her prime."

I started paying attention again because I figured the back-and-forth had finally reached Proxy's choke-point. It had.

"Very entertaining." She didn't sound entertained. "But what does all that have to do with *Eros Rising*?" It says a *lot* about Proxy that none of the males on the call came close to chuckling at that question.

"Not certain," Andy said, absolutely dead-pan, "but anytime you put a little black dress and a little black book together, you've got a chance for pillow talk, blackmail, and back-door influence. That stuff might come in handy if you're working some kind of international scam involving a pricey pic."

Time for me to chime in.

"That same stuff could come in handy if you were trying to rig bids on a gas pipeline or subvert a central Asian government. I'm the one who brought von Leuthen into the conversation, so I feel a little responsibility here. Do we have anything except a Pittsburgh lawyer's intuition and a Vienna cop's question to me to make us think that Alma von Leuthen has something to do with the painting we insured?"

Absolute silence for five seconds. Seriously, you could have heard crickets chirp. Then Andy spoke up.

"Well...yeah."

"Well yeah, what?" Proxy asked.

"I mentioned that she has a fine arts degree and she's an arty type. She's a painter. She paints."

"Oh," I said.

"She paints," Proxy said.

"Shit," Quindel said.

"Yeah, she paints," Andy said. "You know, like Hitler."

"Oooo-KAY." I imagined Proxy block-deleting the emails she'd undoubtedly been reviewing while we chatted. "Thanks to all of you for your helpful input. Jay, I'll call you right back."

Click! Eight seconds later my phone buzzed. Proxy. I answered.

"Jay, I think you need to track von Leuthen down and have a talk with her."

"Got it." I said that as if I had some idea of how I was going to find a foreign national Andy hadn't managed to locate. "By the way, how did you manage to dump the budget hit for Andy's work on Quindel?"

"That's right, I haven't told you yet, have I? The Museum wants a quote for insuring *Eros Rising* against loss, theft, or damage while it's on loan to a museum in Vienna and traveling back and forth. Quindel's department has to rate the risk."

"On loan to a museum in Vienna. Sounds like the deal Nesselrode floated when we were there."

"Yeah, it sounds a lot like that."

Oh.

Chapter Thirty-one

JAY DAVIDOVICH

How do you find a needle in a haystack? You get a big magnet and make the needle come to you. Or if you don't have a big magnet, a lot of small magents.

I called Dany Nesselrode. No answer, left a message, said it was important. Checked my watch. Still early evening in Vienna, so I had a shot.

I called Jakubek, the shysterette. No answer, left a message, said it was important.

I called Father Utica, the rector of the seminary in Albuquerque. No answer, left a message, said it was important.

I made a list of all the guys I'd known in the army who at some point had found themselves less than six degrees of separation from the State Department. Short list, because I ran out of names after I reached one: Tat Baldwin. I don't think "Tat" is short for anything. Just the name his mom and dad had hung on him. Marine lifer whose last pre-retirement gig put him on the security detail of a U.S. embassy somewhere in the Balkans.

Ordinarily a Marine veteran wouldn't give an ex-Army National Guardsman the time of day. Tat, though, kind of liked me. During beer call at an Enlisted Personnel Club in Baghdad, one of my fellow PFCs noticed Tat and decided it would be hilarious to refer to a cat house raid we'd done the day before as "Operation Tit for Tat." If you're a guy, you can make fun of another's guys looks, or his sexual prowess, or his athletic skill, or any number of other things without getting anything more than verbal pushback. But there are two things you don't make fun of: a guy's mom, and his name. So the second time I heard the "Tit for Tat" thing I told the perpetrator that I thought he'd exhausted the comedic potential of the idea. (I didn't put it quite that way.) Tat appreciated that, because otherwise he would have had to kill the guy, which might have gotten him busted from gunnery sergeant down to lance corporal.

Fingers crossed, I clicked on the number my contact list had for Tat.

"Thank you for calling Pelican in the Wilderness Holiness Gospel Church." Hmm. "'I am like a pelican in the wilderness.' Psalm one-oh-two, verse six. At the tone, please leave a brief message including the nature of the ministry you require and a number where you can be reached. May God be with you, and have a blessed day."

Beep!

"Hey, Tat, blast from your past. Jay Davidovich. Listen, I need to talk—" I didn't get any farther because Tat's voice interrupted my message.

"Davidovich! Man, that brings back memories! Where are you now?"

"Transoxana Insurance."

"Thank God you called! It's *so* hard to get life insurance when you have leukemia!"

"I'm not in sales."

"Yeah, that doesn't come as a complete surprise."

"I've got a name for you. Alma von Leuthen. I'm wondering whether she ever showed up on a list of people embassy staff shouldn't play footsie with when they're out sightseeing."

"Hmm." Tat let that syllable hang in the air for a second or two. "Believe it or not, you're actually on to something. They did circulate what they called a DCM List every month when I was in Belgrade. DCM stands for Deputy Chief of Mission.

He's the pro, even if the ambassador is a political appointee. Or she, I guess. The names on that list belong to people who, when you're around them, your lips and your fly both stay zipped."

"Alma von Leuthen's name ever show up, that you can remember?"

"Oh, man, that list wasn't for the likes of me. That was for real foreign service officers. And I wouldn't remember anyway."

"Can you ask around?"

"Sure, but it'll cost you."

"Name your price."

"First, you have to 'Like' Pelican in the Wilderness Holiness Gospel Church on Facebook."

"Can do."

"That's just for starters. The big one is you have to go to www dot chapultepecanniversary dot org. There's an online petition there to make September thirteenth a state holiday in Virginia, in time for the one hundred-seventieth anniversary of the American victory in the Battle of Chapultepec in the Mexican War."

Rang a bell. I recalled mentioning Manifest Destiny to an Austrian cop not long before. Still…

"Are you yanking my chain, Tat?"

"No, sir, I am most certainly *not* yanking your chain. I am as serious as a hernia exam about this. You get the point, right?"

"No."

"That's where the 'Halls of Montezuma' in the Marine Hymn comes from. Chapultepec. Sons of Virginia such as George Pickett and Harley Grafton were heroes in that battle."

"Tat, like every American, I've heard of the Halls of Montezuma. And I've heard of Pickett's Charge at Gettysburg. But who in the bloody hell is Harley Grafton?"

"The great-great-grandfather of a particularly prosperous member of our congregation who is a great believer in both Gospel holiness and in celebrating this battle."

"Comes the dawn. Done, Tat. I will sign the petition."

"Okay, then, I'll call you back when I've got something."

"I'd appreciate a call-back for sure, Tat, but the main idea is to put von Leuthen's name out in this connection to as many people as possible."

"What will that accomplish?"

"If she wasn't on any of those lists, it won't accomplish a thing. But if she was on, say, one or two of them, some ambitious desk officer is going to get the bright idea of circulating an email to a long list asking for information about von Leuthen's whereabouts."

"Well, I hope you know what you're talkin' about, 'cause I surely don't. But I'll start the ball rolling."

"Much appreciated."

"Remember that website, now."

"Will do."

I quick-stepped over to Rachel's computer table in the dining room to find something I could use to write down Tat's website while I still remembered it. Murphy's Law operated in its usual way, and I knocked a manila folder on the floor in the process, scattering its contents onto the rug.

Nuts.

I scooped the pages up to replace them in the folder. All of sudden I found myself looking at a print-out of the head-and-shoulders shot from Cynthia Jakubek's website. Plus a lot of other stuff about Cynthia Jakubek, with yellow highlighting over words like *Harvard Journal of Law and Public Policy*, "federal court clerkship," and "Calder & Bull." Hmmm. Nice to have your spouse take an interest in your work, but even so…

Well, I had other things to worry about, so I went back to worrying about them. Such as, what's the connection between the computer hacking investigation I'd abandoned and the *Eros Rising* matter? Because the more I thought about it, the more it seemed there had to be a connection. Did someone wonder why Jay Davidovich had been called into the *Eros Rising* mess, instead of some other loss-prevention specialist who wasn't already busy on something else? Getting the answer to that question made at least as plausible a reason for trying to grab

Proxie's attaché case as the long-shot chance of diverting a wire-transfer payment.

Forty minutes later I hadn't come up with an answer, and nothing else important had happened. I checked my emails. Some genius in Hartford had blitzed a Transoxana directory list that included my name to ask, "Is anyone licensed to practice law in Nevada?" Someone else had hit REPLY TO ALL and answered, "Yes, several thousand people. I'm not one of them, but good luck!"

It came as a great relief when Nesselrode returned my call. After something in Yiddish that I didn't understand he asked what was so important.

"Alma von Leuthen."

"What about her?"

"She's a painter, or at least she knows how to paint."

"That's like saying someone in Nashville knows how to play guitar."

"Someone who knows how to paint could forge a painting. She got out of Vienna just before a guy who was supposed to take you and me to a forged painting was killed. Plus, one of the American players in the *Eros Rising* sweepstakes was in Vienna at the same time, and I heard von Leuthen's name from his lawyer. I don't believe in Santa Claus, but it's beginning to look a lot like Christmas."

I heard the distinctive *whoosh-click* of a butane lighter being fired up and then snapped shut. I waited. Nesselrode finally rewarded my patience.

"And so you're looking for her?"

"Yes, and I'm not the only one. I need to talk to her."

"And you think I can help?"

"Yes."

"Why?"

"Wild guess." I hate it when guys play dumb—especially smart guys. "Look, Dany, Transoxana is a great big multi-national company, and one of the places it lives is Austria. We can't afford a rep as a bad corporate citizen there. I've got a typical, head-up-his-ass, by-the-book corporate careerist telling me we should whisper Frau von Leuthen's name to the Vienna cops. I need a good reason not to do that, and the only way I can get one is to talk to her."

That was not, of course, strictly speaking, true. But Quindel *would* have been telling me that if he'd had the street smarts of a crack mule, and sooner or later even he was going to figure it out.

"Okay, Alma von Leuthen has nothing to do with either the original or any forgery of *Eros Rising*. I know this with absolute certainty, and I give you my word on it as a diaspora Jew."

"Dany, your word is good enough for me. End of the day, though, it's not my call. So let me make a suggestion. If, by some wild chance you find yourself in contact with von Leuthen in the next couple of days, please ask her to give me a call. Meanwhile, I'll try to stall the numb-nuts up in Hartford."

"'Couple of days.' Wait a minute." Dead air followed for ten seconds or so. "Look, I'm coming to New York on Monday. We could talk face to face on Tuesday evening if you could get up there. Can you stall him until then?"

"'The difficult we do immediately; the impossible takes a little time.' Sure, I can stall him until then."

"Thank you."

"And how do you know about Nashville and music?"

"Everyone in the world knows about American popular culture. That's why they hate you so much."

"Thank you for explaining that."

"Also, I'm sorry I cursed you the last time we saw each other. I was drunk."

"No problem. Forget about it."

Yes, Dany, you *were* drunk. I tried that excuse on Rachel once and her answer was, "*In vino veritas*"—which, roughly translated, means, "Drunks tell the truth."

The Second Thursday in April

Chapter Thirty-two

CYNTHIA JAKUBEK

I picked up Davidovich's message at eight o'clock the morning. I was shouldering my way through a throng of drunks, wife-beaters, hookers, street-hustlers, first-offense (sure) shoplifters, and bar brawlers in the hallway outside Branch 2 of the City of Pittsburgh Municipal Court. I got the "it's important" part, but it wasn't as important to me as stalking a client, which is what had brought me to this Hogarthian hallway.

Not that I had any interest in Muni Court work. I'd do insurance defense before making a career out of that. George Fenzing, however, wasn't your average Muni Court defendant. A Pittsburgh cop had clocked him doing fifty-two in a thirty-five zone, and he'd find himself right on the edge of a license suspension if things went too far south this morning.

None of which mattered a whit to me. All I cared about was that his company, Shear Genius Precision Cutting Tools, Inc., had just had a high six-figure judgment entered against it in a suit by a distributor claiming wrongful termination. This morning I planned to bump into Fenzing, introduce myself, shake his hand, wish him luck, and scoot back to my office. That way, I could email him later in the day that I'd handle an appeal of the verdict on a straight contingent fee basis—no fee if I lost—without breaking the rule against solicitation, because I'd be contacting an "acquaintance" instead of making a cold call.

No Fenzing in the hallway. Nuts. Inside the courtroom I spotted him in deep conference with an early-fifties white male who was probably his lawyer and a mid-twenties African-American woman with all the earmarks of an overworked assistant city attorney. Talking plea bargain, no doubt, so I'd have to bide my time.

I decided to stay in the courtroom to keep my eye on him. Mistake. Judge Monica Childress promptly took the bench. Fenzing *et al.* adjourned to somewhere less public to continue their discussion. Childress' clerk called "City v. Washington" and a slight, aging African American male in clothes straight off the Goodwill rack stepped forward to answer a citation for "loitering or prowling." Translation: a cop had decided Washington was up to no good when he wandered onto a parking lot. The clerk asked him how he pled. "Not guilty!" he shouted angrily. "And I wants a lawyer!" Not clear that he had a right to one, but Judge Childress didn't go in much for legal research. Gripping her gavel at the hammer-end like a pistol, she pointed the handle's tip straight at yours truly.

"Congratulations, Counsel, you just got a new client. Ten minutes to confer. Call the next case."

No point in arguing. I took my client and a postcard-sized arrest report out into the corridor. Twenty seconds to read the card and another forty to get Clarence Washington's story: "I'm walkin' to the river, kickin' a can along the sidewalk, and the can go into this parkin' lot, see? I goes in to get it, an' I sees a pack o' cigs. Or I thinks it is. Turned out it was empty. Next thing I know Bull Connor in there is cuffin' me." So I was ready for trial with nine minutes to spare.

"Got it," I told Washington as I took my phone out to speed-dial Willy.

"You know who Bull Connor was?"

I tapped Willy's icon and glanced up at Washington.

"Sort of. Top cop in, what, Birmingham or maybe Selma during civil rights demonstrations in the early sixties…Hey, Willy, this is CJ."

"Yo. What's up?"

"You think we gots a chance? 'Cause I can't pay no fifty dollah," Washington said.

"Just a second, Willy."

I turned my face back to my new client. I looked into eyes where rage, despair, and resignation fought losing battles with each other. I kicked myself in the butt for acting like an asshole. *This is your CLIENT! Treat him like one!*

"The odds are ten-to-one against us, Mr. Washington. The judge already thinks you're guilty. We'll have to move her off that."

"Can you do that?"

"Don't know, but I'm going to give it a shot."

He gave me a decisive nod, as if this were good news. I went back to Willy.

"Sorry about the interruption, tiger. Here's why I called. Transoxana has keyhole peepers looking for the lady we discussed."

"von Leuthen?"

"That's the one. We'd like to find out what they find out."

"Damn right we would."

"So the game is I'll-show-you-mine-if-you-show-me-yours. What dope can we give them in exchange for theirs? If whatever you wanted to see her about is off the table, what else can we tell them that they don't already know?"

Long pause, accompanied by the sound of a lengthy exhale.

"I don't know," he said at last. "I'll have to think about that."

"Can you think about it between now and...let's see... ten-thirty?"

"Sure. Your office?"

"Yes. And bring Amber."

Reholstering my phone, I returned my attention to Clarence Washington.

"What was the can?"

"Wha'?"

"The can you were kicking. What was it?"

"They wants us back in the court."

He pointed to an open door where a bailiff was gesturing to us. I grabbed the threadbare serge coat that had once been half of a suit.

"Can, Mr. Washington. What was the can you were kicking?"

"Oh. Sprite, I guess. Yeah, thass it. Sprite."

Okay.

"Nice of you to join us, Counsel," Judge Childress said thirty seconds later as we strode up to the bench.

"Ready for the defense, your honor."

She scowled over at the assistant city attorney who'd drawn Clarence Washington's case.

"Call your first witness."

The arresting officer stood to the city attorney's left, facing the judge. No witness stand in this courtroom. He took the oath and said he'd spotted the defendant casing cars in the fenced-in parking lot of a private company and had arrested him because he couldn't give a plausible reason for being there. Feeling Washington's eyes on me, I leaned a little to my right so that I could look the officer in the face while I cross-examined him.

"Mr. Washington identified himself to you when you asked him to, officer?"

"Yes."

"And he gave you his correct name?"

"Yes."

"He did give you an explanation for being in the parking lot, didn't he?"

"He tried one on me."

"You just didn't buy, it, right?"

"You got that right. In my professional judgment based on seventeen years as a law enforcement officer, he was there casing cars."

"By the way, this 'fenced in' parking lot had openings in the fence so people could walk in and walk out, right?"

"Yes."

"You didn't have to open a gate or climb over the fence to get in, did you?"

"No."

"Hurry it up, Counsel," Childress said impatiently. "This isn't Trial Practice One-Oh-One."

"When you arrested Mr. Washington, you searched him, didn't you?"

"Yes."

"Reviewing your report, I don't see any mention of a slimjim or a tire iron or a heavy wrench that someone might use to break into a car. Did I miss something?"

"No, I didn't find anything like that."

I glanced at Washington to draw the judge's eyes to him so that she could try to imagine the smallish man breaking a car window with his bare hands.

"Did you look for an empty soda can?"

"I didn't see one."

"My question was did you look for one."

"Not specifically." He looked a little nervously at the judge as she bristled.

"One more question, Counsel," she said icily.

"Very well, Officer, one more question. In your seventeen years as a law enforcement officer, how many well-dressed white men have you arrested for 'loitering or prowling'?"

"All right, that's it," Childress said. "The witness is excused."

Washington then told his story. He even remembered to say he'd been kicking a Sprite can. The city attorney was new at trial work, so his cross-examination consisted of having Washington repeat the story. Childress instantly found Washington guilty, making some crack about how, "the game here wasn't kick the can but liar-liar-pants-on-fire. Forty-dollar civil forfeiture. You have—"

"Waive reading of appellate rights." I snapped that instead of just saying it. "We'll file an appeal for trial *de novo* in the Court of Common Pleas and a jury demand by nine o'clock."

Childress gave me a look that could strip chrome from a semi's bumper.

"Counsel, you realize that the appellate filing fee is fifty dollars, right?"

"Yes, your honor."

"And that it is non-refundable, even if you win?"

"Yes." Oops. Actually, I hadn't known that. But I was in way too deep to back out now.

"Why are you going to spend fifty dollars to try to overturn a forty-dollar fine?"

"On the record or off the record, your honor?"

"Off the record. I want to hear this."

"Because your ruling pisses me off."

"First straight answer I've gotten from a lawyer in six months." She shook her head. "Submit a chit and I'll sign off on half-an-hour for your work this morning. I don't think your appeal has substantial merit, though, so good luck with getting a *per diem* on that one."

Well, if I end up handling it pro bono it'll be a thousand years off my time in Purgatory—and I can use it. I managed not to say that out loud.

As I was showing Washington out into the hallway, I spotted Fenzing and company in back of the courtroom, presumably waiting to tell the judge about their plea bargain. Judging from his expression, Fenzing didn't think much of the deal his lawyer had cut. Introducing myself to him right now looked like a low-percentage play. Washington had a major glow on, but it was wasted on me.

Even so, I let him get it out of his system—"Man, I gots *Perry Mason* up there! How'd she rule against us, anyhow?" I told him what the whole appeal thing meant. The main thing it meant to Washington for the moment was that cops couldn't run him in for not paying an outstanding fine just because he struck them as an unsightly blot on a downtown sidewalk some afternoon.

I gave him my card and we parted company. I turned back toward the courtroom and waited for Fenzing and his lawyer to come out. When they did, Fenzing looked like an eight-year-old who'd just been spanked in public. A world-class chewing out from Judge Childress can do that. Some survival-of-the-fittest instinct must have alerted his lawyer to what I had in mind. He moved smoothly in between me and Fenzing.

"Nice job in there playing a tough hand. Call it a moral victory."

I like to give people the benefit of the doubt, so I decided to go provisionally with the ten percent chance that this guy was a genuinely empathetic professional colleague instead of a condescending prick.

"Thanks, but I'm not a great believer in moral victories. If a case goes to decision you win or you lose. So far I've lost, but the fat lady hasn't even warmed up her voice yet."

Fenzing brusquely pulled his lawyer out from between us.

"Do you handle all kinds of cases, or just stuff like this?"

"General corporate and commercial trial and appellate work and counseling."

"Do you have a card?"

"Sure." I handed him one.

"Thanks. Before much longer I might be looking for a lawyer with some balls."

Chapter Thirty-three

JAY DAVIDOVICH

Father Utica and I were wrapping up his call-back when the shysterette's call came in. I figured Jakubek really wanted to talk to me and the *padre* was mostly being polite, so I decided not to cut our conversation short.

"It doesn't particularly surprise me that the Vienna police had my name," he said as the shysterette went into voice-mail.

"Why is that?"

"I spent a term at a school in Linz called Katholisch Theologische Privatuniversitad, taking advanced scriptural studies. German scriptural scholarship is world renowned. For almost fifty years, the seminary where I'm rector now has been sending promising students there if they have a little German."

For some reason the university name sounded familiar, and I couldn't think of any reason why it should have. I had a witness to locate, though, so I went on with my conversation.

"Your studies there had to be quite a while ago."

"Well over thirty years. But Austrian police are very thorough."

I shook my head. I'd give you six-to-one under a full moon that the Vienna cops had gotten Father Utica's name from something they'd found on or near Ertel's body, not from a local college's foreign student records. No sense arguing with a source who's trying to be helpful, though, and I thought Utica was.

"Thanks, Father. Listen, would you mind texting me the name of that university?" Including a phonetic spelling that would look like gibberish in the report I sent Proxy would ruin her day. Might even cause her to indulge in an extra carrot stick as comfort food.

"Certainly, Mr. Davidovich. I'll get it to you within the hour. Please feel free to call me again if I can be of further help."

I thanked him again and hung up. Something he'd said was tickling an overworked neuron somewhere in my brain. I was anxious to talk to Jakubek, though, so I couldn't fuss with it right then.

"Thanks for calling back," I said when I reached her. "von Leuthen is an interesting lady. I'd like to have a little heart-to-heart with her. Any idea how I can get in touch?"'

"Nope. I've got something else for you, though, if you're willing to tell me what's so interesting about her."

"Sure." I yawned and stretched. "You go first."

"The Taser used in that elevator job was stolen from my client's condo."

"What?" I sat up straight in a hurry.

"It gets better. The guy who stole it was bidding on the bill of sale that Transoxana ended up buying."

"And who is this guy?"

"No name, but a description. Amber, you're on."

"Okay," a different female voice said. "So. I surprised him while he was doing the place. He busted me one, but I got a look at his head. Black hair cut real short, like a soldier's, and brownish skin. But not real dark brown like a black guy's skin. 'Cause his face looked like a white guy's face, not like a black guy's, you know what I mean?"

"Yes."

"And there's one more thing. He'd gotten a pretty good clop in the chops not long before. His nose was swollen and bandaged, and he had a black eye. I mean, someone clocked him a good one. You know what I mean?"

"Yes." Someone like me, for example.

Amber's description could have covered the wheelman who'd picked up Ertel after I'd relieved him of Proxy's attaché case. Of course, it could have covered a thousand other guys as well. But I didn't see any way Amber or Szulz or Jakubek would have known about our little dust-up, and no one ever went broke betting against coincidence.

Fair's fair. I told Jakubek and Amber (and, I assumed, Szulz) what I knew about Frau von Leuthen.

"She sounds interesting more in a *Letters to Penthouse* sort of way than in a fine arts hustle kind of way," Jakubek said.

"I don't think she high-tailed it to Geneva when she did to get a watch fixed. Do you see an innocent-bystander explanation for that?"

"It doesn't leap out at me."

"Me, either. I'm developing a theory. I know there are things you can't tell me, so why don't I just spin it out as a hypothetical and see where we are?"

"Go ahead."

"First point: if Taser-guy in the elevator was bidding for the bill of sale, then he had a partner. That partner happened to pass away just before I could talk to him in Vienna, and just after von Leuthen left. Second point: I'm ninety-eight percent sure your client was in Vienna that same night. Third point: your client has to be on pretty thin ice, what with a cop getting nailed with his Taser."

"Where are we going with this?"

"I'd like to know why your client was in Vienna and whether it has anything to do with Alma von Leuthen."

"Tell you what," Jakubek said, "can I put you on mute for a few minutes?"

"Sure."

A few minutes is a long damn time on a silent telephone. I put the muted phone on speaker so that I could tell when Jakubek came back on, and started reviewing emails. Nothing worth opening until I got down to one from Proxy that led to an extended dialogue:

Status on AVL contact? PVS

Nothing yet. JD

Leads? PVS

Negative. Not really going the leads route. JD

What route are you going? PVS

I replied with an eight-line response that explained the magnet theory: you get several different people sending out feelers on her from different angles, sooner or later it gets back to her—and when it does, you have a fifty-fifty chance that she contacts you just to get it over with and make the searches stop.

Okay. Keep me posted. PVS

Will do. JD

Hearing an upsurge in white noise over my speaker I picked the receiver back up.

"Okay," Jakubek said, "I'm going to go the hypothetical route with you, just like you did with me."

"Fine. I'm betting your hypothetical starts with, 'If Willy was in Vienna.'"

"If Willy was in Vienna that night, it would have had nothing to do with *Eros Rising*. His interest in Alma von Leuthen, if he had any, would relate to an entirely different matter."

"And I'm taking his word for this, right?"

"Well, you can verify it by talking to von Leuthen, if you can find her."

"I suppose I could."

"So I've got a deal for you. We'd both like to talk to von Leuthen. Let's agree that if you turn her up, you'll cut us in on the deal, and if we turn her up, we'll cut you in."

I felt like a rube in New York City being offered a Rolex for fifty bucks. Alarm bells went off in my head, but that watch sure looked shiny.

"I'll need to think about that one," I finally said.

"Fine with us. While you're thinking about it, let me finish my hypothetical."

"Sure."

"If Willy had been in Vienna that night, there's a pretty good chance he would have seen C. Talbot Rand there too. Have a pleasant day."

The Third Monday in April

The Third Monday in April

Chapter Thirty-four

CYNTHIA JAKUBEK

"Yo! Juice! Over here!"

The heavily tattooed white dude who barked this instruction snapped his fingers above his head in case I couldn't hear him from fourteen feet away. I moved in his direction, taking my time about it. St. Benedict the Moor Open Door Café, third Monday of the month, Cindy on the drink line.

I take attitude like his as part of the deal. Some guests act grateful, with lots of smiles and thank-yous. Some seem grudging: "Yeah, I appreciate this but, frankly, it's the least you could do." Some deeply resent needing help, and therefore resent you for helping them. And some apparently just plain feel entitled.

Reaching the formica-topped table that looked like something out of June Cleaver's kitchen would have if she'd been on food stamps, I poured thin, orange stuff into a plastic cup in front of an unambiguously phallic snake inked onto the guy's forearm. He had cut the sleeves off a denim shirt at the shoulder, so the snake looked *really* long.

"About goddamn time."

"Watch your mouth!" This from black lady across the table. "You gettin' a free meal! Be blessed!"

Tattoo boy opened his mouth, but he shut it quick. A glance up told me why. Sister Luanga was making her stately way from the meal service area to the table. Her ebony face glistened under an ample white veil that complemented her royal blue, ankle-length dress. She didn't have a ruler, but she might as well have.

"If you must abuse someone, then abuse me as you think best," she said in lilting English with a distinctive West African accent. "But please do not take the name of our Lord in vain, for it wounds me to the heart when you do."

The tattooed guy looked sullenly down, muttering, "Sorry." Even the snake looked a little sheepish. I distractedly filled a couple of other cups on my way back to the coolers and coffee urn that defined the drink line here. I had my mind on something less noble than giving drink to the thirsty.

Willy's little bombshell about thinking he'd seen Tally in Vienna had provoked a succession of unpleasant thoughts. Willy had a motive to kill the guy in Vienna. Hijacking the bill of sale, though, made sense for him only if it was phony, and I wasn't buying that. I couldn't see how the Vienna murder accomplished anything at all for Tally. He wouldn't want the Museum to lose *Eros Rising*, but he wouldn't stick his own neck out to save the painting, and one thug more or less didn't figure to change that equation much anyway.

But what about my good client Sean? I didn't know about Austria, but he'd sure been in Europe at the right time. And he'd told Willy more than he should have, which might have something to do with Willy appearing in Vienna. Suppose Sean killed the thug with the idea of framing Tally for the murder? Might that make Tally more flexible on the annulment negotiations? On the other hand, wouldn't committing cold-blooded murder just to have a church wedding qualify as the ultimate unclear-on-the-concept move? That leaves out the Abbey factor, though. I'd seen the adoring gaze that Sean laid on Abbey. For all values of y and x, if y is male and x is female and the question is whether y would kill for x, the answer is: don't bet against it.

I shook my head. *Ridiculous.* I saw someone else asking for orange goop and ambled toward her. *Yeah, keep telling yourself that, Cindy. It's ridiculous.*

As I headed back to the drink line I noticed a reed-thin, older white woman in a black habit. Not as full a habit as Sister Luanga's. The veil stopped short of salt and pepper hair at the top of her forehead, and the skirt came only to mid-calf. But I could tell she was a nun. She stood beside Sister Luanga, looking directly at me. Didn't recognize her. As she gestured toward me, Sister Luanga caught my eye and nodded. After setting my pitchers on the counter, I walked over to them.

"Sister Bettina Fouts, St. Scholastica Abbey." She held out her right hand while I still had a good four feet to cover. "Are you Cynthia Jakubek?"

"Yes, Sister." I shook her hand. "Happy to meet you."

Her introduction puzzled me. St. Scholastica Abbey is a Benedictine Convent about sixty miles outside Pittsburgh. "Benedectine" as in the original St. Benedict, not St. Benedict the Moor, who was named after him. The convent had nothing to do with the parish church that ran the Open Door Café.

"I've driven someone over here who's anxious to speak with you."

"No kidding. Who's that?"

"Her name is Alma von Leuthen."

HELL-O. I glanced at my watch.

"Well, I still have about half an hour here. Can Ms. Von Leuthen wait—"

"No worries." Sister Luanga brushed my left arm reassuringly. "We will cover for you. Run along with Sister Bettina."

"Rectory?" I asked as we headed upstairs.

"No. Father Larry is letting us use the reconciliation room."

That floored me at first. Not quite like using the sanctuary of the church for a spelling bee, but close. Then I thought it over for a second. Reconciliation rooms are where priests hear confessions these days. The one at St. Ben's is about the size of a small office. Basically soundproof, but with a window in the upper half of the door so that no one will think any hanky-panky is going on inside. For a meeting like the one coming up, it made a lot of sense.

Not sure what I expected von Leuthen to look like. Cliché from a 1930s movie, maybe: six-inch cigarette holder, *faux* hauteur of faded aristocracy, clothes with old, elegant labels inside and threadbare hems outside. The tall, slender woman Fouts introduced to me didn't bear the slightest resemblance to that image.

If I hadn't known she was in her sixties I would have guessed her age at something south of forty-five. Hints of silver-white here and there made her golden hair somehow more striking rather than less. Her pale blue eyes laughed in a secret-joke kind of way, against a background of wistful resignation: *Yes, the human condition is tragic, but as long as we're all here, let's have a drink.* She wore an ivory silk blouse and a charcoal gray wool skirt that struck me as comfortably *soigné*. Leather dress gloves matching the skirt lay in her lap. Pale, delicate complexion; simple gold earrings, understated but pricey watch, no other jewelry.

She didn't shake my hand when she rose to greet me. She took it and grasped it confidingly while her eyes held mine with a gaze that mutely pled for something I couldn't figure out—maybe that I wouldn't disappoint her. We both sat down as von Leuthen glanced at the nun.

"Would you be so kind as to leave us, Sister?" She spoke English with just enough of an accent to sound charming.

"Certainly."

Sister Bettina stepped outside. I gently closed the door. Miss von Leuthen and I sat in the only two chairs the room offered.

"So, Ms. Jakubek, you are Willy Szulz's *avocat*."

"Yes. He and I have worked together on various things for almost a year."

"I require a favor from him. He is making inquiries about me, trying to track me down. I must ask him to stop this. That kind of attention could cause people to think I have something to do with the dispute over *Eros Rising*. When you are talking about expensive art, wrong impressions can be dangerous."

"Fatal, in the case of a guy named Ertel in Vienna."

"Excellent example."

She leaned forward, smiling. If my reference to a recent homicide jolted her, she didn't show it. Without making any effort that I could see, she drew me in, giving me the feeling that she found me absolutely fascinating—a warm, pleasant feeling that I wanted to go on having. Instant and total empathy. It was as if, for her at that moment, I was the most important human being in the world.

"I have no idea how he thinks you could help him on the painting thing," I said, "but perhaps if you talked to him you could satisfy him that you can't."

"Oh, he knows that. He wants to talk to me about a matter that has nothing to do with the painting."

"Namely?"

"As his lawyer, perhaps you should ask him. All I am asking you to do is to take a message to him: I know what he wants. I do not know whether I can get it for him. If I can, and I decide that I should, I will get in touch with him. In the meantime, I must ask him to stop pushing. His persistence could get me killed."

As I bathed in the melancholy smile that continued to brighten von Leuthen's luminous face I abruptly realized something. *She's truly beautiful. Not hot or sexy, necessarily—I'm the wrong demographic to poll about that. But stunningly, classically beautiful in a way that defies age and time.*

"I must be sounding melodramatic, and I regret that," she said then. "But I am perfectly serious. Avrim Halkani is a very dangerous man. He won't hesitate to kill. He's done it before."

"Who is Avrim Halkani?"

"He's the partner of Ertel, the dead *schlager* you just referred to. Was the partner."

I have zero German, but I could figure out *schlager* from the context: thug or gangster or something like that. Halkani, though, baffled me.

"Halkani sounds Lebanese. I thought Ertel and his partner were Palestinian."

"Ertel was Palestinian. Halkani is Israeli."

"Odd couple." I said that because saying something seemed like an improvement over sitting there with my mouth open.

"I'm no expert, but I've been told that cross-border partnerships aren't unheard of in the Israeli underworld. For someone with no conscience, you can see the advantages. So. Will you take my message to Szulz?"

"I will, but I'm not sure it will do any good." I had to make a tactical decision. Surprise is generally a good tactic, so I decided to tell the truth. "Look, cards on the table. Whatever Willy wants your help with, I have no idea what it is. But I don't think he's the one behind the skip-trace you're talking about."

"Skip-trace?"

"Legal slang. It means trying to get contact information for someone who has left town."

"I see. But someone is behind it."

"Yes, and I think I know who." Actually, I was certain I knew who, but why overplay my hand? "It does involve *Eros Rising*, and I'll be happy to tell you all about it. But first I need to know what's going on with Willy and you, because I can't take a chance on undermining my own client."

She picked up her purse the way women do when they're about to get up and leave in a huff, but then I guess she thought better of it. A little snap colored her tone when her next words came out.

"All right. Very well. I suppose there is no other way."

Keep your mouth shut. I bit my tongue and waited in silence. It's one of the most effective interrogation techniques in the world—but hard to do. It worked.

"To begin with, I assume you have been briefed on me."

"I have."

"Well, don't believe everything you heard. If I'd slept with all the men those stories claim I have, I wouldn't have had time to piss."

The casual vulgarity startled me, the way seeing a nun smoking would have. Nothing all that shocking about it, but it just didn't go with the polished manners and continental style. I continued my silence. Why change a hit?

"There's an old European saying: "I've never cheated on my husband—kings don't count.' My variation on that has been, 'Genius doesn't count.' I have had affairs with men of genius—geniuses of power, mostly."

"Okay." I shrugged. No way I'd be lecturing anyone on unchastity.

"So I have committed many sins. But in my entire life, I have only done one thing that I consider truly wicked, one sin that I am still deeply ashamed of."

"And that is—" I made little circular gestures with the fingers of my right hand to prompt her to continue.

"It was more than twenty-five years ago. I met a boy in Vienna. An American. Early to mid-twenties. I don't know why I went after him. He was no kind of genius. I suppose I was just showing off."

I thought I saw real remorse in her eyes just before she looked down for a moment at her lap.

"This doesn't sound like the kind of thing where your penance would involve flogging, even before Vatican Two. I'm having trouble finding 'wicked' in there."

Her smile this time combined indulgence with condescension. I gathered that my American *naiveté* was showing. Shaking her head, she looked back up at me.

"I'm not a collar robber."

Huh? Never heard that one before. I must have looked blank, because she immediately explained.

"He was a seminarian. A collar robber is a woman who causes a candidate for the priesthood to realize that he has not been called to a celibate life, as the Church puts it. He didn't want a fling, an afternoon dalliance now and then for a couple of months. He wanted a passionate affair that would cross oceans and span continents and go on forever. He left the seminary. Such a child. Such a precious little child. Even now, after all these years, thinking about it breaks my heart."

I let it sit there for close to a minute. Even mediocre lawyers can generally tell when someone is lying. That's easy: they're almost always lying. The hard part is knowing when someone is telling the truth. And on the soul of my sainted mother, I *knew* at that moment that Alma von Leuthen was doing exactly that.

"Well," I said, "I can't imagine any way Willy could hustle that into enough money to justify a trip to Vienna, but I guess I should ask him about that."

"You will have to. I simply have no idea. I know what he wants, but I don't know why he wants it."

"Okay. A deal is a deal. The guy who is trying to track you down is a loss-prevention specialist with Transoxana Insurance Company. I don't have his number with me, but in an hour or so I can email it to you."

"No!" Alarm washed over her face. "Nothing with computers! Hacking into computers is child's play for Halkani."

"All right, then. Would you prefer that I talk to the Transoxana guy for you?"

"Yes. That would be very kind."

"Fair enough."

I opened the reconciliation room's door. Sister Bettina jumped up from a nearby pew and hustled over to join us.

"Back to St. Scholastica, Ms. von Leuthen?" she asked.

"Thank you, but no. If it would not be too much trouble, please take me to the airport."

Chapter Thirty-five

Jay Davidovich

"Do you think Jakubek is right about von Leuthen telling the truth?"

Proxy asked this as I shifted the phone to my left ear. I'd gotten off the phone with Jakubek less than two minutes before I'd called Proxy to tell her what Jakubek had told me. By now, both ears were sore.

"I do think she's right, but it doesn't really make any difference."

"Why not?"

"Because what Jakubek told me is a hundred percent of what we're going to get from von Leuthen. My plan smoked her out, she got her story together, and she told it—except to Jakubek instead of me. Ain't gonna change. If I managed to surprise her in the sack with the French prime minister in a hotel room in Strasbourg and interrogated her, I'd get the same stuff she just fed Jakubek."

"The Catholic Church must not hold grudges over corrupting seminarians," Proxy said. "Why do you think she rates the shelter and chauffeur service?"

"I've been giving that some thought. Trying to come up with some link to the seminary in New Mexico getting hacked. Don't see it. Jakubek said that giving shelter to people who need it is one of the things Benedictine monks and nuns have been doing for, like, fifteen-hundred years. It's at the core of their tradition—von Leuthen contacts a Benedictine abbot in Austria, he calls a mother superior near Pittsburgh or whatever, bingo. I don't think it's any more complicated than that."

"Maybe. I can barely tell a rosary from a pyx, but I'm thinking the abbot would need a better reason than pious tradition to make that call."

"Proxy, what in the *hell* is a 'pyx'?"

"One of the greatest Scrabble words ever. Now, focus: better reason."

"How about that her life really is in danger? There's probably a rule about that somewhere in all those books the Church has."

"Fair point." She sounded surprised. "We know independently that she was plugged in with some important people. That theory even adds credibility to her story, because it means that someone else who probably isn't an idiot believed her."

"Damn. I'm even smarter than I thought I was."

"Look, Davidovich, I'm sorry, but I missed lunch. I don't usually do this, but I'm going to nibble on some rabbit food while we talk."

"Go ahead. It's the kind of thing I'd do, except with real food."

While Proxy worked on her celery stalk or whatever, I wondered whether 'plugged in with' was an intentional *double entendre*. I hadn't decided by the time she spoke again.

"So what do I tell Quindel about selling the policy?"

"If it's up to me, tell him if he even thinks about selling that policy he's a fucking idiot, because there's at least one chance in five of some major shit going down between the time *Eros Rising* leaves the Pitt MCM and its return."

"Right." Nibble nibble. "You mean, of course, that in your judgment there is a material prospect of an insured event taking place, resulting in a risk-quotient that, even after discounting optimistically for likelihood of occurrence, would substantially exceed any plausible premium."

"Yeah, something like that."

"I'm trying to imagine Quindel reading that in a memo and then walking away from three hundred thousand dollars a year for three years."

"Not likely, huh?"

"Hard to say. He's a smart guy, and he knows how to run numbers. But nine hundred thousand dollars is real, and your qualitative judgment is—well, not so much."

That sounded right to me. To a numbers guy, anything you say after "in my opinion" is just making stuff up.

"Tell you what," I said. "Nesselrode is in New York, I assume on some fund-raising boondoggle. He wants to see me tomorrow so he can talk me into leaving von Leuthen alone. Why don't I go ahead with the meeting, tell him that I've called off the dogs, and feel him out about some of this stuff? Not exactly a regression analysis, but at least we'd have one more piece of solid data for Quindel."

"Are you confirmed for that meeting? When and where is it supposed to happen?"

I picked up the most expensive two and a half by six and a half-inch piece of stiff paper I've ever held in my life and ran my thumb greedily over its slick surface. A Post-It on the thing read "B4BP."

"I got a FedEx package this morning from the organization that I assume he's coming to see. The only thing in it was a ticket for Tuesday night's game between the Yankees and the Orioles. Luxury suite three twenty-eight. I think he plans on seeing me there just before batting practice."

"Not bad." Proxy whistled. "Luxury suite tickets at Yankee Stadium cost more than Kim Kardashian spends on shoes in a month. No guarantee you get any real information, but it might be worth a shot."

"Not only that, you could probably put the plane ticket and hotel room on Quindel's budget."

"I love this plan. Take no prisoners."

She hung up. I sat there at the kitchen table that passes for my home office. I rehashed our conversation. *Yep. Proxy's double entendre was* definitely *intentional.*

Chapter Thirty-six

CYNTHIA JAKUBEK

I was polishing off a discovery request in Clarence Washington's case—all City of Pittsburgh Police Department loitering-or-prowling arrest records in the last three years—when Willy finally returned my call. I gave him the von Leuthen rundown.

"No kidding. Wow. Sonofagun. Maybe you coulda called me on your way to see her, huh?"

"I didn't know where we were going until we were almost there. Plus, I didn't think of it. Sorry. Probably would have just scared her off if I had, though."

"Yeah, you're prob'ly right."

"Besides, I'm betting you haven't been in church too often since your baptism. You probably don't even know what a reconciliation room is. Might have taken you all afternoon just to find it."

"You got that right. Speaking of that, what *is* a reconciliation room, anyway—basically a squeal room with nicer furniture?"

"Close enough. Bottom line, whatever you want from von Leuthen, my guess is that the only way to get it is not to go after it any more. The stunt Transoxana pulled has the lady seriously spooked, and for all I know she may still be blaming you for it."

That's when it happened. The little hesitation, the moment of calculation. I'd done it myself a dozen times with mom. Normal pre-dinner conversation, then just a hint of a pause: *Casually work the detention into our chat, or let it go and hope for*

the best? Who knows, maybe my getting home an hour later than
usual won't come up.

"Hey, I'm not the CIA," Willy said. "I can't track this round-heeled broad down if she doesn't wanna be found." Short but clearly perceptible pause. "By the way, where is that reconciliation whatever at St. Ben's?"

"If you're facing the altar, it's along the wall to your left, directly opposite the ends of the last six or seven pews. Why? You thinking of going to confession?"

"Who knows? Never can tell about me. When do they hear confessions these days?"

I am NOT buying this. Not for a second. But what was I going to do? Threaten to drop him as a client unless he stopped bullshitting me? Yeah, sure. This is Pittsburgh, not Hollywood. I played along.

"Saturday mornings right after eight o'clock Mass. And Monday through Friday at various times. I don't know what they are, but you could find them in the bulletin."

"So, basically, every day except Sunday."

"Yep. They lock the church up right after everyone clears out following ten-fifteen Mass."

"Okay." Note of finality. "I think you're right about not pushing her anymore. If she decides to come across for me, she'll prob'ly do it through you."

"And then I'll know what this is all about. That's a hint, by the way."

"Tell ya what," he said. "Next Monday. Week from today. How about that?"

"Is that a promise?"

"More like a hope, but I'd call it a pretty good bet. See ya."

Click. Why would Willy want to know when confessions were heard at St. Ben's? Of course, he didn't want to know that. What he wanted to know was when they *weren't* being heard. I should have seen that. Thigh-high fastball on the inside corner—a pitch like that shouldn't have gotten by me. But it did. I didn't see the obvious until it was damn near too late.

The Third Tuesday in April

The Third Tuesday in April

Chapter Thirty-seven

JAY DAVIDOVICH

I hate to sound like my dad, but why would anyone watch a baseball game from a luxury suite? Swordfights to the death in the arena—yeah, I could see that. *Hey, nifty throat-slash—which reminds me: how about some of that steak tartare from the warming pan?* To enjoy baseball, though, you have to concentrate—and a luxury suite is basically a thousand cubic yards of distraction.

I got to Suite 328 about the time the grounds crew was hauling a portable batting cage into place behind and looming over home plate, signaling the official start of batting practice. The handful of souls in the stands ninety minutes before game time seemed lost in the stadium's vastness. Yankee-blue canvas hung slackly from the cage's framework of aluminum fence poles, to stop any batted ball that wasn't headed for the field of play. I love watching BP. It reminds me of getting to Red Sox games way early with dad so that we could catch the last ten or fifteen minutes. But nostalgia had nothing to do with tonight.

"How do you like it?"

Looking over my shoulder at the sound of the voice, I saw Nesselrode striding into the suite. He spread his arms expansively, as if the thing had been in his family for six generations.

"Magnificent."

Nesselrode had already squatted in front of a mini-fridge to dig out two Guiness ales. He tossed one to me.

"Sorry." He shrugged at me. "The only alternative is Budweiser."

"I'm easy to please. Thanks for the ticket, by the way."

"Trust me, you'll earn it. Hate to skimp on foreplay, but we'll be having lots of company in forty-five minutes or so. We need to discuss things while we still have some privacy."

"It's your party."

I followed him to the two rows of leather-cushioned, theater-type seats at the front of the suite, where you'd sit if you actually wanted to watch action on the field. He gestured toward the two seats at the far end of the first row. Didn't like it. Minimum visibility, zero mobility, maximum vulnerability. I sprawled into the end seat anyway. He sat down next to me, taking a long hit on his Guiness as he did.

"We need to make a deal."

"I'm game." I tried to look game. "What are the terms?"

"Terms. Yes." He took another deep swallow. "Clause one: I will give Transoxana Insurance Company some extremely useful advice at no charge."

"Sounds good so far."

"Clause two: Alma von Leuthen is off the table for good. No gumshoes, no keyhole-peepers, no *et ceteras*."

"Transoxana is already out of the Alma von Leuthen business."

"I need it to stay out. Drink up, I feel conspicuous."

I swallowed a respectable measure of crisp ale.

"I can take a no-Alma guarantee up the ladder, Dany, but I'm a very small cog in a very big machine. If Transoxana puts another loss-prevention specialist on this case tomorrow morning, he could reopen the von Leuthen can of worms without a by-your-leave from me. Or she could, if there were any shes in TO's Loss Prevention Department. Which there aren't, but anything can happen."

"Ah, so you're not Transoxana's CEO. That disappoints me." He drank some Guiness, and I felt weirdly compelled to do the same, as if I were sixteen years old again and we were down by the quarry after midnight. "I'm joking. What you can promise is that you will tell me whether Transoxana has rejected the policy the Museum wants to buy; and also whether you've picked up any hint that it's looking at von Leuthen again."

"I suppose. That's not exactly in the employee manual, but I can play an angle here and there and try to stay in the loop."

He grabbed my right bicep in a fierce, steely grip. Hard enough to smart. I snapped my head toward him and found myself looking into intense, burning eyes.

"No 'suppose' about it, Judas Macabeus Davidovich. There is no 'try.' There is only 'will.' I need your word on your honor as a Jew that you *will* find a way to let me know if Transoxana goes back on von Leuthen's trail."

"Dany, for starters, let go of my arm."

He relaxed his grip and sheepishly dropped his hand.

"Sorry."

"Now, I'll give you my word on whatever you want that I will do my damn level best to let you know about any developments on the von Leuthen front. But no guarantees. I'm not going to overpromise."

"Thank you for that. Half-a-loaf is better than bullshit, as Americans say—or would say, if you had a little more imagination."

"The best way to keep Transoxana on the sidelines as far as von Leuthen is concerned is for you to give me a bullet-proof reason for us not to issue the policy."

"Yes, yes, you're absolutely right." He finished his Guiness, crushed the can in his right hand, and tossed it over his shoulder in the general direction of nothing in particular. "I promised you valuable advice, and I'll deliver. First, though, I need another libation—and perhaps one for our new arrival."

As Dany sprang nimbly to his feet, I looked back into the interior of the suite. The new arrival, whom Dany must have heard even though I hadn't, was wearing a black coat, black trousers, black hat, white shirt, and black beard dominated by ringlets of hair. Standard Hassidic male outfit, except for a recently damaged nose that wasn't in any hurry to heal.

"Jay Davidovich, Aram Himmelfarb." Nesselrode said this in a perfunctory voice as he cruised past "Himmelfarb" and headed for the mini-fridge. "Aram Himmelfarb, Jay Davidovich. The 'J' stands for 'Judas'. Jay's full given name is Judas Maccabeus. So don't give him any shit."

I worked my way out of the seating rows to three leather sofas arranged in an open square around a glass-topped table to form a conversation space. "Himmelfarb" had parked himself on the couch at the bar side of the square.

"You're the loss-prevention specialist Dany has been telling me about?"

"On the nose, Reb Himmelfarb." I touched my own nose as I spoke.

I would have spotted Halkani even without the injured nose. As disguises go, a fake beard falls somewhere between mediocre and pathetic for someone with any cop experience at all—and I'd had all I wanted of that. Halkani gave me the kind of hard look that Warner Brothers used to hand out from its prop box to actors in gangster flicks. It lasted a nano-second before he managed to smear a smile over it. Nesselrode slapped a beaded can of Guiness in Halkani's hand and remained standing while I sat down opposite the guy.

"Question," Nesselrode said. "Suppose Transoxana refuses to insure *Eros Rising* on this Vienna boondoggle. Could the Museum find some other insurer?"

"Yep."

"Suppose that insurer asked Transoxana why it had turned down the policy. What would Transoxana say?"

"'Go to hell.' We'd put it a little more politely. 'Company policy and concern for the privacy of the insured precludes us from making any comment except to confirm the fact and dates of past coverage.' But, basically, go to hell."

Nesselrode nudged Halkani's shoulder with the back of his left hand.

"So you see, Himmelfarb, *someone* will insure the venture, and as long as the insurer isn't Transoxana, neither the amateurish bullshit up to now nor the sudden pursuit of von Leuthen should interfere with anyone's plans."

"A master of subtlety—just what you'd expect from the son of a diplomat!" Halkani rolled his eyes theatrically and shook his head. "What are you going to do next—hand him ten thousand dollars in a white envelope?"

"Of course not. I'm going to hand him something else in a white envelope."

Nesselrode drew a standard business envelope from inside his suede sport coat. I noted with considerable disappointment that it was way too thin to hold a hundred C-notes. Instead of tendering it to me he held it horizontally a couple of inches below his chin. No name on the outside.

"You know Willy Szulz?"

"I've met him."

"The document inside this envelope is for him. It is very important to him. I am asking you to put that document into his hands. Not in his mailbox, not in his lawyer's hands or his girlfriend's hands: his hands."

"This would be clause three of the deal you want to make?"

"Yes."

"When do I get the bullet-proof reason for my employer to blow off a high six-figure premium?"

"You've already gotten that, you dumb goddamn yid," Halkani said. "What have you been doing for the last ten minutes— watching batting practice?"

"Thanks for the hint. I was hoping for something a little more concrete."

"Use your imagination."

"I'm trying. I'm imagining that there's a coherent connection between giving a piece of paper to Willy Szulz and saving Transoxana a fifty million-dollar loss. I'm not getting anywhere."

"There is no connection," Nesselrode said. "That's the whole point."

"Then the point is way too sophisticated for an American *putz* like me."

Halkani sighed. He set his Guiness, still unopened, on the table. Leaning forward and resting his forearms on his thighs, he looked directly at me.

"Let me tell you a parable."

"Okay."

"There was a *shiksa* who had a way with men—especially men who were powerful or famous."

"You're missing an excellent opportunity to keep your goddamn mouth shut," Nesselrode muttered.

"One day, she happened on a man who had no fame whatever but, in his own way, had a modest but impressive kind of power. This man happened to be a Jew."

"Feel free to ignore him," Nesselrode told me. "He's one of those Israelis who like to play 'I'm a better Jew than you are.'"

Halkani continued unperturbed, as if Nesselrode hadn't said a word.

"Well, this thing went on as these things do, and by and by the woman got herself knocked up and discovered that she had conceived a son. Not an immaculate conception—apparently only Jewesses have those. The powerful Jew was the boy's father—with the catch, however, that he would stop being powerful very quickly if it got out that he had been whoring with the *goyim*."

Nesselrode bristled. Halkani and I simultaneously flicked our eyes to see whether Nesselrode was about the throw a punch. No, as it turned out, but it struck me as a pretty close question.

"This *shiksa*, for some goddamn reason that I can't imagine, didn't abort her pregnancy. When the half-breed was born, she took him to a rabbi for a little knife-work on his tiny *schvance*. She managed to find a family that, for a reasonable price, would raise him as a good Jew. She arranged for his father to see him now and again when he wasn't too busy protecting the Temple Mount."

I kept my mouth shut, with one eye on Nesselrode and one on Halkani. If I had been Nesselrode, either Halkani or I would have been on his way to the hospital five minutes ago. Or the morgue. Did Nesselrode's restraint come from cowardice or calculation? Or both? Or something else?

"As you would expect in light of this background, our boy has spent most of his life overcompensating for his mother's lack of Davidic genes." Halkani raised his eyebrows and flicked his head toward Nesselrode. "Any second now he's going to say, 'Fuck you.' That's his idea of snappy patter."

"Very interesting." I kept my eyes focused on Halkani. "Tell me something: Where were you Wednesday and Thursday of last week?"

Halkani threw his head back and laughed like I'd just told the knee-slapper of all time.

"Nowhere near Vienna, my friend. Since the World Trade Center attack, I've found it prudent not to leave the United States unless absolutely necessary. Getting back in can be an adventure." He leaned forward and favored me with what I think was supposed to be an earnest expression. "Look. This is what we do. You and I. This is business. Our business. Take a punch, throw a punch. No hard feelings, right?"

My policy is actually *Throw a punch so you don't have to take one*, but I figured saying so might seem impolitic. So instead I nodded and said, "Sure."

Nesselrode strolled a few feet away, then turned back to Halkani and me. Some random light penetrating the suite caught one of his onxy cufflinks just right and flashed a little starburst at us.

"You know what I find interesting about the completely fucked-up attempt to steal that bill of sale from you at the Museum? How could anyone possibly have imagined that it would work? And yet, it almost did. It's as if Caleb, the spy that Moses sent into Canaan, were a blithering *klutz* who made it back safe and sound anyway."

I stood up. Halkani started to do the same, but apparently thought better of it. I held out my right hand toward Nesselrode.

"I'll take the envelope. I'll get the document to Szulz."

Nesselrode gave me the thing. I folded the envelope in half and stuffed it into my rear trouser pocket, next to my comb and handkerchief. Then I headed for the door. I glanced over my shoulder on the way.

"Thanks again for the ticket. Enjoy the game."

As I reached the door I heard feet moving rapidly toward me across the carpet. I pivoted, halfway expecting that I'd have to block a flying fist. Halkani, though, stopped just outside of effective range for either of us.

"Can I give you a ride back to your hotel, Judas Maccabeus Davidovich?"

"No, thanks, I'm in a hurry." You can get almost anywhere in New York City faster on foot or on the subway than you can in a car.

"Fair enough. Before you leave, though, let me tell you a parable."

"Okay."

"Fuck with me I'll kill you."

Chapter Thirty-eight
JAY DAVIDOVICH

Once past the guard desk as I exited the luxury suite area, I transferred the envelope from my back pocket to the right side pocket of my khakis. Making my way in a bustling, self-important hurry—in other words, like a New Yorker—I took two flights of stairs down to ground level and then scampered to a window-fronted counter inside the special entrance for people with suite tickets. Lettering above the circle in the glass window read VALET PARKING.

At that point I slowed down a little. I handed one of my Transoxana business cards to a grizzled African-American who had "retired cop" written all over the features under his fuzzy, salt-and-pepper hair.

"What's this supposed to be?"

"Hi. Jay Davidovich from Transoxana. Could you call a taxi for me?"

He gave me that puzzled/intrigued New Yorker look—the one that says, "Is this asshole just jerking me around, or could there possibly be people in the world this fucking stupid?"

"Sir, do you have a car valet-parked with Stadium Parking Services?"

"No, that's why I need a taxi."

"We don't do taxis here, sir. Call nine-one-one and tell them you're a mental case."

I raised the first two fingers of my right hand to my right eyebrow for a mini-salute.

"Thanks a lot. I really appreciate it."

I strolled casually out the door to the driveway where the valets pull up cars they're returning to their owners. While pushing through the door, I dug out my wallet to search for a five as if I intended to give someone a tip. I crossed the driveway, turned back toward the suite-ticket entrance, and nodded casually at a couple of dudes in valet-parking jackets. They nodded back, but I got the feeling they didn't really have their hearts in it.

I got to feeling real conspicuous about forty-five seconds into the charade. I sucked it up. Finally a car pulled up to be valet-parked for the big shot driving it. The moment it came to a full stop I turned around and started down the sidewalk, heading away from the suite-ticket entrance. Three more or less normal strides, and then I clicked into full run. It took me less than a minute to reach the subway entrance. Tokens ready, through the gates, down the stairs, on the platform, waiting for a train that would take me back to midtown Manhattan.

It would have been a nice gesture for New York to have a train pulling into the stop just as I reached the bottom of the stairs, but the city apparently had other things to worry about. I had a three-minute wait. I used the time constructively. Specifically, I kept my eyes laser-focused on the stairs leading down to the platform, seeing if I could spot anyone who looked like he (or, in theory, she) had gotten a cell-phone call about spotting the tall blond guy and looking for an opportunity to knife him and relieve him of a compromising envelope—and who hadn't been led astray by my Oscar-caliber performance at the valet parking station, and who could then somehow keep up with me while I was running like a scalded chicken.

None of the eight people who came down during the wait fit the bill. None of them even glanced in my direction. When the train arrived I held back. All eight of them got on, even though they couldn't know which car I'd choose. So, ninety-nine-point-nine-percent chance I was home free.

Even so, a tenth of a percent ain't zero. I boarded the last car, sat with my back against the bulkhead at the far end, and kept an eye on the door leading from the car ahead. No one came through during my twenty-five-minute subway ride. That didn't mean it was time to let down my guard. I got off a stop early and walked the rest of the way to the Millennium Broadway Hotel.

Almost certain that Nesselrode's envelope handoff had surprised Halkani. Almost no chance that Halkani would have had some accomplice ready to do unpleasant things to me if the need happened to arise. Almost. But I'd seen that sonofabitch's eyes. Not stone cold. Lively and excited, as if he were enjoying himself. He wasn't some wounded soul working out pent-up hostilities beaten into him by abusive parents or ass-grabbing uncles. He was just your basic greedy bastard with his eyes on a big payday and quite ready to kill to make it happen. So until I was inside the hotel room with the door bolted, I'd be on Defcon Four.

TV Voice: "...played winter ball with Harry and I in the Dominican Republic after last season. Man, they *love* baseball down there!"

Rachel: "Or '...played winter ball with Harry and *me*,' as educated people sometimes say."

Weird. As if I'd somehow triggered this snarky little dialogue just by carding open the door to Room 1125. Taking the kind of deep breath you do just before going out for a full dress inspection, I opened the door all the way and strode into the room. Rachel had flown up to New York with me to share this trip, and apparently she'd brought a dose of Rachel-tude along with her. I snapped the security lock into place.

"Hi, I'm back."

"...see him lying prone on the field on the tape there."

"Hi. Excuse me a second. '*lying supine* on the field,' you semi-literate cretin. He's on his *back*, and what he's doing is *intransitive*. How was the game?"

"Hasn't started yet—which is why MSG is still running that inane pre-game blather you're savagely criticizing."

Rachel scissor-legged nimbly off the bed and ran over to me. Wrapping me fiercely in her arms and ungently pulling my torso down toward her level, she serially kissed me: lips, cheekbone, chin, eyelids, then lips again—the second one long, slow, deep, and hungry. It must have taken her half a minute before she came up for air on the last one.

"I'm glad you're here." She gulped breath.

"I can tell. Grammatical errors must really turn you on. I'll file that for future reference."

"I'm just trying to help them with their work." Her eyes danced with light and life as she smiled.

"You understand that they can't hear you, right?"

"That's just a rumor spread by the government to suppress dissent. A writer named Bill Vaughan said that in the newspaper once, so it must be true."

I pulled her hard against my body, intoxicated by the scent of shampoo in her hair and of fresh soap on her face, basking in the gentle pressure of her blond head on my right shoulder and the needy grip of her fingers digging desperately into my ribs. *God I love this woman. All the shit, all the mishigas, even the occasional impulsive slap—I don't care. Doesn't make any difference. I love her. I love her so much.*

"So," she said, stepping back from me but keeping her hands on my shoulders. "We're in New York. Maybe not the greatest city in the world anymore, but one *hell* of a lot better than Alexandria, Virginia. What would you like to do?"

Now, a rookie husband would probably have blown that question. He would have suggested some New Yorkish adventure or (even worse) said something like, "Whatever *you* want to do, beloved."

I'm no rookie. I fielded it cleanly. Got my butt down, eyes level with the screaming one-hopper, and snagged the ball backhanded in the webbing of my glove just before it would have gone skittering down the left field line. I picked Rachel up, left arm under her shoulders, right arm under her knees, and carried her giggling and squealing to the bed. While getting my shirt off I might have mentioned something about it being a silly question, but I really don't remember.

◇◇◇

A little over two hours later, I stood in the darkened room in front of a window looking over Broadway. Rachel slept contentedly, emitting occasional little lady-like snores that reminded me of an agile cat purring. I had the room phone on speaker as I poured a blow-by-blow account of my suite adventures into Proxie's voice-mail. I kept my hands free so that I could use both of them to hold a towel dampened with hot water against my back. Eight distinct scratches there, each an inch or so long. Nice passion trophy, but about twenty minutes ago they'd started to sting.

"No doubt after tonight," I told the phone. "Suspicion confirmed. *Eros Rising* is the target of a carefully planned theft that hinges on lending the thing to a museum in Vienna. Most likely scenario is a flush-and-switch. They get the thing into the open by arranging for the transfer, then somewhere on the way to Vienna they substitute a forgery for the real painting. They can probably count on weeks before someone suspects the forgery, but even if it's caught while the painting is being readied for display, the thieves will be okay. The catch is that Nesselrode wants to turn the painting over to heirs of the original owner as some kind of vigilante Holocaust reparation gesture, and Halkani wants to turn it into five million dollars or so—probably by selling it back to us so we can cut our loss, if we're stupid enough to insure it. Assuming I can reach Szulz's lawyer tomorrow about turning over the letter, next stop will probably be Pittsburgh. Stand by for updates, you know the number if we have to talk further."

I slung the towel over the shower-curtain rod in the bathroom, then came back out and just stood beside the bed, gazing at Rachel. In the subdued light she radiated a loveliness that took my breath away. Radiated a lot of other stuff too, of course: need, guilt, anxiety, insecurity, nauseating panic that I won't find her desirable any more once her belly gets really big. Stuff that had played at least as big a role as lust in her come-on a couple of hours ago. But that was okay. Marriage is a package deal.

Kicking aside trousers and underpants along the way, I walked back over to the desk where the phone sat. I picked up the letter Nesselrode had given me. I'd promised to put the thing in Szulz's hands, and I intended to do exactly that. But I hadn't said anything about the envelope. No promise about not reading the letter before I turned it over.

Except, of course, that I don't read German. It was addressed to "Alma." Penmanship okay, like a guy's, instead of exquisite, like a chick's. Dated something like twenty-five years ago. Signed "Tabby."

The room phone rang. *What the hell?* I hurried to answer before the polite burring could awaken Rachel.

"What does the letter say?" Proxy's voice.

"It says a lot of stuff in German. Proxy, are you seriously still at your desk after ten-fifteen on a Tuesday night?"

"No, I'm at LAX before seven-thirty local time. I'm waiting for a flight home, checking my iPad for a PDF of a letter in German, and not finding one."

"No wonder you didn't get my fax."

"*Fax?* I thought the Berlin Wall fell on the last fax machine left in the world. Don't they have scanning capacity in the business center at whatever hotel Quindel found for you?"

"They barely have a business center. The next option after fax was Pony Express."

An exasperated little squeal told me how frustrated Proxy was. Her next words confirmed it.

"Raindrops on roses and whiskers on kittens!" (This is Proxy-speak for *Shit!*) "There's a rush meeting in Hartford tomorrow night, because the window is closing on the Pitt MCM opportunity."

"Please tell me I'm not invited." *Please please PLEASE!* I haven't prayed for anything so hard since my third date with Rachel.

"You're the guest of honor. Command performance."

"Raindrops on roses and whiskers on kittens."

"Try to say something constructive, Davidovich. Quindel's last memo called this a five million-dollar decision. That would be one of the emails sitting in the in-box that I'm guessing you haven't checked in the last twelve hours."

"Okay, steady soldier." I covered my eyes with the heels of my hands and ran my fingers through hair that, frankly, could have used some Head 'n Shoulders. "There has to be an all-night Federal Express/Kinkos somewhere in midtown. I'll get the thing copied, scanned, and emailed to you in the next ninety minutes or so. If you don't get it before your flight takes off, you can sleep on the plane and read it while the limo is taking you from La Guardia to Hartford."

"Maybe…" Proxy's voice trailed off in grudging displeasure.

"Tell me something." The new voice startled me. I glanced over to see Rachel out of bed and slipping into a white, Millennium Hotel robe. "Why do people just assume that all Jews can read German?"

"I don't think anyone assumes that, Rache."

"Who's that?" Proxy demanded.

"My wife, Rachel."

"It's like assuming that all white people have natural rhythm."

"I don't think you'll get much buy-in on that one, either."

"WHO?" Proxy again. "Are you sure?"

"Give me the letter," Rachel said.

"Okay, Proxy, I'm gonna put you on speaker. Unless I'm mistaken, my beloved wife—not a call girl, not a hooker, not a spicy little bundle of expense-account padding but *my wife*, Rachel Davidovich—is proposing to favor us with a sight-translation of this little missive."

"Go ahead." Proxy's audible sigh chilled three thousand miles' worth of electrons.

I gave the letter to Rachel, who gazed at it dubiously while she flipped the room lights on.

"Okay. 'My Dearest and Most Tender Alma.' We begin badly, with a cliché from Young Werther's copybook, but no matter. We heroically continue. 'I approach the glorious day when I can rid myself of the final constraint and think of joining you again. You have never left my thoughts, true heart. I know you don't believe me. You thought me bound by a chain I could never break. I have proven you wrong.' *Proven!* Underlined with an exclamation point, if you please. 'I enclose a copy of my *Acta Formalis Defectionis.*' That last part was phonetic. The words aren't German. They look like Latin, and I don't know what they mean. 'I submitted it to my' something-something, can't tell, superior, maybe, 'to my superior yesterday morning. Now you know! Now there is no going back for me, dearest heart! For me, or for you either! I count the minutes until I can lay my poor eyes on you again. Ever, ever, *ever* yours, Tabby.' I hope that was helpful. If you will both excuse me, I am now going to go vomit."

"Thanks," Proxy said as Rachel returned the letter to me.

"Proxy, before you ask me whether the envelope Nesselrode gave me had any enclosure with the letter, which it didn't, I have to know who the hell 'Young Werther' is. Or was."

"Title character in a lushly romantic novel by Goethe." Proxy said this as if it were something even guys whose only degrees were in civil engineering should know. "I'd love to see what 'Tabby' enclosed with the letter, because I'll bet that was what Szulz spent the cost of a round-trip ticket to Vienna to get his hands on."

"Well whatever it is, I don't think it's a game plan for an art heist twenty-five years in the future. I'll sound out Szulz when I give it to him."

"You're going to have to hustle to get that thing to a guy in Pittsburgh and still make it to Hartford, Connecticut, in time for a meeting at six tomorrow night."

"If it was worth a trip to Vienna for him, it ought to be worth a trip to New York. I'm planning on hopping a limo for Hartford at La Guardia at, say, three tomorrow afternoon. If Szulz wants the thing that badly, he can get to La Guardia by then. Twelve-to-five he shows."

"No bet," Proxy said. "Sleep well, and spend Quindel's money wisely."

The Third Wednesday in April

Chapter Thirty-nine

Cynthia Jakubek

"Seriously? You're telling me at seven forty-five in the morning that if my client can drop everything he's doing and get from Pittsburgh to New York by three this afternoon you'll give him a document that he'll otherwise receive whenever you get around to it?"

"That's about the size of it," Davidovich said.

"That's the most high-handed thing I've heard since the last time I was in court."

"Yeah, I've been working on my self-esteem."

"All right, I'll pass it on."

"Have him try to let me know either way, okay?"

"Sure, Davidovich." I couldn't quite keep the sarcasm out of my voice, maybe because I didn't try very hard. "We always strive for courtesy."

Exasperation undoubtedly showed as I punched END CALL. How in the hell was I going to present *this* to Willy? He deeply appreciates *chutzpah*, but only on his side of a deal.

I dialed his number and got Amber, whispering—which probably meant that Willy was still snoring blissfully a few feet from her. Before I could tell her that she'd better wake him up for this one, I heard his groggy voice in the background.

"That's okay, I can take it. And how about some coffee?" Then, much more clearly, "What's up?"

I told him. I'll say one thing: the news sure woke him up. The last time I saw that fast a transition from grumpy to giddy, controlled substances were involved.

"Really? You serious? Holy shit…What time is it?"

"Seven-forty-nine."

"Almost eight…Shit. Lemme get my computer on. This is the big Jew, right?"

"Yeah, Willy, the tall dude."

"Let's see…Eleven-ten, gets in by twelve-thirty…Little tight at this end but, maybe, let's see, no luggage…I can do this! Made in the shade! No sweat! C.J., you're a genius!"

"Right now I feel more like a messenger girl, but I'll take it. You have a pen handy? I want to give you the big guy's mobile phone number so you can call him and confirm the hook-up."

"Do me a favor, C.J., text it, can you? I gotta fly. I don't even have my boxers on yet."

TMI, Willy, TMI. I smiled anyway. Couldn't help it.

"Can do on the text thing, Willy. Have a safe trip. And, if you think about it, sometime maybe you could tell me what the hell is going on."

"Monday for sure, Counselor, like I said. Take it to the bank. Gotta go."

I shrugged, remembering one of my mom's old lines: *You can laugh or you can cry, so you might as well laugh.* I checked my watch: seven fifty-one. One-tenth of a billable hour—on the nose.

Chapter Forty

Jay Davidovich

"This legit?"

Szulz looked at the letter to von Leuthen that he was holding in his left hand, and then at the envelope in his right. We'd just completed the hand-off: two-twelve p.m. at LaGuardia International Airport's livery service area.

"No idea. I'm just the messenger."

"This envelope was already open when you gave it to me."

"Yeah, I couldn't read the letter while it was still in the envelope."

"So you know what this says?"

"Yep."

"And you kept a copy of it?"

"No, Willy, I memorized it. *Of course* I kept a copy of it."

Szulz gave me a long, searching look. Not a hard look. No anger in his eyes, no twitching in his facial muscles, no teeth-clenching. Just appraisal. Was I dumb or did I have the best poker-face east of Vegas? That's the question I read in his expression. In Szulz's opinion, apparently, that letter should have made me smack my forehead with the heel of my hand and blurt out that it explains everything. Well, whatever it was I sure hadn't figured it out yet. So I guess I'd have to go with dumb.

If you have to get from LaGuardia to Hartford, Connecticut, an air-conditioned Chrysler Imperial driven by someone else is the least unpleasant way I know of to do it. Plenty of room to stretch out my long legs. Cold MGD to take the edge off parting with Rachel earlier than I'd planned. Some old horse opera on TCM, muted so that I could enjoy one of Sirius XM's jazz channels while I watched guys in white hats and guys in black hats blaze away at each other with smoking, soundless six-shooters. At times like this, loss prevention ain't a bad gig.

I reached the Transoxana campus in Hartford around five-twenty. Not the beehive of activity that you'd see on a weekday morning, of course, but not just a corporal's guard standing watch either. Transoxana has local offices and billions of dollars at risk in every time-zone on the planet. It manages all of them from Hartford. Transoxana HQ doesn't completely close for Christmas and New Year's, much less for weekday evenings.

After the usual badge-flashing and log-signing, I found myself alone in a conference room heavy on mahogany and set up with real and decaf coffee, four varieties of soda, and bottled water. I figured Proxy would have called if she'd wanted a pre-meeting. She hadn't, so I grabbed some real coffee, found a side seat toward what I assumed would be the foot of the table, and booted up my laptop to check emails. I had twenty-seven, but only one of them mattered much:

> Where are we on interviewing von Leuthen?
> Advise ASAP.   —Quindel

I stared at the thing for seven seconds, not quite gaping but with my mouth slightly open. I couldn't believe it. Could not believe it—because it couldn't possibly be true.

Could Quindel have not bothered to read the memo Proxy had undoubtedly sent him reporting my von Leuthen scoop? Not likely, but not beyond the realm of human possibility. Could he have read it and completely forgotten it? I wouldn't bet much on that one, either, but I suppose it could have happened.

But no way Quindel would have sent an intra-corporate communication outside channels. No way he would have contacted me directly, circumventing Proxy. We'll find a loophole in the Second Law of Thermodynamics before that happens. Quindel is a lot of things, some of them unprintable, but dumb and lazy are two things he ain't.

Chapter Forty-one

Jay Davidovich

I was still going over the Sent From data on Quindel's email to see if I could spot anything that seemed off about it when Proxy came in and started briskly setting up for the meeting: laptop booted up, mobile phone off and out of sight, mini-legal pad beside the laptop. That reminded me to update my voice-mail prompt and then turn my own mobile phone off—ironclad protocol for a Quindel meeting. Then I showed Proxy the message.

"Holy…" She choked off the vulgarity—habit, I guess. "Thousand-to-one Quindel didn't send this."

"Agreed—and I wouldn't give you a thousand-to-one on the outcome of a North Korean election."

"So apparently someone has hacked into Transoxana's computer network."

"Or at least into the marginal ganglion of the network that connects to my laptop."

"They'd have to get past fourteen firewalls to do any real damage to the system." Proxy's lips pursed fetchingly in concentration. "Forward this to Tech Support—no, wait. Do you mind if I just jump on your machine and do it myself?"

Not really a question but for form's sake I said, "Be my guest." I had to admire the Proxygram she tapped out for the benefit of whichever techie had the short straw tonight:

Analyze message below and report to pvs@transoxusa *only*. Do *not*, say again NOT, reply to forwarder or original sender. Implement standard security protocols but take no action, say again NO ACTION, transparent to original sender.

She almost hit SEND without asking me but remembered just in time. I nodded. *CLICK!*

The table had now started to fill. Andy Schuetz, our ex-FBI guy. Some gray-hair from Legal with that I'm-a-lawyer-and-you're-not look all over him. A Quindel flunky in a khakis-and-polo-shirt outfit. And a senior secretary whose presence meant that we'd have official minutes for this meeting—in other words, *All right, Ms. Shifcos, let's see how you perform under pressure.* Finally Quindel strolled in, trailed by another flunky in charge of carrying his briefcase. Quindel was wearing blue jeans and a dress shirt with French cuffs. I'm serious. True, they were designer blue jeans that probably cost about four hundred bucks, but even so. We all seated ourselves and—no other word for it—came to order.

From the head of the table Quindel smiled. Good-looking guy. Early forties and, just a hunch, feeling a tiny bit threatened by Proxy. Six even, trim body you'd expect of someone with a personal trainer, nice tan, and slightly curly salt-and-pepper hair that looks like it costs fifty bucks a crack to cut. Radiates confidence. Says "metrics" when "numbers" would do just fine. Has a tendency sometimes to call other people's opinions "unmitigated bullshit," which always makes me wonder what mitigated bullshit is like. The CEO of the company could scream at him for ninety seconds about what a moron he was and he wouldn't bat an eye or pop a bead of sweat. He'd just wait out the tirade and then say calmly, "Let's get some metrics." Wouldn't want him walking point for me on a patrol, but maybe that's just me.

"Thank you all for taking time out of your evening for this meeting. I realize it's an imposition. Unfortunately, we're looking at a hard stop. As in Chinese Wall. We have until noon tomorrow to give Pitt MCM a firm quote on art-exchange insurance. The insurance premiums will be funded by an NEA grant, so the Museum is going ahead with the exchange regardless of anything we say. At stake for us are premiums totaling almost a million dollars if the exchange runs its full three-year course. Even more important, it's likely that we'll lose our existing account with Pitt MCM for its standard insurance package if we refuse to quote. So looking at, say, ten-year metrics, we have a five million-dollar decision to make."

He smiled again and swept the table's perimeter with his eyes. He lingered for an extra fraction of a second on me. I think he was daring me to compute how many years of my salary five million dollars amounted to. Then he got down to business.

"With that background, Mr. Davidovich, keeping in mind that your job is *loss* prevention, not *sales* prevention, please explain why Transoxana Insurance Company should blow five mil off its bottom line."

"Because five is less than ten and we face at least a twenty percent risk of losing fifty million. Professional bad guys have criminal designs on *Eros Rising*. We've dodged the bullets so far but we can't expect to keep that up forever, because they're getting inside help from someone at Pitt MCM."

"Which orifice did you pull that out of?"

"Nesselrode's crack about how amazing it was that the attempted snatch at the Museum almost worked even though it shouldn't have had a chance. The only way it had a chance was if someone at the Museum decided to add aiding and abetting to his job description."

"Someone like Rand?"

"Maybe him, maybe someone else." I shrugged. "Doesn't really matter."

"Maybe Jennifer Huggens, the executive director." Andy Schuetz contributed that one.

"Explain." Quindel shot laser-eyes at Schuetz.

"The Museum has something called a deaccession committee. 'Deaccession' is a fancy word for selling stuff. That committee has been looking at unloading some of its paintings to build up a sagging endowment and help cover budget deficits that it's been running for several years. Donors are getting tired of chipping in to cover the gap, so you can see where fifty million or so would come in handy."

"So what? If they sell the thing we're off the risk. It's their painting. They can sell it if they want to, can't they?"

"Not that simple." Proxy jumped in. "Museums can sell paintings to raise money to buy other paintings, but not to cover operating expenses—like Ms. Huggens' salary—or to make their balance sheets look better. Apart from possible lawsuits by heirs of donors, Pitt MCM could go on a black list if it pulled that, meaning other museums wouldn't engage in exchange programs with it or include it in touring exhibitions."

"So far it sounds like their problem, not ours," Quindel said.

"Our problem is the Museum's possible solution to its problem." Keeping his hands folded in front of him, Schuetz leaned forward for emphasis. "Namely, for the Museum to collect fifty million for *Eros Rising* from us instead of selling it."

"Which it could do," I said, "if the painting were switched with a world-class forgery while it was on its way to Vienna."

"Easy." Quindel shrugged. "We drop fifty thousand on air-tight security. Ex-Blackwater guys are going for a dime-a-dozen these days."

"Ain't no such thing as airtight."

"Fine." Quindel tried to look like he was getting hot under the collar. "Let's say Loss Prevention falls down on the job and the bad guys pull the switch. They've got the real painting. They can't sell it to an honest buyer, so they sell it back to us for ten million. Or less. That's what art thieves almost always do unless the victim doesn't have insurance. At your twenty percent risk assessment, the discounted value of our risk is two million. Two is less than five."

Three words into Quindel's comment I'd noticed an eerie stillness come over Proxy. I felt a vibe of puzzle-pieces falling into place in her brain, as if she were on the verge of a *Eureka!* moment.

She was. She waited a couple of extra seconds after Quindel had finished speaking before she swung her eyes first toward me and then back in his direction.

"Except that they won't sell it back to us. They won't have to. This isn't just a snatch, it's a scam. We'll be on the hook for the whole fifty million."

Quindel looked straight at Proxy, daring her to break eye-contact. After a few too many seconds of that malarkey he spoke. "Well, I really want to hear this. It ought to be good."

Chapter Forty-two

JAY DAVIDOVICH

"No actual switch will happen." Proxy spoke with the casual certainty of Vin Scully explaining that you could expect a fast ball on a three-two pitch with the bases loaded. "That's the elegance of the plan. The bad guys don't have to sell it to anyone. A few weeks will pass—no more than three months. Then one of the heirs of the original seller will hold a press conference in Jerusalem."

"And say what?" Quindel asked.

"Some variation of what Nesselrode told us. When the original owner saw the forced sale coming, he had someone gin up a copy and sold that, hiding the real painting and then inconveniently dying before the war was over without telling anyone where he'd hidden it. The heir will then say that the original painting has now been found. He and his co-heirs are donating it to a museum in Jerusalem."

"But if people buy that, it means the Museum had a forgery all along. A little celebrity value, maybe, but nothing with six or seven zeroes after it."

"That's just the point." Proxy's voice suggested infinite patience with a slow learner. "A lot of people *won't* buy the story. All the high profile cops-and-robbers stuff has been window dressing all along. It's intended to make it look like the bad guys must have found a clever way to switch the paintings, à la some caper flick, even though they didn't."

Quindel nodded a couple of times—*I get it, but that doesn't mean I buy it.*

"What if we put some microscopic chip on the painting before the Museum sends it over? Then we can prove that whether the painting that comes back is real or fake, it's the painting the Museum sent—which is the one we will have insured."

"If the mastermind behind this is really a Museum insider," Schuetz said, "the Museum won't let us do that. They'll say it would impair the integrity of the painting. They might even be right."

"The Museum will make a claim under the policy." Proxy gave Quindel's nod right back to him. "Also a claim against the museum in Vienna and its insurer. Maybe against the heirs and the Jerusalem museum as well, just for good luck. All this time, of course, Pitt MCM will have been using the exchange arrangement and the hands-across-the-sea stuff as a fund-raising hook, and the painting lent by the Vienna museum as an attendance-booster. When we deny the claim, the Museum will sue everyone and his twin brother—starting with us."

"Cluster fuck," the gray-hairs from Legal muttered.

"You say that as if it were a bad thing." Quindel smiled modestly at his *mot.*

"Not a bad thing for me. I get to ship a three-million dollar retainer to someone I went to law school with. The department that has to come up with the three million dollars might take a different view."

"Still simple." Quindel raised his eyebrows in what I guess was supposed to be a meaningful way. "Win the lawsuit and we're still ahead."

"As a rule, insurance companies don't win lawsuits, they settle them." The lawyer shook his jurisprudential head. "Experts disputing each other, all the sympathy with the Museum, and no way to know which expert is right except to ask a jury of laypeople who couldn't tell Giotto from Jasper Johns the best day they ever had. Which we can't risk doing. So we'll settle."

"What good *are* you people, anyway?" The exasperation coloring Quindel's voice seemed genuine, for once.

"We're good at transferring wealth from other people to lawyers. We really shine at that."

"Pitt MCM keeps *Eros Rising.*" Proxy said that in a back-to-the-point tone. "The forgery claim remains ultimately unresolved. That generates continuing curiosity and publicity for the Museum. And Pitt MCM uses our settlement payment to jack up its endowment and cover its budget deficit."

Damnation! She nailed it! She's absolutely right! I'll bet everyone in the room thought exactly the same thing. Everyone except Quindel.

"Great plot for a made-for-TV movie. But here in the real world, exactly what do the bad guys get out of all this?"

"A piece of the settlement, probably." Schuetz threw that in. "Plus a chunk of change from whoever gets the tax deduction for the Israeli museum donation."

Quindel sat still for maybe fifteen seconds, face raised but eyes hooded. Then his eyes snapped open.

"Not buying it. Too many moving parts. *Way* too complicated, *way* too many contingencies. If this theory is right, these guys are running around committing felonies totally on spec."

"Well," I said, "they're sure as hell running around committing felonies, so they must at least think this way-too-complicated plan could work."

"Thank you for your insights and input." Quindel handed his legal pad to the briefcase-carrier and recapped his lapis-lazuli pen. "They have been very helpful. At the end of the day, though, this is my decision."

"Yes it is." Proxy said this in full ice-queen mode as she glanced at the senior secretary furiously taking shorthand. "Please note that if your decision is to bid on the policy, you will have made it against the recommendations of Risk Management and Loss Prevention."

I could tell that Quindel was about to offer Proxy whatever suit-speak for *fuck you* is when the door opened after a polite knock. A woman with a telephone-earpiece and associated wiring parked on her head leaned in.

"Excuse me. A detective from New York City is trying to reach Mr. Davidovich. He says it's urgent."

"Put him through to the conference room phone," Quindel snapped. "Put that phone on speaker."

Thirty seconds later I heard a white-noise hum from a speaker inlaid in the table's center. I spoke in its general direction.

"Davidovich."

"Sir, are you Jay Davidovich?"

"Yes."

"Sir, this is Detective-Lieutenant Stornmonth with the NYPD. Do you know Moshe Hillel?"

"Name doesn't ring a bell."

"Well that's very interesting, sir, because someone with your cell-phone number has called his cell-phone several times in the last week."

"Description?" I sipped coffee to warm up the cold spot suddenly spreading through my gut.

"Five-ten, one-seventy, dark olive complexion, hair—"

"Yeah, yeah." I rolled my eyes at the ceiling. "Hair black, eyes dark brown, all that stuff. How about distinctive body markings?"

"Tattoo of a wristwatch on his left wrist."

Gut punch. Hit me right across the seams. Did *not* see that one coming.

"He sounds like someone I know under the name Dany Nesselrode. What's happened to him?"

"Victim of a hit-and-run about two o'clock this morning in the Bronx. He's taking a nap in intensive care. We're calling it attempted murder."

"Lieutenant, you and I need to talk."

"Yes we do, sir. Now would be convenient."

"Now won't do. Give me a number where I can reach you in fifteen minutes."

He rattled off ten digits as I checked my watch. Then he said, "Fifteen minutes. Not sixteen."

After the dial tone had sounded, Quindel cocked his head at the note-taker.

"Only 'attempted' murder. You got that part, right?"

Chapter Forty-three

Jay Davidovich

Apparently Proxy wasn't sure that last crack was just Quindel's idea of humor.

"There's something on Jay's computer that you should see," she told him.

"Have you been sandbagging me, Ms. Shifcos?" Quindel's eyebrows arced toward his scalp as he headed toward us.

"Came in just before the meeting." I wouldn't exactly call that answer *No*.

I had enough sense to pull up the email string that included Proxy's forwarding message to Tech Support as well as the original email. It took Quindel about two-point-three seconds to absorb the words and grasp their significance.

"Why are you telling them to report to you and not to me?"

"Because we have to assume that your email address has been compromised—and we don't want them to know that we know."

"Right. We know, but they don't know we know. Very good. Absolutely right."

Translation: "Greetings, Jay Davidovich. Your draft status has just been changed to BAIT." Quindel looked down at me.

"Remind me of why the bad guys care so much about this von Leuthen dame."

"Because they think she has inside information on where the real painting or the really-good fake painting can be found."

"But she doesn't have any such information?"

"Can't be sure, but I don't think so."

"If you're right, then she must have some other connection with this circus, or the people involved in it."

"I agree."

"Namely—what?" Quindel put a challenging little nuance into the question.

"Don't have the faintest idea. All I know is that without realizing it I somehow got them all hot and bothered when I dropped the seminary-hacking case and jumped feet-first into this one. And a long time ago she apparently had a little romp with a seminarian."

"How can you possibly imagine putting those pieces together?"

"Still working on that. Something I can't put my finger on is nagging at me, but I haven't come up with it yet."

Quindel strolled back to the head of the table, as if he were in his den at home, going to get an interesting book to show us. I didn't pay a lot of attention to watching him think. In nine minutes I had to call a detective in New York, and if I ever got off the phone with him I had to call what's-her-name, Jakubek, the shysterette in Pittsburgh.

Finally, Quindel came out of his private little thought world and looked at the rest of us.

"Okay, here's how we're going to play it. First thing tomorrow morning we'll bid eight hundred-fifty thousand for the first year of exchange insurance, four-hundred for the second, and six hundred-fifty for the third. Because the risk is higher when the painting is in transit. If that scares them off, so be it. More likely, though, they'll shop around a little and then come back to us to try to bargain us down. That buys us some time to see if we can smoke out the malefactors. If we do, we can bring our price down and maybe save the business."

I glanced at my watch. Quindel noticed.

"Loss Prevention has to call a cop, so if there's nothing else we'll adjourn."

"One other thing," the lawyer said. "Do we share our suspicions about inside collaboration with the Museum?"

Quindel looked at the secretary, who stopped writing.

"No. Fuck 'em."

The Fourth Sunday in April

Chapter Forty-four

JAY DAVIDOVICH

"Holy shit!" I exploded.

"What happened after the Last Supper, Alex?"Rachel did an eyes-right to get a look at me as she swung the Suburban onto our street. "Although I guess Jews shouldn't make jokes like that."

"Doesn't sound like especially promising material for Christians, either."

"You're right. From now on I'll limit myself to jokes about serial killers. They don't have an anti-defamation league. Yet. Why did you almost drop our bag of bagels just as I started the turn?"

"I realized something. All of a sudden. It's been gnawing at my brain for days, and then *bam!* It just hit me."

Rachel pulled into our driveway and navigated smoothly to the back of the house and then into the farther stall in our garage.

"So what was it that nailed you like that?"

"*Katholische Theologische* something."

"Is that some outfit you're going to report my blasphemous joke to?" Rachel did a nice job of flashing *faux* alarm as she asked the question.

"No. That's a place that the priest running the seminary in New Mexico that had a hacking problem mentioned. He said his seminary sometimes sent students there for a term to pick up some kind of world-class scriptural study."

We were out of the car now and exiting the garage to start walking toward the back door. Rachel hungrily eyed the bagel bag as she got her key ready to open the door.

"Okay, I'll bite," she said. "So what?"

"I'll have to check the briefing packet on my hacking case to be sure." I set the bagels on the counter and opened my computer. "But I'm right at ninety-nine percent already. The name sounded familiar when the priest said it, and I couldn't figure out why."

"I'll die of suspense, but not until after I've had a bagel. You want one?"

"No, thanks," I murmured. *We finished breakfast less than twenty minutes ago, for crying out loud!*

I clicked on the icon on my computer for the hacking case file and scrolled through the beginning part of it—the part that I'd just skimmed on my flight to Albuquerque. Most of it was the kind of inessential background detail that gets translated into pixels when a loss-prevention support assistant empties her notebook into a computer. But not all of it.

Bingo. There it was. I unholstered my phone and speed-dialed the shysterette's number. Voice-mail. Sunday morning, figures. I started to talk before the beep was over.

"This is Davidovich, otherwise known as muscle. Before I got called into the Pitt MCM thing, I was working on a computer-hacking matter at a seminary in New Mexico. It was the second insured computer-hacking loss at a Church-related university in the last two months, so Transoxana put Loss Prevention on it. Last week I was talking with the rector of the seminary in New Mexico, and he mentioned that for decades they've been sending students to an Austrian university called *Katholische Theologische Privatuniversitad.* Probably butchered the pronunciation, but you get the idea. This morning I finally realized why the name rang a bell: KTP was where the *first* hacking-loss claim came from. Thought you should know."

Chapter Forty-five

Cynthia Jakubek

"It's like you're setting me up for one of the top-ten dumbest cross-examination questions ever put to a witness."

"By looking at my watch?" I glanced at Phil—yeah, we'd gotten from "Schuyler" to "Phil" without wasting any time about it—as I took a semi-final sip of coffee.

"Yeah. Actually happened once during cross-examination of an alibi witness. Supposedly. 'Question: You say you were talking with the defendant at six minutes of eight at least a mile away from where the mugging happened at eight a.m.?' Answer: 'That's right.' Question: 'How can you be so sure of the exact time?' Answer: 'Because it was Sunday morning and I remember looking at my watch and thinking if I didn't get a move on I was going to be late for Mass.'"

"I'd never heard that one."

"We use it to scare baby prosecutors. 'Don't ask one question too many.'"

"Well, it's eerily appropriate. I'm lectoring at the ten-fifteen Mass at St. Ben's this morning. Lectors are supposed to show up in the sacristy fifteen minutes before Mass, so I need to get on my way pretty soon."

Late breakfast with Phil at the Omni William Penn's sidewalk café. *New York Times* split between us and eagerly read with running commentary on both sides. Good talk. Flattering gleam in his patrician eyes and, to tell the truth, more than a dab of lust-light in my own. Not carried away in transports of ecstasy as I had been a few years ago by a guy who turned out to be using me, but comfortable. And happy. Verging on mellow. How would I like doing this on a regular basis—say, roughly every day? I would like that a *lot*.

We split the bill—don't want to fall into any bad habits—and I headed for St. Ben's. I had my reading prepared. Something from Paul, as usual. No need to turn off my mobile phone, because I hadn't turned it on yet this morning. You have to draw lines, and that's one of mine. I get Sunday mornings off. Period.

At ten on the dot I walked into the familiar sacristy scene: Father Larry vesting, sacristan making sure the ribbons in the jumbo missal the priest will use are at the right places, one server getting ready to light the sanctuary candles, my co-lector running a bit late, and Sister Luanga looking for the other servers who hadn't wandered in yet. She sighed with visible relief when she spotted a second server stroll into the servers' room and start looking for an alb and cincture to put on.

"How are things going, Cynthia?" I looked over my shoulder at Father Larry, who'd asked the question.

"Keeping the balls in the air. So far. Hey, maybe there's something you can help me with. An insurance guy I'm working with on a case mentioned a Latin term I'd never heard before: *Acta Formalis Defectionis*. Do you know what that is?"

"Something I hope you never sign. The full title is *Acta Formalis Defectionis de Ecclesia Catholica*. It's a formal renunciation of membership in the Catholic Church. Does that help?"

"Well, I'm ahead of where I was fifteen minutes ago. Thanks."

I checked my own reading in the Lectionary—someone should have scolded Paul about his penchant for run-on sentences—and took a look at the first reading as well, just in case my co-lector didn't show up and I had to handle that one too. By the time I'd finished that, the second server had reached our area. His alb—basically an ankle-length gown made out of white cotton—looked okay. The knot in his cincture, though—not so much.

A cincture is a braided fabric rope tied around the waist of an alb to serve as a belt. The two free ends are supposed to hang down from the left hip, where the knot is, to well below the knee. This kid had a lumpy mess where the knot was supposed to be, and the ends barely reached the top of his knee. It looked like he'd knotted the strands one at a time and had just kept tying them until he figured he had something that would hold. With some amusement, I watched Sister Luanga struggling valiantly not to laugh at the thing.

"Here," she said to the fifth-grader instead of chuckling. "Let me show you a trick with that cincture."

The boy laboriously untangled the green rope, took it off, and handed it to her. She doubled it and then pulled it out nearly to arm's length, holding the loop in her left hand and the two free ends in her right. She moved her right hand up to a foot or so above the free ends. After a pause to make sure she had the server's attention, she began her instructional.

"When you put this around your waist from the back, you hold the loop just in front of your left hip and bring the free ends across the front of your waist over to the same hip." She did this, except that she kept the entire cincture in front of her where he could see it. "Now, here is the tricky part, you see. You bend the loop backwards on the outside, and then take the two strands, well up from the free ends, and push them both through the loop, so now you have a double loop."

She demonstrated this. Her hands worked with almost magical dexterity as she made the move look easy. Then she pulled the strands out and did it again much more slowly, so that the boy could see every step.

"You see?"

"Yes, Sister."

"Now all you must do is put the two loose ends through the new loop you have made, and you have a nice, clean knot."

Demonstration by Sister Luanga, nod from the server. She undid the knot and handed the cincture back to the server.

"Now you try it."

He did. Epic fail on the first effort because he intuitively slipped the first loop in between the two strands instead of putting the strands through the loop to make a second loop. Sister Luanga explained this to the server, who tried again. This time he got it. And not a moment too soon. Father Larry was antsy for us to hustle to the back of the church for our procession up to the sanctuary.

All the way through Mass something kicked at me, tickling the back of my brain, tantalizing me like a Friday *New York Times* crossword clue that you think you ought to have but you can't quite grasp. I gave special attention to my reading, hoping for some Pauline inspiration to clear up the puzzle. No luck. He must have been thinking of something else when he dictated this one to some hapless secretary while both of them waited for hammering at the door that would mean armed men and unpleasant tomorrows.

Mass over. Up to the sanctuary for the recessional. Trek to the rear of the church in a tidy little procession, then back to the sacristy to straighten things up. By eleven-thirty I'd made it to the sidewalk outside the church. Life felt good. Pleasant sunshine, clear sky, unseasonably warm temperatures, and a nice little six-block walk to the building that housed my office. I'd parked my car—well, technically, dad's car—in the ramp there. I figured to be sitting down to Sunday dinner in ninety minutes.

I decided that almost eleven forty-five was close enough to noon to justify turning on my mobile phone. I promptly heard a tonal *beep!*, telling me that some voice-mails would appreciate my attention. I looked at the first. Davidovich. I punched it up. I listened to it. And just like that the dominoes started falling in a cascading free association that would have made Rube Goldberg blush.

Davidovich/collar robber/seminary-computer-hacking/ art-heist/dead-guy-in-Vienna/Insider-at-the-museum/

Tally-hustling-Sean-and-Abbey/collar-robber again/Willy-in-Vienna/Acta-Formalis/Tally-in-Vienna/Von-Leuthen/reconcili-ation-room/Willy-worming-out-of-me-that-confessions-weren't-heard-on-Sundays/Willy promising to tell me the whole story tomorrow...Hoo-boy!

I wheeled around and sprinted back toward St. Ben's. Reached the church in four minutes flat. Front doors locked. Figures. More than half-an-hour after the end of the last Mass. I raced around back. The Open Door Café would start serving at noon, and Sister Luanga would be getting ready. No key, but she'd recognize me. Around the corner to the back of the church. Line of hungry homeless already formed outside the door. Adrenaline racing, heart pumping, blood pounding my temples, sweat streaming, fear gripping my gut. A voice came from behind me as I whistled past the waiting men.

"Hey! Hey, hey!"

I looked toward the voice in the line and saw a blur.

"Later! Sorry!"

Passing the door that would be opened in a few minutes to the guests, I stopped at the service door leading directly into the kitchen. Sister Luanga stood like an answered prayer at a stainless steel counter inside. My rap on the window drew an impatient backward jerk of her head, telling me to go to the other door, but then she saw me. She hustled over to open the door.

"*CYN*-thia! What is it?"

"Something upstairs!"

I pushed in and scampered by her toward the basement's main hallway. I'd barely found enough breath to get the words out. I run ten miles a week (except when I don't), but running is one thing and hurtling like you have a rapist with herpes chasing you is something else.

Hallway dimly lit to save money but I knew my way around. Twenty loping strides to the stairs that led to the church. Up the stairs to the servers' room, behind the wall on the left side of the sanctuary. The door leading to the front of the nave was locked from the inside, which is the side I was on, so no problem getting through that one. I should now be diagonally across from the reconciliation room on the other side of the nave, near the back, but I couldn't see it in the almost lightless church.

I decided to run across the front of the nave, directly in front of the sanctuary, and then down the side aisle outside the pews. My flats sounded to me like thunderclaps on the terrazzo floor. So much for the element of surprise. Tough. Keep going. Careful turn down the side aisle. Moving a bit more cautiously now, but still making enough racket to startle the stained glass saints in the windows above me.

By the time I reached the reconciliation room my eyes had adapted to the near darkness and I could make out the door. No light showing behind the pane of glass. I peered in, but all I saw was a deeper shade of darkness. Couldn't hear a hint of a sound from inside, of course.

I tried the door. Open! If I'd had the tactical sense that God gave geese, that would have told me something important, but I don't and it didn't.

Now I heard something. Labored, choking breaths and thrashing body movement, like you'd expect from someone having a nightmare. Found the light switch and flipped it on. Willy! Lying on the floor, purple-faced, twitching spastically—and with a thin, beaded cord constricting his neck—secured with a slip-knot exactly like the one Sister Luanga had taught the server that morning.

Dropping to both knees, I attacked the thing. Thank God for short nails. I managed to work two fingers underneath the top two strands and get a little separation. The would-be killer hadn't finished the job, and I didn't want to finish it for him. He'd probably heard me clumping through the church like a lummox and scooted out of the room to hide somewhere until he figured out what I was doing there. *Which meant it was ten-to-one he was still here.*

No time to think about that now. The purple discoloring Willy's face seemed to deepen as with agonizing slowness I gentled the strands free. Got the first two strands pulled up enough that I could start delicately tugging them out of the loop and simultaneously pulling the outside of the loop toward me. Finally the tension gave and the whole cord went slack.

What next? Nine-one-one or CPR? CPR.

Kneeling beside his body, I interlaced the fingers of my two hands and put the heel of my right hand roughly between where the nipples of his breasts figured to be. Push, hard, going for a two-inch compression. Repeat. And again. Thirty times. Pause. Face as close to his mouth as I could stand to check for any sign of normal breathing. *Nada.*

Deep breath for me. Pinch Willy's nose shut with the thumb and index finger of my left hand, pull his mouth open and pin his tongue down with my right, and blow air into that mouth, hoping enough of it would get into his bruised windpipe to open it all the way back up. Head-up, exhale, repeat. The summer before my senior year in high school a perky little fifteen-year-old had taught me basic CPR so that I could get a lifeguard job at a municipal pool. Toward the end of the summer, I'd taught her how to smoke, so I guess I got the better of that deal. She'd called the two mouth-to-mouth efforts "recovery breaths."

Back to the chest compressions. Thirty times. Pause. Hint of real breathing, but not enough. Two more recovery breaths. Halfway through the next round of chest compressions I sensed his torso start to heave a little. Checked his mouth. I got the blessed odor of Marboros and black coffee—blessed because air brought me the odors. Willy was breathing again. I sat back on my heels, hoping and praying that I'd brought it off.

"I've already called nine-one-one."

I jumped like a six-year-old watching a horror film as I heard Tally's voice behind me. I jerked my head around to look at him, framed in the doorway with looming darkness behind. *Think fast, Cindy. Pretend you're in court.*

"Tally, thank God you're here!"

"This gentleman and I had an appointment. His idea of a joke, I suppose, choosing St. Ben's for our meeting. Got here before Mass was over, looked around, and then waited forever, but we didn't connect. Then I saw a chap who looked a little dodgy slipping out the door as if he didn't want to be seen. Thought I should investigate. Slow work with nothing but my cell-phone as a flashlight. Didn't even think of looking in here. I'm glad you somehow stumbled over him."

Thank God for long-winded egotists. Tally's nervous logorrhea gave me time to come up with something.

"Okay. If you've called nine-one-one, you'd better go push the front door open and wait there to let them in. The doors are locked."

His skull might as well have been transparent. I could see the metaphorical wheels turning. *Was she really that dumb? Buying the generic bad-guy line?*

"You're right," he said at last. "I'll wait for them. You'll stay with Szulz?"

No, you moron, I'll just pop down to PNC Park for this after-noon's ball game.

"Yes, I'll stick with Willy."

He backed up about three feet, then turned to his left. Trying to make it look good, I suppose. That gave me all the room I needed. Quick arch backward, stretched my left arm out and back until it hurt, caught the edge of the door and slammed it shut. And punched the little button that locked it.

I sensed Tally wheeling back in indecision, but I couldn't really see him anymore. Did he think about banging on the door, trying to force his way in? Good luck with that one. Ever hear about the seal of the confessional? Whatever, he ended up not doing it. He probably figured that he'd give me maybe three minutes and then come hustling back, yelling that the EMTs were here.

I called nine-one-one, because Tally sure as hell hadn't done it.

"What is your emergency?"

"Attempted strangulation at St. Benedict the Moor Catholic Church." I rattled off the address. "Victim is near death and needs immediate attention. Pulse weak, respiration shallow, eyeballs distended."

"What is your—"

"Cynthia Jakubek. Victim is in immediate danger of death, repeat, *immediate* danger of death."

"Dispatching."

I gave her thirty seconds, then spoke up again.

"Now listen carefully. The front doors of the church are locked. Call Father Larry in the rectory and tell him what's happened. Have him meet the EMTs outside with the key when they arrive."

"Is the perpetrator still in the vicinity?"

"Don't know."

"Are you with the victim?"

"Yes."

"Are you in immediate danger?"

"No."

"Stay where you are."

"Count on it."

Seemed like two hours later when I finally heard sirens in the distance, but it couldn't have been more than three or four minutes. It gave me time to fish the much-folded von Leuthen letter out of a pouch in a money belt that Willy had concealed under his shirt and waistband. Right on cue, maybe thirty seconds after the first audible klaxon, Tally appeared in the window, rapping on it and mouthing *They're here! They're here!*

Sure they are, Tally. Pulling my phone up, I punched dad's number.

"Jakubek residence, this is Vince."

"Cindy, dad. I'm gonna be running late. Don't hold dinner."

Chapter Forty-six

CYNTHIA JAKUBEK

Did I actually bring this off? Really?

Those questions ran through my head as the EMTs wheeled Willy away and the cops snapped their notebooks shut over my story and Tally's. Had Tally bought my little act, my pretending to believe that a bad guy matching Halkani's description was running around Pittsburgh, and thank God Tally had shown up like a white knight?

A pleasant hope but, as my dad taught me, "Cheer from the heart, bet from the head." Three-to-two I hadn't fooled Tally. Maybe longer odds than that. So I needed a Plan B.

Tally and I followed the others out toward the central door and the brilliant sunlight beyond it. Father Larry stood in the vestibule, jingling the keys the cops had returned to him. I shot him a glance over my shoulder.

"I'll get the doors, Father."

A puzzled look splashed for a second across his face. He knew that the church's doors locked automatically when they swung closed unless you push an obscure button on the bottom of the brass case that houses the latch-end of the inside push-bar on each door. He's a savvy guy, though. After one look at my face he wiped his baffled expression away and nodded, as if my comment made sense.

I held the door for him and Tally. As they exited, I surreptitiously found the button with the middle fingers of my left hand and pushed. The *click!* sounded to me like it could have been heard in Ohio, but Tally didn't seem to notice. I joined him on the sidewalk, watching the others move away toward their different destinations.

I did a quick run through alternative options, which in my view basically sucked. No way the EMTs would let a non-relative ride along with Willy in the back of the rescue squad truck. I had nothing concrete to tell the cops, and they heard donuts calling them. If I started spinning theories they'd tune me out and tell me a detective would be in touch. Pushing eighty, Father Larry didn't strike me as promising human shield material, so improvising a spiritual crisis to talk to him about didn't make much sense.

Zero for three, leaving Tally and me *mano a mano* with a surreptitiously unlocked church door as my only plan. Under the circumstances a banality seemed to be in order. I turned toward Tally and came up with one.

"Quite an adventure."

"Certainly was. May I accompany you back to your car—you know, just in case?"

"Actually, I'm gonna head around back and see if they need any help at the café in the church basement. Plus, I have to check the church doors like I promised Father Larry."

He responded to that by giving me a long, shrewd look. A little unnerving. Okay, a lot unnerving. When he spoke his tone seemed matter-of-fact, almost jovial.

"You know, don't you?"

So much for my thespian skills.

"Yeah, Tally, I know." I sighed at the sheer tawdriness of the whole thing. "I know that you were a Catholic seminarian who slipped the traces after you had a fling with a charismatic lover and turned her into a collar-robber."

"Lost my vocation." A rich whiff of irony wafted from his words.

"God be praised for *that*. You have about as much business in ministry as I do in air-traffic control. I know that you formally apostasized because you thought that would impress your lover. No one formally defects from the Church unless he's already part of it. You filed the paperwork after your marriage to Abbey Northanger, so that nuptial is invalid on its face. Catholics can't get married by an Elvis impersonator in an ersatz 'chapel' on the Las Vegas strip."

"They can't get married by the Archbishop of Canterbury in Westminster Abbey without a dispensation—and we sure didn't have one of those."

"That shoots your plan to shake down Sean and Abbey all to hell. All that trouble—having some thug-hacker destroy seminary computer records in New Mexico and Austria so that your enrollments in those places couldn't be documented, all the gratuitous 'free-thinker' comments to throw people who thought about your background off the scent, the clever idea of having Sean bribe you with a share of his next deal instead of hundred-dollar bills in an attaché case—all wasted. Of course, you still have the *Eros Rising* scam. Maybe you can bring that one across the finish line. Unless Halkani wakes up one morning and decides that it's kill-a-redundant-gentile day."

"I think we have some things to talk about—in a less public venue."

So he thought he could bribe me, and through me, Willy. I wonder if he could have—if I had a price for something this important. I don't think so, but to tell you the truth I can't be certain. I guess we'll never know for sure.

I was exhausted. Physically, mentally, emotionally, and morally. Hungry. Thirsty. And at the moment disgusted with life. I couldn't imagine digging down into my soul for another chase at the best-actress Oscar. I wanted to just spell it out for him, scream it at him.

It's over, Tally. You strangled a guy in Vienna, using a knot that would be second-nature to an ex-seminarian. You tried to strangle Willy the same way, and you failed. Even if you got him from behind he'll know it was you. The Halkani story won't hold up for fifteen minutes once the cops start talking to Willy. You engineered a scam putting the Museum at risk because you knew that if the deficits kept piling up, sooner or later they'd have to cut staff—and inside counsel always seem dispensable. Halkani couldn't have gotten on top of that elevator car unnoticed without your help, or known when to be there without your telling him. You're done. Finished. It's over.

But I didn't. I plunged into my guts again. Felt a little like dumpster-diving.

"You're right, Tally. We should have a talk. How about my office?"

His eyes lit up. He swallowed my gullible/greedy chick act hook, line, and sinker. To him, my office would be absolutely perfect. Total privacy. He could do anything there that he wanted to. *Buy her if you can; kill her if you have to.*

"We can take my car."

"Sure. I'll double-check the church door and we'll be on our way."

I started moving before he could get an objection out. I knew I hadn't sold this one. Not completely. I'd only put eight feet between me and him, with a good ten feet before I'd reach the door, when I heard his voice.

"Here, let me help you."

That did it. A whisper of scraping pant-legs, meaning he was coming after me. *Hammer down, Cindy.* I broke into a sprint. Reached the church door in three loping strides and a stutter step. Lost a precious second swinging the heavy door open but still made it inside before he could grab me. Couldn't count on the door closing fast enough to lock before he reached it, so I didn't bother to fumble with the button.

With his longer legs, Tally figured to be faster than I was. Bigger and stronger, too. I do my ten miles a week at eight-plus minutes a mile, but we weren't going to be running a mile. Best case, we might run a thousand feet. I had one advantage, though. I knew the inside of the dark church and he didn't. Built for an era when people would be crowding the aisles at each of three Sunday Masses, the church featured a main body of pews separated by a wide center aisle, with a set of mini-pews across narrower aisles on the outsides of the main pews.

I sprinted through the vestibule and up the main aisle. Tally had apparently worn soft-soled shoes, but I could still hear faint *slaps* against the floor—and not all that far behind. *Assume he has a gun. Running in a straight line makes you an easy target unless he can't see you in the dimness—and the longer we're in here, the more his eyes will adjust.*

Time for a calculated risk. Halfway down the main aisle I pivoted at close to full speed and dove headlong to my right, onto one of the pews. Slid almost half its length on the lovingly waxed oak, worn smooth by a century of poor and working class fannies. Rolled to the floor, scrambled to my feet, took two cramped strides, levered myself on a kneeler some worshipper had forgotten to put up, and vaulted over the back of the next pew, gaining a couple of yards toward the far side.

The maneuver had gained me a few seconds. Tally had lost sight of me. I'd made plenty of noise, but with the sounds echoing off stone vaults and stained glass, the racket wouldn't help him much. I clambered on all fours across the pew's seat. A lacerated shin and a banged hip provoked some fiercely whispered blasphemy, but I made it to the end and scooted onto the floor.

Back to my feet and running straight ahead again. Breathing shallower. Diaphragm felt hollow. Tally sounded like he was roughly abreast of me, but separated by the entire length of the main body of pews on our side of the church. Only about twelve feet from the stairs leading down to the basement now. I tried to remember if I'd heard the door at the bottom of those stairs re-lock when it closed behind me on my way in. Couldn't be sure, so I had to assume that it had. Anyway, with only about thirty feet between me and Tally, betting the other way was too big a risk.

With a slanting right pivot I headed for the side door to the parking lot. Five churning strides and I slammed through it. Not an instant too soon, either, because Tally had already made up some serious distance. Suddenly awash in dazzling sunshine, I raced for the rear corner of the church building, maybe sixty feet away. If I could get around the corner I'd be within sight of the Open Door Café entrance, and anything Tally tried then would happen in front of a dozen eyewitnesses.

His footfalls seemed to slam in my ears. I felt like I could feel his hot breath on the back of my neck. Panicky fear. *Not gonna make it.* Managed a small scream, but I didn't have much breath to give it and, anyway, screams don't qualify as anything special in this neighborhood. *Don't look back!* Ten feet from the corner. His left arm grabbed my left bicep, but with the help of the streaming sweat that had soaked through my blouse and suit jacket I managed to snatch my arm from his grasp.

But that felt like my last bullet. One decent stride from rounding the corner, his right hand grabbed my collar at the nape of my neck and jerked me backward. Spinning me around to face him, he grabbed a fistful of the front of my blouse. I saw a fetid combination of pure hatred and raw fear in his reptilian eyes, and thought I could actually smell their stench. His left hand administered an ear-ringing slap to my right cheek, followed by a backhand to my left cheek. Okay, fine. I've been slapped before. Hurts like hell, but I can handle it. I was opening my mouth for a lustier scream than my last effort when his left hand darted toward his belt and I suddenly saw his fist filled with a gun.

No. Not a gun. A Taser. Through some irrational impulse, it scared me more than a gun would have. The thought of however many volts zapping me, of smashing to the pavement and twitching spastically, seemed even worse than dying quickly of lead poisoning.

"Now listen—carefully." His menacing whisper suggested complete control. "We have to talk. We can walk to my car together, or I can zap you with this thing and carry you to my car as if I were rescuing a damsel in distress."

Tempting. God, how tempting it was. Fought the good fight, run the race, all that stuff. Now stop banging your head against a wall. Growing up with two older brothers I'd thrown punches and taken punches, but I didn't have an ounce of technique. Not ten seconds of hand-to-hand combat training in my life. All I had was eight years on parochial school playgrounds, and I'd only learned two things there: never quit, and kick 'em between the legs.

That's what I did. Got him pretty good. Not dead center, but close enough to bring that telltale green tinge to his jowls and slacken the grip he had on the front of my blouse. That let me back a little toward the corner. He had to come with me a few steps to keep from losing me altogether.

We'd made it past the corner when I screamed. I don't remember exactly what I called him, but I should probably mention it at my next confession. I tried everything—thrashing, twisting, bucking, weaving—but I couldn't pull free of that damned right hand of his. *All right, you didn't quit. That's something.* I figured that would be my last coherent thought for awhile. Then, off to my right, I heard a voice and the *smack-smack-smack* of feet running in what sounded like slow motion on the pavement.

"Hey! Whachu doin', man? That my moufpiece!"

As he glanced to his left I thought Tally couldn't have looked more astonished if he'd seen ET peddling toward the sky on his bicycle. Couldn't blame him. Clarence Washington, in all of his tiny wispiness, five-feet-nothing and a hundred-twenty pounds soaking wet, was charging forward like a chihuahua with designs on raping a St. Bernard.

Tally raised his left arm to level the Taser at Washington. I took advantage of the distraction to bang my head into Tally's sternum, in the wild hope of spoiling his aim. Washington, of course, took off his right shoe. I mean, that's what anyone would do, right? Just slow up for a second and slip your right shoe off.

Not sure if I spoiled his aim, but Tally had apparently figured out that he didn't need any Taser to send Washington to the emergency room. He turned the weapon back toward me. Didn't see much I could do about that, so I held my breath and braced for the zap. Then, instead of a thousand strobe lights exploding behind my eyeballs, I saw a flash of black as Washington whizzed his shoe at us..

Tally screamed. Tortures of the damned kind of thing, with a tinge of astonishment coloring the pain that echoed from his screech. The Taser clattered against the pavement, falling next to the shoe that had dropped there after smashing Tally's wrist. Tally's face turned white. Releasing my blouse, he grabbed his left arm with his right hand.

Hopping gingerly now, Washington covered the rest of the distance separating us. He peppered Tally with indignant questions as he approached.

Tally's eyes wildly swept the perimeter, which at the moment pretty much consisted of Washington and me. After a half-hearted move toward the Taser—I had my foot on the thing by now—he began scuttling away. Washington started after him, but I grabbed the sleeve of his coat and held him back. "Away" was exactly where I wanted Tally right now.

I bent over to pick up Washington's shoe. It felt like it weighed ten pounds, with most of the weight in the heel.

"Steel plate?" I asked him.

"Yeah, sure enough is."

"You could do a pretty good number on a car window with that."

"I wouldn' know 'bout that." He shook his head earnestly. "I sure enough wouldn't."

The Fourth Monday in April

Chapter Forty-seven

Cynthia Jakubek

Monday was the greatest day I've ever had practicing law.

Sunday, not so much. We'd drawn the same pair of cops who'd come when I called in Willy's near-death experience. The one who'd talked to me seemed unhappy about my not mentioning Tally's dubious activities the first time around. All I could do was shrug.

"Theories aren't facts. I didn't know for sure he was hip-deep in two scams until he came after me."

"Lame." The cop had shaken his head as he scribbled.

"Best I can do."

"DA might think you took so long to put it all together because you wanted to see how much he'd offer you to forget your theories." He'd given me that cop-look, right in the eyes.

"If I'd been playing this for a payday, I wouldn't have run away from him, would I?"

That had shut him up. As Edmund Burke once said, though, you haven't convinced a man just because you've silenced him.

The other cop hadn't had much more fun with Washington. Somehow Washington had gotten confused about which shoe he'd thrown and handed the cop his left shoe—the one without the heavy steel plate in the heel. And somehow that hadn't registered with me in time for me to correct the record. Just not paying attention, I guess. Bad girl, Cindy. I'd made a mental note to slap my wrist when I had time.

We'd taken all this down to the kind of assistant district attorney who draws the Sunday afternoon shift. I'd made it as simple as I could for him, but his eyes had glazed over four minutes into my exposition. He'd waited for me to finish, not absorbing a particle of what I was saying as far as I could tell. Then he'd leaned forward in his chair and put his forearms on his desk blotter so I could tell he hadn't dozed off.

"Do you want to swear out a complaint?"

No, let's just chalk assault and battery and attempted kidnapping up to life in the big city.

"Yes. And one of the officers might want to swear one out for obstruction of justice by glomming on to a Taser that *C. Talbot Rand knew had been used to shoot a Pittsbugh cop.*"

That last line had sounded snarky to me as soon as it came out of my mouth, and I'd immediately wished I'd said it more politely. I swear, though, if I hadn't thrown it in I don't think the lazy oaf would have bothered even to ask the duty magistrate for a search warrant, much less an arrest warrant. By the time he'd gotten around to it, of course, Tally could have been halfway to hellandgone.

All that and warmed over potato salad for dinner when I'd finally gotten home. As mom had once said about an undeserved swat she'd given me, "Offer it up."

Monday brought a vast improvement.

The first email I opened had a PDF of a complaint filed on Friday against Shear Genius Precision Cutting Tools by a disgruntled distributor—obviously a copycat who'd read about the first case and was now yelling, "Me too!" The message from Shear's inside counsel wondered if I could join a conference call at ten that morning to see if I had any ideas. Yes, I could—and after ten minutes with the complaint, I had some.

While reviewing the complaint I left a voice-mail for Sean, telling him that I thought we had the annulment thing nailed and wondering when he and Abbey could stop by to discuss it. I knew I'd be talking to them before lunch.

Then came an answered prayer. Jerry Lysander, a senior assistant DA who actually knew writs from Shinola, called. He had drawn Tally's case. Sorry about the short notice, but could I possibly skip lunch and pop by over the noon hour? That would be yes.

"Good. The Taser confetti shows it was the same as the one used in the attempted Museum heist. Rand's prints are on the Taser and yours aren't. So he's basically screwed and you're officially on the side of the angels."

That sounded sweeter than a choir of Franciscan nuns singing Evensong.

"I'm glad to hear *that*. Do you need a complete rundown—?"

"Yeah, eventually, but I'd rather get that in writing, if it's not too much trouble."

"I'll get it to you by close of business tomorrow."

"Should be plenty of time. Rand has flown the coop, of course. We couldn't find a computer in his house or office, and it looks like he used a lot of paper files for a bonfire, so he's guilty as hell of something. It's just a question of tracking him down. He's an amateur, so it shouldn't take long, even with the head start the lazy fuck downstairs gave him."

"So what do you need from me at noon?"

"I want you to think about how you'd defend this thing if you were his lawyer. No one has defrauded either the Museum or Transoxana yet. The annulment thing ain't exactly a textbook crime: 'Pay me or I *won't* disclose truthful information that would help you.' Not sure that one fits the matrix."

"Well, there's Willy."

"Yeah, haven't talked to him yet. Still in critical condition."

"So aside from the Taser, that leaves slapping me around and trying to take me someplace against my will."

"Right." Lysander sighed. "It leaves that. Think about how you might defend him."

Translation: Tally is going to claim, what? Oh that *I* tried to extort money from *him* with some crazy-chick/bent-lawyer story about art fraud and Catholic divorce or something. When he blew me off *I* pulled out the Taser, which I'd been handling with gloves or a handkerchief or something, but I dropped it and he picked it up to keep me from threatening him with it. Then my low-rent client with a police record helped me break Tally's wrist and he had to run for his life. What about the wild chase? Let's see. Got it! *What* chase? No one saw it, did they? Tally and I were walking through the church, earnestly discussing my shakedown effort, and then just after I got outside I pulled the Taser on him.

What Lysander wanted to know was whether I was ready to handle that. Sit up on the stand and tell my story, knowing that some prince (or princess) of the Pittsburgh criminal defense bar was going to try to make me look like every crooked shyster in popular culture, starting with Saul from *Breaking Bad.*

Hmm. Interesting question. Answer not clear. There's brave— and then there's stupid. Plenty to think about between now and lunch.

After four-tenths of a billable hour of sustained work, Sean called. Could they come up at eleven? Clock check: nine-oh-two. Yes they could, subject to a ten percent chance of a conference call still being in progress at that point. I keyed the appointment into my computerized schedule. *Damn!* Suddenly my calendar was filling up, almost as if I were a successful lawyer with quality clients demanding my attention.

I joined Shear's inside counsel on the conference call at nine fifty-eight. Shear's current outside counsel didn't sign on until ten-oh-three, so inside counsel and I got to exchange small talk for five minutes. Part of the exchange made me very happy.

"What's your standard retainer?"

"I don't require a retainer for a quality client like Shear Genius." I could tell he liked the sound of that.

Outside counsel joined at that point. I recognized the condescending voice of the chap I'd met outside muni court after picking up Washington's case. Not so condescending now. For roughly thirty-five minutes we had a little back-and-forth. The term "embedded jurisdiction doctrine" came up as a way of forcing the case into federal court. I got the impression that current outside counsel didn't have an intimate relationship with that arcane notion. The last thing inside counsel said before we ended the call was that he wanted me on the case as co-counsel—not second chair, co-counsel.

Damn! I might have to hire a law clerk.

Sean and Abbey showed up promptly at eleven. I gave them the good news. The letter alone might not be enough, but the letter told us there had to be other documentation: a baptismal certificate, a confirmation record, first communion, application to the seminary. And some of those records would be old-fashioned paper filled out in Palmer Method longhand, still gathering dust in pre-digital age folders in an antique filing cabinet somewhere. Just a question of time, now. And money.

"We have plenty of that. I'd rather spend five hundred thousand on archival research than give that low-life a hundred thousand dollars' worth of the Woodshed Project."

"How's that going, by the way?" I asked.

"I came up with a hook." Abbey blushed with unwonted modesty. "A *gotcha*. Something to grab initial interest, so that the food can sell itself from then on."

My desk-phone *burred* into this jollity. The caller ID box showed ALLEGHENY CTY DA. Lysander.

"Excuse me. Sorry." I picked up.

"Never mind our noon meeting. We just found Rand hanging from the top arm of an abstract sculpture by someone named Yaacov Agam. Time of death between one and four this morning."

"Can you excuse me for just a minute, Jerry?"

"Sure."

Cupping my right hand tightly over the phone's mouthpiece, I glanced up at Sean and Abby.

"Never mind searching for Tally's baptismal certificate. Sacramental or not, the marital bond doesn't survive death. The only document we'll need now is a death certificate."

"So he's burning in Hell," Sean said with what I thought was unbecoming satisfaction.

"Let's not be judgmental, dear," Abby scolded him. "Perhaps he's burning in Purgatory."

I uncovered the mouthpiece.

"Murder or suicide?"

"Not sure yet," Lysander said.

"Describe the knot."

"Nothing special, judging from this screenful of digital shots. I'd call it lumpy but serviceable, like a beginning Boy Scout might tie before they teach him the square knot."

"Murder," I said.

The Fourth Tuesday in April

Chapter Forty-eight

JAY DAVIDOVICH

"Abort. Terminate the project." A rare redundancy from Proxy, so she must be either excited or pissed off.

"Fine by me, but why?"

"Don't you read the local papers?"

"Only if the headline has 'Israel' or 'nude' in it. Plus, I'm not even in Pittsburgh yet. Rachel and I just got to La Guardia, complaining to each other about having to take separate planes to different places. What's up?"

"The *Eros Rising* exchange thing just went blooey. Officially toxic. Rand either killed himself or was murdered, and the first round of back-story facts pretty much take him out of the running for patron saint of lawyers. The Museum has its hands full of damage-control. That painting will stay where it is."

"*Ergo* no chance to sell exchange insurance, so why should we care about bad guys skulking in elevator shafts and hacking into computers?"

"Bingo."

"I haven't felt this elated since the last time I did something that's none of your business. Great news, Proxy. After I get to wherever I end up going next I'll circle back to you on the seminary hacking thing."

"Not clear yet, but it looks like that may have gone away too."

"Better and better. Let's talk this afternoon."

Since Sunday afternoon Quindel and I had been trading phony emails about my supposedly seeing von Leuthen in Pittsburgh on Tuesday—today. We did this on the assumption that Halkani was reading our mail. What Proxy termed "the project" called for me to come to Pittsburgh today and drive around for four hours. Two other Transoxana loss-prevention guys would follow in a chase car about a hundred feet behind and equipped with one of those tracking things. I'd stop at various plausible meeting places and move on after, say twenty minutes. Sooner or later, in theory, we'd smoke Halkani out. If we could grab him and then persuade the local guys in white hats to cuff him and charge him and hold him without bail—four gigantic "ifs"— then we could dramatically cut the premium for the exchange insurance we wanted to sell the Museum.

Yeah, I didn't think much of it either. Quindel, though, is your basic bottom-line guy, and a million bucks is a million bucks. Now it was zero bucks any way you slice it, so 'abort'—YESSS!

My elation carried me through the tedium of changing tickets and the purgatory of the security and boarding processes. Still floating on it during the flight down to Reagan National, and feeling the same vibe from Rachel. The glow lasted until we were about three fourths of the way through our drive home. That's when my mobile phone rang. I answered it, halfway expecting Proxy. It wasn't.

"Mr. Davidovich, this is Sue Ann from the Blenheim Security call center in Hendersonville, Tennesse. We have an alarm report from sector six of your home."

Funny thing, that didn't bother me too much. Probably a false alarm, right? Still...

"Sector six is the sliding door from the deck to the sun room, right?"

"That's correct, sir. Do you want us to notify the police?"

The sliding door is a wobbly thing, so a really strong wind could have moved it enough to trigger the alarm. But better safe than sorry.

"Yeah, you better go ahead and call them."

"Very good, sir. Calling D.C. Metropolitan Police."

"No! Not D.C. Metro! Alexandria! Alexandria, Virginia!" I smacked the dashboard in frustration. D.C. Metro would answer a call in Cleveland, Ohio before it got around to Alexandria.

"Yes, sir. Checking the listing. Your home is listed as 'D.C. area.'"

"There must be seventy-five police departments in the 'D.C. area'! *Baltimore* is in the 'D.C. area', for crying out loud! Just—" (For the record, my voice sounded like exclamation points because of exasperation, not panic.)

"Yes, sir, calling Alexandria Police Department…Sir, confirmed that APD is dispatching to your address."

"Thank you. Let's hope they get there before the burglar gets away with the kitchen sink."

"Actually, sir, I think police are already on scene."

"Now I'm worried, because that's way too fast."

"No, I mean before. We called your home number first. A man answered. He said he wasn't the homeowner but a police officer who'd been called to the scene by a neighbor who heard the alarm."

"Thanks."

I ended the call and got ready to smack the dashboard again. Rachel laid a soothing left palm on my right bicep.

"Take a deep breath before you say something that you'll have to put four hundred dollars in the swear jar for."

"Since when have we had a swear jar?"

"We don't technically have one yet, but we'll have to start one as soon as our baby comes."

"I guess that's right." Brave little pinpricks of sunshine pierced the storm clouds lowering in my head. "But we're changing security systems first thing next month."

The cops beat us to our home, but not by much. Two of them. They'd made their way in through the sliding door the burglar had jimmied but they hadn't gotten through to Blenheim Security to turn the alarm off yet, so I turned it off myself. When I told the older one about the burglar posing as a police officer already in the house, he nodded with world-weary resignation. I nodded right along with him. I mean, how can *that* trick possibly work?

"I'm surprised he bothered," the cop said, turning his r's into uh's, Southern style. "Looks like it was just a quick hit. You hear the alarm, you figure you've got five to ten minutes, so you grab the first couple of things you see and beat it. Looks like he made you for a couple of items that used to be plugged in under your TV. Didn't even bother with your desktop computer, sitting out there in plain sight in your kitchen."

Belly-drop. I mean big-time. 'Cheap-ass electronics to make it look good.' 'Didn't even bother with your computer.' Suddenly I remembered the look in Halkani's eyes when he'd said, "Fuck with me and I'll kill you." Eight-to-one that Halkani saw the sudden cratering of the *Eros Rising* exchange project as me fucking with him.

Foreboding shadowing every step, I sidled to the elegantly compact work table in the dining room where Rachel keeps the desk-top computer that she uses only for her legal work. Still there, but that didn't surprise me. I opened the right-hand drawer. I saw what looked like half a pack of computer paper, and two replacement ink-jet cartridges, but I didn't see the thing I desperately wanted to see: the notebook where she writes down every blessed code and password we have. She knows she shouldn't do it. I know she shouldn't do it. Hell, everyone knows you shouldn't do it. But I'll bet that almost everyone except Proxy does do it.

I palmed the cops off on Rachel as soon as I decently could and speed-dialed Proxy's number. I had a problem. As I counted the rings I started tabulating the arguments I could use to convince Quindel that my problem was Transoxana's problem. By the time Proxy answered, I was up to none. So I tried something else.

"Shifcos. What's up?"

"Listen, Proxy, even with the exchange program off the table, the heirs' claim that the Museum doesn't legitimately own the painting is still in play, right?"

"Sure, I guess."

"So that's not just a million-dollar opportunity cost, it's a fifty million-dollar out-of-pocket risk for us, right?"

"Where are you going with this, Davidovich?"

"Quindel was ready to absorb eight hundred bucks a day times three for loss-prevention personnel, plus the cost of two rental cars and three plane tickets. Suppose I email Quindel that I've completed the von Leuthen contact and we can pick up the asset at such-and-such a place this weekend. Quindel will know the email is a fake, but maybe Halkani won't."

"Are you just making this up?"

"Not completely. Unless I miss my guess, Halkani has gone to a lot of trouble to re-establish the computer tap that Transoxana tech support probably spent most of the morning negating."

"'Asset' being the real painting?"

"Yes—or so Halkani will think."

"So he shows up at the such-and-such a place, ends up under arrest, and our fifty million-dollar risk looks a lot safer."

"You've convinced me, Proxy."

Silence. That meant Proxy was actually thinking this idea over. When she finally spoke, I heard skepticism in her voice.

"Huge cost-factor here, Davidovich. By picking a place, we make it a target. So we can't just go for, say, the Hays-Adams hotel in D.C. Has to be isolated so innocent bystanders don't get clipped in the cross-fire if the plan works. It'll have to have a top-of-the-line security system. And it will have to pass the smell test."

"How about the model home outside Vegas?"

Transoxana Insurance Company is the largest single residential property owner in the State of Nevada. Not by choice. Back in the go-go days before the bubble burst we had invested lots and lots and *lots* of money with developers building new single-family homes in larger and larger semi-circles outside Las Vegas. Then came the crash. The contractors went broke, the developers went broke, the developers' banks went broke, the banks' banks went into receivership, and Transoxana Insurance

Company suddenly had hundreds of empty, mostly finished houses on its hands.

We'd love to sell them wholesale to a speculator, but if you can find a non-mob speculator in Vegas who still has two nickels to rub together, you're better at it than the two guys and one gal we have on the job. So we're trying to sell the damn things one at a time. We rigged up one as a model home, with running water and functioning electricity and boomer-bait furniture. Ever since, we've been waiting for lightning to strike.

"That could actually work," Proxy said. "Do you think Quindel will bite?"

"Selling this to him will be so easy I'll be ashamed of myself after I do it."

I figured Proxy had only one possible answer for that one. I was right.

"Go for it."

The Fourth Friday in April

The Fourth Friday in April

Chapter Forty-nine

Jay Davidovich

Paperwork.

One Declaration of Unloaded Firearm(s) in Checked Luggage, Bureau of Alcohol, Tobacco, and Firearms Form ATF-06-1978, disclosing inclusion in baggage to be loaded aboard Delta Flight 0870 from Reagan National to Las Vegas, Nevada, of one unloaded and dismantled Remington Model 870 12-gauge shotgun for use by passenger at destination.

One authorization for guest admission to Crosby Trap and Skeet Shooting Range in Pender, Nevada, for the one-week period beginning the next day, together with a receipt for the three hundred-fifty dollars Transoxana had paid for the thing.

One Transoxana Corporate authorization for occupancy by J. M. Davidovich of the Model Home in Lot 23 of Plat 8 in the Kroft Development outside Las Vegas for the same one-week period, plus tonight.

I had exchanged all of this documentation by email, ostensibly with Quindel, to give Halkani a chance to read it. In other words, we'd created a paper trail so wide a blind man could follow it. We might as well have posted billboards up and down the East Coast: COME ON, PUNK: HIT ME WITH YOUR BEST SHOT.

At eleven-thirty that Friday morning, Rachel and I loaded a roller bag, a large backpack, and a Winchester triple-lock high-impact fiberglass firearms transport case into my Chevy Tahoe's cargo bay. We quickly put our cheerful little red brick neo-Federal home in Alexandria in the rearview mirror. At twelve-eighteen we—well, strictly speaking, I—unloaded this stuff onto the sidewalk outside Terminal 1 at Reagan National. The skycaps had apparently all just won the lottery, but Rachel and I managed to schlep the load inside to the ticket counter and then, except for the backpack, to the TSA secure area. By one-oh-five we were in line for security. The travel vest that I'd used in Pittsburgh actually did speed up the security process a bit. We reached our gate at one-twenty, almost an hour before boarding was scheduled to start.

Now came the scary part. Shouldering the backpack, I fortified myself with a deep breath as I turned toward Rachel.

"All right, angel, here's where we part company. If things go as planned, I'll see you in Vegas sometime Saturday night. Otherwise, I'll pick you up back here at Reagan National Sunday night. Either way, you will have had a weekend in Vegas."

Rachel's patented pout came right on schedule.

"Vegas has nothing but hookers, strippers, and gambling."

"One out of three ain't bad. Vegas is batting three-thirty-three, so if it were a baseball player, it'd make the all star team."

"Very funny." Sulky line, but she couldn't help chuckling. "But what if this *golem* Jew, whoever he is, actually takes your fake and sashays out to Las Vegas in search of this famous real/fake painting that probably doesn't exist at all?"

"Then he'll try to burglarize Transoxana's model home in the ill-fated Kroft Development. He'll find four veteran Transoxana loss-prevention specialists who'll specialize for three minutes or so in beating the living shit out of him before turning him over to the first guy with a badge who's willing to take him off their hands."

"But you don't think he's going to do that?"

"No. He's a jackal, not an idiot. He's on the hook for criminal conspiracy to commit fraud, the attempted murder of Dany

Nesselrode, and the actual murder of C. Talbot Rand. Not to mention the murder of his partner, which was actually committed by Rand but which they might try to hang on Halkani just for good luck. He may still have the *Eros Rising* scam somewhere in the back of his mind, but job-one for him right now is tying up loose ends."

"Like Alma von Leuthen."

"Like her."

"And you."

"Don't inflate my sense of self-importance."

"Don't bullshit me. He'll track you to a place where he thinks you're going to buy a painting from her so that he can kill her there. And, incidentally, you."

"That's one theory."

"Not a very comforting theory."

"The idea is to kill more of him than he does of me, if it comes to that."

"Does Quindel know this is a kill mission?"

"I said if it comes to that. Besides, we're an insurance company. We don't do kill missions; we do early policy terminations. I'll try to shoot the gun out of his hands first."

In an eye-blink Rachel's expression did a startling one-eighty. One second I was looking at a petulant teenager who'd just been grounded for prom night, and the next I saw the fiercely burning eyes of a Jew whose people had been living under the shadow of genocide for going on four thousand years—a Jew who would have slit her own children's throats at Masada to spare them Roman crucifixion. She took my right bicep in her left hand. It hurt. A lot.

"Take no prisoners."

Funny, when Proxy says that, it's a metaphor.

Chapter Fifty

JAY DAVIDOVICH

The cab from Reagan National dropped me and my backpack at Town Centre Shops, a strip-mall roughly four hundred yards north of the block Rachel and I live on and, more important for my immediate purposes, about two hundred feet above it. Cross the street bordering the parking lot and you come to a wooded downslope. Maybe I should say "technically wooded." Stunted scrub pine, mostly, with nothing much over eight feet tall. You'd have to work at it to stage a lynching there. Used now mostly for dope-smoking by kids who think they're fooling someone.

Point is, if you go about halfway down that slope with decent binoculars you can get a fair view of Jay and Rachel's manse. If you're wearing OD digicamis—excuse me, olive drab pants and jacket with digital camouflage coloring—like the ones I'd changed into from the backpack, someone near the house would have to be both sharp-eyed and lucky to spot you.

After side-stepping an abandoned baby carriage and a grocery cart lying on one side in the mud, I flushed a couple of fourteen-year-olds who were actually smoking tobacco. Almost as transgressive as pot these days, but such an important Virginia crop that it practically seemed patriotic. I stumbled over a pretty good-quality aluminum ladder that some idiot had left in the underbrush to keep the stroller and the cart company. Settling in behind a juniper bush with incongruous purple flowers, I brought the binoculars up and started a slow, painstaking pan from the opposite side of the street in front of our property to the back fence.

You can disable most residential security systems without triggering the alarm by cutting two widely separated wires at the same moment. That requires two people working closely together, and Halkani's partners tended to die young, so I wasn't putting a lot of chips on it. Even so I checked every wire coming out of our house. No cuts. No sign of forced entry. So it didn't look like Rache and I had company yet.

Next decision: Wait until twilight or go in right now? Now. First stop: garage. I retrieved a Colt Combat Commander 9 millimeter semi-automatic pistol from the locked glove compartment of Rachel's Camry, where I'd stashed it this morning just before we left. Chambered a bullet. Put my thumb on the principal safety. I had satisfied myself that Halkani wasn't in our house— but that wouldn't be much consolation if I were wrong and he turned out to be sitting inside big as life with an Uzi trained on the kitchen door.

I approached the door in a crouch low enough to keep my head below the window in its upper half. Blood pounding at my temples, adrenaline pumping through my veins like horny sophomores streaming into a mixer. Key in my left hand, pistol in my right. Insert the key. Awkward because of the crouch, but I got it done. Turn the key, hear the click, turn the knob, push the door open with the key still in the lock. Hear the steady *beep-beep-beep* of the alarm, telling me I had thirty seconds to punch in our code and keep the alarm from sounding. No burst of fire from inside, no sound of shoe soles scraping on linoleum.

I dove full length through the opening between the door and the jamb with my pistol leveled. Nothing. Scrambled to my feet, made it to the alarm console, punched in the code. Almost got the third digit wrong, but caught myself just in time. The *beep-beep-beep* stopped.

I exhaled. And this was just the beginning.

Chapter Fifty-one

CYNTHIA JAKUBEK

Amber called me with the news just after eight in the morning. Willy was out of ICU. No longer in immediate danger. Able to see visitors.

"And, uh, C.J.?"

"Yes, Amber."

"Willy was wondering if maybe you could come see him? And he's, like, sorry but, you know, right away?"

"On my way."

I dropped everything and hustled over to Woodland Memorial Hospital. I found him and Amber in a semi-private room with no roommate. Willy had a heavy bandage around his throat and another one on top of his head. The skin on his face sagged in crepe-paper folds. Aside from that he didn't look too bad, considering that it was Willy. His first question didn't surprise me.

"They caught Rand yet?" Aside from a bad-cold rasp, his voice sounded fairly normal.

"Someone did. He's dead. Murdered. Hanged by the neck."

"Nuts." Willy turned his face away from me as palpable disappointment washed across it. "I was looking forward to icing him myself."

"Into each life a little rain must fall. On the bright side, I managed to save Tally's letter to von Leuthen. I have it in the safe at my office. You can't sell it to Rand any more, but Sean McGeoghan might appreciate the effort you made to get your hands on it."

He looked sharply at me, eyebrows rising in surprise.

"That's right, I never told you what was going on with that, did I?"

"That would be no."

"No way I was selling that puppy to Rand. Plan was, if he saw it and wanted it, that would prove it was real, and that he was 'Tabby'."

"Well, it was real and he was 'Tabby'."

"See, what I really wanted was the acta defection whatever itself. That was the mother lode document. Hang that paper on him and we're home free. Couldn't find it, but I figured I could forge one to dangle in front of Rand anyway—you know, con the conman. But a real letter is way better than a forged document. And the sonofabitch bought it."

"I'd say he did." *And you almost 'bought it' too.*

"Way I figured it, see, I flash this paper at Rand and he bids something for it. That proves he was Catholic when he married McGeoghan's squeeze, whatshername, so that 'marriage' wasn't no marriage, way the Church sees things, so what's Rand got to squeeze McGeoghan with? Nothin', that's what."

"And Sean would show his appreciation by dropping a few bills in your collection plate." I tried really hard to sound non-judgmental.

"Absolutely not! That'd be a cheap Brooklyn grifter move. Not to mention against the law."

"As to cheap Brooklyn grifters, I defer to you—but I'll handle the legal conclusions."

"All I wanted was a piece of the Woodshed project. Not a free piece, like Rand. I just wanted McG to let me in with only a hundred K. I mean, I was actually going to put up the money. The hundred K. Minimum buy-in for a McGeoghan project is usually a quarter-mil, but I thought he might make an exception if I, like, did this favor for him."

"Not a bad bet."

"Turns out I'm in. Whatshername talked to Amber. So it worked."

"Abbey," Amber said with an earnest nod. "You really gotta remember her name if her future husband has a hundred-thousand of our money in his pocket."

Willy's eyebrows arched heroically at "our." For once in his blessed life, though, Willy self-censored. He kept his focus on me.

"Thanks for comin' over ASAP, C.J. 'Cause I need you to help Amber with something."

"Shoot."

"You've got to talk whoever is in charge here out of my car keys and help Amber get the Sable back to the condo. I parked it on Fourth, as close to St. Ben's as I could get, when I came there to meet Rand. So that was how many days ago?"

"Five."

"Right. It prob'ly has a Brazilian rainforest worth of tickets on its windshield by now."

"They blew me off when I checked," Amber said. "Told me they didn't have any keys. There's a spare set at the condo, but I don't want to leave Willy any longer than I have to."

"No choice, because they really don't have any keys here." These words came from the door behind us. "No keys with Mr. Szulz when the ambulance brought him here. Plus, the Sable has been stolen."

Just after I glimpsed the *oh-shit* look that flashed across Willy's face, my head jerked around fast enough to give me whiplash. I saw a guy who looked like he should've been in a hospital as a patient instead of a visitor. Under six feet, compact build, bloodshot eyes, at least a two-day growth of beard, and an odd tattoo on his left wrist.

"I saw you with that big tall Jew in Vienna," Willy told the visitor. He made it sound like an accusation.

"He knows me as Dany Nesselrode." The guy shambled the rest of the way into the room. He moved so stiffly that it hurt just to watch him.

"Who stole my Sable? I really love that thing—and it's paid for."

"Avrim Halkani stole it. Actually, Rand stole it first. He's the one who relieved you of your keys. Halkani took it from Rand, who had no further use for it after Halkani stretched his neck for him."

"And you know all this—how, exactly?" Willy asked.

"Because some time ago, after that *putz* had convinced himself that you could lead us to Alma von Leuthen and therefore to useful information about an expensive painting, he planted a transmitter-tracking device in your car's undercarriage. During the brief interval between when I hooked him up in New York with Davidovich—'big Jew' to you—and when he tried to kill me, I managed to get my hands on the receiver tuned to the tracking device."

"So you know where the car is?" Willy sounded a lot more urgent than clear title to a twelve-year old car would seem to warrant.

"It's somewhere near Washington, D.C."

"You're bullshittin' us pal. The only tracking dealies with range like that are owned by the CIA."

"The device he installed was standard issue. I know where the car is because I know where Davidovich is, and I know that a close encounter with Davidovich is on top of Halkani's to-do list."

That one left Willy fresh out of wisecracks. It sobered all of us up. But Nesselrode wasn't done.

"The *Eros Rising* thing is *kaput*, at least for now. Even Halkani has to realize that. But he wants Davidovich dead for queering the deal. He wants von Leuthen dead for knowing too much. He wants me dead because it turned out we had different agendas and, besides, he hates my guts. And he probably wants you dead, Mr. Szulz, just for the hell of it. He believes in cleaning up his own messes."

"All right." I blew out a long, long breath. "Time to call the police."

"No, thank you very much. I have three broken ribs, a punctured lung, a buzz in my head that won't go away, and a right knee that doesn't work properly. I should be in the hospital where they took me after Halkani creamed me with a Tacoma SUV he'd stolen. I left without waiting to be discharged because I can't afford to be sitting still—in a hospital with nurses, in a squeal room with cops, or anywhere else—until Halkani is accounted for."

Bullshit. You bailed from the hospital because you didn't want to be lying there when the New York cops finally remembered where they'd put the FBI's phone number.

Willy favored us with a long, world-weary sigh. He had that expression people get when they have to ask you for a favor they don't want to ask.

"Biggie, C.J."

"Shoot."

"I need you to see if you can get the Sable back before it reaches a police impound lot."

I took a look at Amber, then at Nesselrode.

"Could you two take a hike for about five minutes?"

They looked at each other—quizzically in Amber's case, skeptically in Nesselrode's. Amber shrugged. Nesselrode scowled. Then Amber came over to Nesselrode to give him some support as he limped out of the room with her.

"Okay, Willy," I said, returning my attention to my client, "I have to know the deal with the car."

"You sure you wanna know this?"

"Have to whether I want to or not."

"All right. I smelled a con the second you told me about that 'free-thinker' crack Rand had made to you at the Museum. Had no idea what the con was, but bullshit is my business and I know it when I smell it."

"Well, you're ahead of me."

"So I checked the fucker out. Not just Google. Had a Jersey p.i. who's pretty good do a work-up on him. Found out that a fancy Austrian university he attended for a term was a place

American seminarians sometimes get sent to. So I knew something was up, but I still couldn't put it together. Then McG mentions Rand being in the middle of a marriage scam, and I started to get some inkling of why Rand was so anxious to keep people from wondering if he was Catholic."

"You mean you flew to Vienna on intuition?"

"No, I went to Vienna to talk to an old friend of dad's. He's the one who put me onto Alma von Leuthen. But that looked like a dead end. And that acta document stuff—I didn't know any of that."

"Yeah, you somehow never struck me as a canon law expert."

"Amber was the one came up with that. She knew the basic rule about how marriage outside the Church doesn't count for Catholics, but does count for non-Catholics. Which I didn't. That last part, I mean. She talked to this priest she goes to for confession, and learned enough from him to pin down the acta document stuff on the net."

"But you hadn't come up with it in Vienna, and no telling where you might find it."

"Yeah. Tell ya what, I had *no idea* what a pile of shit I was stepping into. Anyway, once I come back from Vienna empty-handed, Amber forged the acta *et cetera*. I took a stab at it. She took one look and told me it was for shit. She said it a lot nicer than that, but that's what it came down to. She forged one that really looked good."

"So Amber can add creative writing to her list of impressive talents."

"The forged acta whatever is in an envelope inside the rim of the spare tire in the Sable's trunk. I wanted it where I could use it with Rand if I had to on Sunday. Didn't quite get that far with him, though."

"In other words," I said, "the Sable is the hiding place for evidence that Amber is the sweetest, nicest co-conspirator you'd ever want to meet. You didn't actually defraud Rand or anybody else. But you and Amber worked together to defraud Rand, and the forged document is an overt act in furtherance of the plan, even though you never brought the plan off. In theory, that puts you both on the hook for criminal conspiracy."

"I know. Stupidest goddamn thing I ever did, bringing her into it like that. I mean, I wouldn't tell *you* what was going on because I wanted to keep your skirts clean, but I couldn't even of thought the thing up without Amber."

"I did say 'in theory.' The potential victim was a bad dude, now he's dead, you never got a penny out of it. Not the kind of thing the average cop would jump at, even on a slow day."

Laying his head back on the pillow and shaking it slowly from side to side, he stared at the ceiling.

"The connection to the art thing makes it a huge deal, C.J. Sure as hell they're gonna say I was in cahoots with Halkani on the whole thing. Which would mean Amber was lying about Halkani stealing the Taser and put me right back in the soup on that deal."

"Something to that, all right."

"Now I can handle that. I'm a big boy and I know the rules. What I can't handle is the Feds threatening to prosecute Amber as a way of getting to me." Wincing with pain as he raised his head, he propped himself up on his left elbow and looked pleadingly at me. "If they get my Sable with Halkani's prints all over it, they're gonna take it apart bolt by bolt and search every square foot of it. They'll take that letter and shove it right up my ass an inch at a time. Same with Amber. She's tougher than she looks and smarter than she sounds, but I can't put her through that."

Willy was begging me. He loved Amber more than he hated begging, and that was saying something. On top of that, I couldn't disagree with a thing he'd said about the way the Feds would come after him and Amber.

I stepped outside to summon Amber and Nesselrode back into the room. I wondered whether Nesselrode was technically a fugitive yet. If Davidovich's theories were even half right, Nesselrode was up to his eyebrows in a large-scale criminal plot—and unlike Willy, he was actually guilty of serious crimes. Noble purposes aren't a defense. Halkani had tried to murder him, but that didn't mean they weren't working together on something that had gotten other people killed– probably made it more likely, if anything. On the other hand, theories aren't facts. So I wasn't technically aiding and abetting—yet.

Nesselrode might have been reading my mind.

"I haven't been charged with anything as far as I know. And when I say I want to account for Halkani, I mean, of course, that I want to find him and identify him to the proper authorities so that they can arrest him and provide him with due process of law."

"Finding him means finding the Sable." Willy contributed that.

I sighed. I looked down. I took a deep breath. My client needed a service. Not, strictly speaking, a *legal* service, but at least arguably not an illegal service either. Willy had been there for me when I was eating Ramen noodles for lunch and wondering whether I'd be able to pay next month's rent. Plus, Davidovich was in danger and might not know it, and I kind of got a kick out of him. And I liked the hell out of Amber. I looked up at Nesselrode.

"Do you have a valid, government-issued identification?"

"Yes."

"Are you armed?"

"No—and I don't plan to be, if that's what you're worried about."

"That's one of several things I'm worried about. Any money?"

"No."

Willy snapped his fingers at Amber. She dipped into her purse and came out with a modest wad of hundred-dollar bills. Instead of just tossing them into my lap she handed them to me. That's Amber. Pure class.

"Okay. We'd better take a cab to the airport. You're in no condition to drive, and I'll be busy finding flight times and booking tickets. Amber can get the spare keys from the condo and meet us at the airport with them."

Willy beamed.

"You are one hell of a lawyer, C.J."

"Yeah," I sighed. "For the moment."

Chapter Fifty-two

CYNTHIA JAKUBEK

It was like traveling in the third world, as Willy might put it. Not really, of course. No one was shooting at us.

On the way to the airport I called the Pittsburgh PD to report the theft of Willy's Sable. I mentioned a tip that the car might be in the D.C. area now. I figured that would generate nothing but a report, and that was all I really cared about. I managed to book two tickets on a direct flight that we could just barely make. Amber got to the airport with the keys and gave them to me. After that things went downhill.

Flying time from Pittsburgh to D.C. is supposed to be one hour and one minute, but that's after you get off the ground. We didn't even get on the plane until ninety minutes after the scheduled departure time. Then we sat on the runway for awhile. After we took off, air traffic control held us up so that there'd be a clear runway for us to land on at Reagan National. Once we landed, we had some more ninth-circle-of-Hell stuff trying to get to the gate. Bottom line, we weren't strolling into the terminal until almost three o'clock.

Nesselrode had put away three mini-bottles of Johnny Walker Red during the flight. He wasn't close to drunk, but you could tell he hadn't been drinking lemonade. When we finally approached the Avis counter, I suggested that he hit the men's room so that the agent wouldn't get too strong a whiff. It worked. By twenty of four we were driving to Alexandria.

With a little navigational aid from GPS we found the culde-sac where Davidovich lived and drove past his house. Looked to me like nobody was home. Nesselrode said he wasn't getting a peep from the receiver balanced on his thighs. I frowned my way through a Y-turn and got ready to exit the culdesac. I still had the frown on when I looked over at him.

"Now what?"

"Now we drive in expanding circles around this area."

"For how long?"

"Until I pick up a signal."

And what if you never pick up a signal? Unconstructive question. No point in asking it. I was pissed off, but so what? I sure didn't have any better ideas.

Traffic in Alexandria sucks. Makes Pittsburgh look like an urban planner's dream. Around six-thirty-seven on this particular Friday night it started sucking slightly less than it had before. I mention the time because that was when I noticed that the same pair of headlights had been in my rearview mirror for a while. With a chilly little gut tingle I wondered if someone was following us. *That's right, Nancy Drew. Off on an adventure in the roadster, so someone must be following you.* Well if they were they sure weren't doing it in a Sable, so I repressed the thought.

We had put over fifty miles on the car and I'd just about given up hope when I heard a *blip* from Nesselrode's receiver. Not a *beep*, a *blip*. I remember filing that away with a mental *isn't that interesting* note attached to it. The dashboard clock read seven-thirty-two.

"How far away is it?"

"Something like four or five miles." For the tenth time he reached for a pack of cigarettes in his shirt pocket and then irritably checked himself. "But it's not like we can drive straight to it. We have to weave back and forth in the general direction and correct when we lose the directional signal."

"So it's not like TV?"

"No. All kinds of stuff can affect the signal. It's basically trial and error. Hope, prayer, and guesswork."

"Well," I sighed, "we have plenty of experience with that. Go ahead and smoke if you want to. I can handle it."

I've never had a more frustrating experience in my life, including *coitus interruptus*. *Blip-blip-blip* and then all of a sudden nothing. Turn back the way we'd come from. Hold our breaths. *Blip-blip-blip*. Repeat. More than two bloody hours of that.

Seriously. It was like following a directional signal in a third-world country.

Chapter Fifty-three

JAY DAVIDOVICH

I woke up at five o'clock after almost exactly two hours of sleep. I'd retrieved my keys, relocked the back door, and reset the alarm. Then I'd thrown sofa cushions on the kitchen floor and allowed myself a power nap with my body resting against the door and the Colt nestled lightly in my right hand. Sleepwise, that would pretty much do it until dawn, roughly twelve hours from now.

I'd given a lot of thought to how I'd proceed if I were Halkani. Maybe he thought I really *was* going to Vegas to lure him there. Instead of walking into the trap, he'd sneak into our empty home and wait here for us to come back Sunday night. Then he'd kill us and make tracks. Or maybe he realized the whole Vegas thing was a feint and that I'd be waiting for him here. In that case, he'd try to find a way to sneak in despite me, kill me, and move on to the next victim on his list. Either way, he'd be coming here unless he really had taken the Vegas fake, in which case my efficient colleagues would take care of him and I had nothing to worry about—but I wasn't betting on that one.

But which night would he pick for the break-in? Small hours on Sunday morning? That would leave him no margin for error if the break-in went wrong for some reason. Small hours Saturday morning—say, seven or eight hours from now—would make more sense. Every minute he spent wandering around Alexandria or cooling his heels in a cheap area motel he risked having some cop spot him as a guy Pittsburgh police and the FBI would like a word with. Much less likely to attract attention once he was inside the house.

How was he planning to get in? He'd gotten the security code. He might not know which code went with the house alarm, but I had to believe he could figure that out with a little study and some educated guesswork. Would he assume that I'd realized what he was up to and changed the code? Probably not. He had a tendency to underestimate me. Actually, he had a tendency to underestimate everyone, but I was the one I cared about at the moment.

All of that argued for the back door. Doing cat-burglar stuff on the roof to come in through a second-story window might not leave him enough time to get downstairs and punch the code in. So, eighty percent back door, twenty-five percent upstairs window, five percent front door.

When Rachel and I travel we always leave a small light on in the entryway off the kitchen, along with another small light over the kitchen sink. Neither of those can be seen from the outside during the day, so they're not a tip-off. We leave three other lights on timers. At six o'clock they came on: one in the living room, one in the den, and one in our bedroom upstairs. They'd all click off at midnight.

One more thing to do before settling down to wait. First thing Friday morning I'd brought a battery powered camp light up from the basement—a rectangular fluorescent tube in a metal frame mounted directly on a big six-volt battery. I put the camp light just inside the linen closet at the top of the stairs, leaving the closet door open. I switched it on. If I were at the bottom of the stairs and suddenly couldn't see the glow from that light, that would mean something had gotten in between me and it: time for target practice.

I started in a squat with my back leaning against the kitchen door. Cozy group: a Magnum flashlight powered by four D-cells, my Colt Combat Commander semi-automatic, and Judas

Maccabeus Davidovich. Just the three of us. Old friends who required no conversation. I'd turned off the entryway light, but in the modest glow from the living room light I could see both the bottom of the stairs and the front door from where I was.

After thirty minutes, I moved to a perch with my back against the front door. Thirty minutes there and I worked out a little route around the first floor that I could crawl, walk, and duck-walk through without being visible to anyone looking from outside. I'd make two or three circuits, then return to the kitchen-door post. You can't think about nothing, so I just went down the checklist for this solo operation: A) kitchen door entrance secure?—Check; B) front entrance secure?—Check; C) second floor secure?—Check. Spot an intruder: A) shoot; B) ask questions.

At ten-oh-seven—I checked—I heard an embarrassed little *tinkle* just above me and to my right as I crouched against the kitchen door. A suede covered elbow gingerly smashed the three-by-three inch lower inside pane of the door's window. Glass shards sprinkled onto my shoulder. My eyes went from open to *way* open. My heart started racing. A black glove worked its way tentatively through the empty frame, feeling for the latch on the back of the door.

No hurry. All the time in the world. I inched out from behind the door, toward a spot against the kitchen wall, about a foot from where the door would open. Pistol, check. Flashlight, check. The latch snapped. Leaving the flashlight on the floor, I stood up, pistol in my right hand pointed toward the ceiling, left hand free. The door swung open by centimeters. *Beep-beep-beep.* Clock ticking, asshole. Better do something.

A circle of light splashed the area just beyond my feet. *Beep-beep-beep.* Then the flashlight beam glared into the middle of the kitchen—as if anyone were going to be standing *there*. *Beep-beep-beep.* Suddenly the door swept all the way open. *Beep-beep-beep.* A male figure shorter, stockier, and darker-skinned than I remembered Halkani being rushed into the entryway. In the pale glow of his own flashlight I could see him swerve away

from the darkness where I lurked and lunge toward the security
control console on the wall. *Beep-beep-beep.* Twenty seconds left.
Absolutely motionless, peering at him from darkness that ended
just beyond my feet, I watched him tensely punch numbers into
the console.

Beeeeeeep! Beeeeeeep!

"Shit!"

I knew the screen was telling him that he'd messed up the
code and had one more chance. He paused. Took a deep breath.
Punched in numbers again. The *beeps* stopped. No alarm
sounded. He blew out a long breath as his shoulders sagged
with release of tension.

I didn't know if he was armed, but I knew he didn't have a
weapon in either hand. I took one step toward him, grabbed the
back of his collar with my left hand, and threw him tumbling,
stumbling, falling, and then skidding across almost the entire
length of the kitchen floor. His head and body slammed into the
cabinet doors underneath the lower leg of our L-shaped counter.
I retrieved my flashlight in time to shine four D-cells' worth of
light in his face while I showed him the Colt's muzzle. Turning
his head away, he brought both hands up to shield his face.

"Hey, man, whachu do that for? Shit."

"Because you broke into my home."

I deliberately kept my voice calm, halfway between whisper
and normal conversation. Alarm crept up his face. I made him
for eighteen or nineteen.

"Shit, man, I didn' know you was here!" His indignation at
the thoughtlessness I had exhibited by living in my own home
seemed perfectly sincere. "You 'spose to be off on vacation in
honkie-heaven somewhere. I mean, lights go on at *exactly* the
same time on two floors an' you tryin' to tell me someone's
home? Bulllllshit. No, that mean folks is gone an' they doin'
sneaky white shit to make everyone *think* they home. Dumb
crackers. Shit. I mean, you got no business *bein'* here. That light
shit, thass jus' false *pretenses*, thass what that is."

"I don't think you're in a position to be making moral judgments."

"Yeah, well fuck you, honkie. An' get that light outta my face."

"Let's start with your name." I kept the light shining full beam on his face.

"Fuck you. No name shit. Jus' call the heat and we start the dance. Make bail, get back wid my baby, see about probation by an' by."

Lifting my right heel a good four inches from the floor I snap-kicked his left kneecap. He grabbed the knee with two panicky hands as pain exploded across his face. He writhed on the floor in a fair imitation of a fetal position if the fetus were balanced on its tailbone.

"OWWWWW! JESUS H. FUCKING CHRIST, THAT HURT! MOTHUH-*FUCKUH*! FUCK YOU, YOU GOD-DAMN HONKIE!"

"Name, son. I need your name."

He thought about it for a second. A determined step forward convinced him.

"All right! Jimmy, okay? My name be Jimmy Whitelightnin'. An' if you broke my knee you in big goddamn trouble. I know my rights, goddammit."

"Okay, Jimmy, we need to talk."

"Fuck you. I ain't talkin' wid no one. You jus' call five-oh so's they can get my ass outta this crazy-ass place an' down to the jail."

I set the flashlight on the counter. I could still see him easily in the glow from the light over the kitchen sink. Retreating a bit, I found our utility drawer. I rummaged around in there until I could grab a fish filet knife with a serrated blade and bone handle that you might take on a camping trip so that you could gut fish over a campfire, or something wholesome like that. I tossed it onto the floor, where it landed about halfway between Jimmy and me.

"Do you know what that is, Jimmy?"

"Yeah, that be a knife. An' I ain't touchin' it."

"That's what police call a 'throw-down'. In the old days, like up until oh, last week or so, cops on tough beats would always carry one or two with them. You run across someone in some dark alley at two in the morning, one thing leads to another, he ends up dead—but the inconsiderate little shit turns out to be unarmed. So you drop the 'throw down' near the body and you've got self-defense all tied up in a neat package."

He did his level best to hide the fear on his face, but no dice. He scooted a couple of feet farther away from me. I shook my head. He stopped.

"Now you jus' go an call the police right now, dammit! Jus' do it! I know my rights! I gots a right to be arrested! I wants a motherfucker wid a badge standing there readin' me my rights in five minutes! Get to it, goddammit!"

"You see, Jimmy, this isn't the District. This is northern Virginia. I think I'm beginning to feel in peril of death or grave bodily injury at the hands of an intruder here in my own home. My castle. From which I don't have to retreat, even at the cost of taking human life. So in sixty seconds either we'll be having a constructive exchange of views, or you'll have your prints on that knife and three or four bullets in your gut—not in that order."

Seconds ticked by. Fear held his face in a nauseating rictus. Finally tears started streaming from his right eye. Maybe his left too, but I didn't notice it.

"I wasn' gone hurt no one." His voice started as a whine and degenerated toward something close to a sob. "I jus' needed a little weekend weed money fo' me an' my woman. Man, I get more'n three months for this an' I'll still be inside when that baby comes. It's our first one, man! She'll be so hurt, I'm not there."

Very good, Jeff; time for Mutt. I came to a squat, resting my right hand with the pistol casually on my right knee.

"I know how it is, Jimmy. I can be a reasonable man. You know what I mean? Thing is, we have to talk. Hear what I'm saying, Jimmy?"

He nodded. He'd gotten control of the tears and now had has face set in an eight-year-old kid's version of hopeless defiance.

"Whachu wanna talk 'bout?"

"Well, here it is, Jimmy. I'm not buying the story about how you happened to notice lights being turned on by a timer, and then figured out all by yourself that no one was home. That's pretty high-level cogitation, and I just don't think you're up to it. So I want to know how you really came up with the idea of hitting this place. Who actually put the idea into your head and explained it all to you? I know you want to tell me I'm full of shit. I can understand that. Totally. But think real hard before you lie to me, Jimmy. This is kind of like final jeopardy. Know what I'm saying? Final jeopardy, except you're betting your life on the right answer."

Watching his face as he clicked through his options and tried to come up with the guts to pick the only one that made sense was like watching a snuff flick must be. Every step in the process seemed to draw blood from his insides.

"Okay." Huge sigh from him. "Like I say, I'm just lookin' for a little decent weed for my baby and me. Walkin' aroun' wid that shorty inside her, thass a lotta stress, y'know?"

"I understand, Jimmy. A man has to provide for the girl he loves."

"Thass right. Anyway, this Hymie/A-rab somethin' track me down, yesterday, say he has his eye on this place. Now this is in the District, okay, in Southeast, so you don't see lotta crackers there, but they be somethin' badass 'bout this mothuh-fuckuh, and don't no one be messin' wid his ass, you know what I'm sayin'?"

"Yes, Jimmy, I sure do. Describe him."

Jimmy provided a fair description of Halkani. I nodded at him to go on.

"So he say he got his eye on dis place, like I says, an' he gots the code for the alarm thing an' shit, and if he sees these lights go on at the same moment that mean ain't nobody home an' the coast be clear, ya hear me?"

"Yep."

"So he tell me to go in, turn the alarm off wid the code, grab this computer that's right on the table and whatever else I wants, meet him up at that shit-ass mall up the hill, an' he drop two bills on me. Plus whatever I gets for what I grabs, ya know?"

"Yeah, pretty much."

"'Cept he didn' say nothin' 'bout no racist mothuh-fuckuh wid no jive-ass cannon be sittin' here waitin' for me."

"Well, Jimmy, I can understand where that's information you would rather have had, and I don't blame you for being upset about this guy's incomplete disclosure of the situation. You can get up now."

He rolled onto his right side, reached laboriously up to get a grip on the counter, and pulled himself to a standing position. He grimaced in pain when he tried to put weight on his left leg.

Claws ripped dutifully at my conscience. If I gave him, say, the AM/FM radio on the kitchen table or our obsolete computer printer to take back to Halkani as proof that he'd completed the burglary and disabled the alarm, the odds of Halkani showing up would improve a lot. On the other hand, fifty-fifty Jimmy would be dead by morning. If I just sent Jimmy on his way empty-handed, then he'd probably go back to Halkani anyway, regardless of any warnings I gave him, because no way he'd leave two-hundred bucks on the table. Jimmy's life would still basically turn on a coin-flip, but Halkani would know something was up. Jimmy versus Jay-Rachel-unborn-child.

"Jimmy," I sighed, "you're not good at this. If you'll take my advice, you'll go tell your grandmother what you've been up to tonight so she can take a whoopin' stick to your sorry ass and encourage you to find another line of work. If you choose to go back to the guy who handed you this shit-gig, you're as likely to get a bullet as a payoff. But it's up to you. Now get out of here before I kick your ass just to get some negative energy out of my system."

I unplugged the radio and handed it to him as he limped out the door.

Chapter Fifty-four

CYNTHIA JAKUBEK

We finally found Willy's Sable a little after ten p.m. in the parking lot of an oversized strip-mall called Town Centre something-or-other. It took some doing even after the receiver ratcheted its *blipping* up to a steady, insistent level to tell us that the car had to be *right there!* One of the mall's anchors was a twenty-four-hour grocery store and the other was a six-screen movie theater, so scores of cars still dotted the parking lot, whose sodium-vapor lights didn't provide excessive illumination. It took a good ten minutes of driving up one row of yellow-striped parking spaces and down another one before Nesselrode finally spotted the thing—with stolen Maryland plates that Halkani had presumably put on it.

"Why in the name of *dreft* would he stash the thing here?" Nesselrode's question came out thoughtful and puzzled, as if he were pondering a tricky acrostic clue.

"Because it will be less conspicuous here than on a residential street?" By the time I said that I had pulled into a parking space about ten slots from the Sable.

"Yes, you're right, that's exactly it. So Davidovich's house must be somewhere within walking distance—no more than a mile."

We both climbed out of the car. I headed for the trunk. Nesselrode reached for his smokes.

"We started our search right outside Davidovich's house. If the Sable was that close all the time, why did we have to drive all over Hell's half-acre before we got a blip?"

"Elevation. The signals from the transmitter go in all directions, but each signal goes in a straight line. They don't go straight for a hundred yards and then dive down an embankment." He pointed to the edge of the parking lot farthest from the entrance we'd used—just about a football field away, if I was any judge. "Twenty to one Davidovich's house is on a street at the bottom of a hill just beyond where the light stops."

Interesting theory. Might even be right. Shrugging, I started to open the trunk. Nesselrode shot me a surprised glare through a cloud of smoke rich enough for me to see even in the near darkness.

"You're new at this, aren't you?"

"Yeah, you could say that. I couldn't find a class on covert operations at Harvard."

"What if a cop doing a routine patrol notices you rummaging through the trunk? Asks for your license? Wonders why someone with a Pennsylvania license is rifling the trunk of a car with Maryland plates? Checks the registration and notices that you don't own the car?"

"I guess I'd suggest that he call Willy."

"Whose mobile phone is in a hospital storage locker and who's probably taking a mildly sedated snooze right now."

"Amber, then."

"Whose name isn't on the registration any more than yours is."

Nuts. He was right. I turned away from the trunk.

"Any ideas?"

"Yeah. Leave the rental car here. Drive the Sable down to Davidovich's block. Maybe even park it in his driveway. Then quietly and unobtrusively do your search away from prying eyes."

What can I say? It seemed like a good idea at the time.

Chapter Fifty-five

Jay Davidovich

I felt better. Not necessarily a good thing. *No battle plan survives contact with the enemy.* Hard to remember helpful adages like that when endorphins start doing threesomes in your cerebral cortex.

Halkani had suckered Jimmy into verifying the code Halkani had come up with. In fifteen minutes or so, even with Jimmy's gimpy leg, Halkani would have that verification. Jimmy wouldn't mention me. He'd blame the knee on a fall going up or down the hill.

Jimmy figured to be spreading this story all over Southeast D.C. within an hour, so Halkani almost had to come in before dawn on Saturday. Suppose he made his move around two in the morning. I'd already figured long odds against a second-story entrance for reasons that still made sense to me, so I had a pretty simple job: Reset the alarm; get a bead on the back door while keeping a wary eye on the front door just in case; and wait.

Making sure that I'd relocked the back door behind Jimmy, I turned to the security console to reset the alarm. Would the broken window pane keep me from doing that? What if the system somehow read the vacant space as an open door? The console's mini-screen would unhelpfully flash ERROR—ENTRANCE NOT SECURE. One way to find out. I punched in the code to turn the alarm back on. SYSTEM ARMED. Now just find a spot to—

Holy shit! The ladder! A panicky tremor shook through me as I remembered the ladder that I'd stumbled over on the hill this afternoon. What if it wasn't just detritus someone had jettisoned? After all, it looked to me like it was in pretty good shape. Head spinning, I realized that I'd bought into a misdirection play as simple as the one I'd pulled on Halkani when I'd conned him into stealing a brushed steel attaché case without the document he was looking for.

Halkani had *not* brought a brainless chatterbox like Jimmy into this deal for a code-verifying dry run. He'd sent Jimmy in to trip the alarm at the kitchen door *so that Halkani could go in through an upstairs window at the same time!* That's why he'd hidden the ladder on the hill, figuring that it would look like discarded junk. Using the ladder to get to the first floor roof, he could smash the pane of an upstairs window as soon as Jimmy's break-in made the *beeps* start. He'd probably jostle the motion detector on the sash, but if he knew what he was doing he could get the metal contacts matched up with each other again before Jimmy turned the alarm off downstairs. From that point he could just sit and wait. Bottom line, I had to assume that *the sonofabitch was in my house right this minute!*

I felt iced right through my pores. Two long strides through our cozy dining room, then I hit the deck, shoulder-rolled into the living room, and swept it with my Colt in the modest light, Nothing.

Thank you, God. Dodged the bullet. Didn't deserve that break, but I got it anyway. Halkani hadn't made his move yet. Why should he? He could bide his time upstairs while I strained every nerve standing watch for hours. Sooner or later, sometime during the day tomorrow, I'd fall asleep or just lose my edge from fatigue.

Okay, buddy. Deep breath. Bad scare, but situation retrieved. I'd actually gained a smidgeon of tactical advantage. Halkani had lost the element of surprise but probably didn't know it.

What now? Going up after him would be stupid squared. Halkani could hide wherever he wanted to and ambush me before I even got a look at him.

Option two: keep watch as long as adrenaline and doses of concentrated caffeine would keep me awake; if he hadn't shown by full light, call the cops. No. I'd be sitting in a static defense, out of direct contact with the enemy, leaving the initiative for hours to him. Didn't work at Yorktown, didn't work on the Maginot Line, didn't work at Dien Bien Phu—didn't work at Masada, for that matter. Hard to like the odds.

No, the right choice was the boring option, the anticlimactic one: get the cops here right away. Yeah, officer, I had a home invasion. Chased the perp away, but I'm afraid he had a buddy who's still hidden somewhere upstairs. Think it might be the same guy who burgled the place a week or so ago.

Think it through. Cop cars pulling up with lights flashing would flush Halkani. Ten to one he'd exit through the upstairs window, across the roof, and down the ladder. If he got away, I'd gone to a lot of trouble and bruised a punk's knee for nothing. But if I got the back door wide open and the yard lights on, I might actually manage a decent shot at him. That could lead to some legal inconveniences, but if it came down to that I'd rather be judged by twelve jurors than carried by six pallbearers.

Seemed like the right answer for sure, but I resisted the impulse to just dive in and call nine-one-one. No need to jump the gun. Maybe there was an option 3-A that I hadn't thought of yet, a Proxy-type option that a little outside-the-box thinking would turn up.

I willed the adrenaline sluicing through my body to chill. I needed to think this through—that and keep my eyes open.

Chapter Fifty-six

CYNTHIA JAKUBEK

Even though we finally knew where we were going, it took us a solid ten minutes to navigate our way back to Davidovich's block. About thirty feet from the turn Halkini whispered an order.

"Cut the lights."

I did. I also slowed way down, without being told to. We eased onto the street and crept along. I noticed three lights on in Davidovich's house, one downstairs and two up. *Hmm. Proves nothing, but interesting all the same.*

I did *not* park in Davidovich's driveway. I went all the way to the end of the cul-de-sac at the base of the hill where I couldn't see either street lights or houselights, and pulled to a gentle stop. Breath I didn't know I'd been holding exploded from my lungs.

Okay, time for round two with the trunk. Opened my door quietly and slipped it almost silently shut. Nesselrode did the same on his side of the car. We approached the trunk as if we were sneaking up on it. When I stuck the key in and turned it, the *thunk* sounded to me as if everyone on the block could have heard it.

Raising the trunk lid turned on a small, white light. I tugged at the near driver-side corner of a cover-cloth and pulled it all the way to my right to expose the spare tire, nestled in a well cut into the trunk's bottom. Except, of course, it wasn't a *tire,* it was a *wheel*, pinioned to the chassis with some sturdy looking metal tubes. Willy had said that he'd stashed the envelope in the tire's rim, but a hubcap that looked like it didn't plan on moving fit tightly above the bead and sealed the rim off.

Now what?

"Allow me," Nesselrode whispered.

Feminist scruples about the big strong man coming to the aid of the helpless female gave way to practicality. I hadn't changed a tire since sixteen, when my dad made me do it before he'd give me keys after I got my license. Nesselrode seemed to think he knew what he was doing.

He did. He was short of breath and panting now, and even in the meager light I could see beads of sweat on his forehead and waves of pain rolling whitely across his face. But with only a bit of initial strain he quickly got the triangular hunk of metal on top turning to the left and inching up, exposing the threads of a very long, thick screw as it rose. When he got the triangular thing all the way off, he flipped one of its sides up, stuck its blade underneath the hubcap, and popped the thing off.

Now I found myself staring at a black wheel with a circular opening just about the size of my hand in each of its quadrants. I hit paydirt on the third hole. I felt smooth paper with a hint of grease. I pulled it toward the hole, got a corner of it peeking through, and then worried it the rest of the way out. Remembering Davidovich's sleight-of-hand at the Museum, I opened the envelope and took out the single page of cursive script that it held. *Bingo*.

"Congratulations," Nesselrode said.

"Thanks. And thanks for your help." I started for the driver side door.

"Where are you going?"

"Back up to the mall. I can get an envelope and stamps at the grocery store and put this thing in the mail to my office. Whatever happens after that, the cops won't find it unless they start searching the U.S. mail."

"Are you out of your fucking mind?"

"Well, I'm standing here talking to you, so you could get plenty of votes for yes."

"Give me that thing!" he snarled, grabbing it from me. He came up with an old-fashioned Ronson lighter and coaxed flame from it.

"Wait a minute!" I grabbed for Amber's forgery and got Nesselrode's iron-hard bicep instead. "I came down here to get my client's document into safekeeping—not to destroy evidence."

"Sure you did," he muttered as a corner of the document caught fire. "Anyway, you're not the one destroying it, are you?"

The point seemed moot, because by now the flame had reduced half the page to a charred crisp, and the other half wasn't far behind.

Then we saw headlights. High-mounted headlights, coming at us fast and then going off suddenly while the truck (or whatever it was) hurtled toward us. *Cops for sure.* Wrong. A good forty feet from us the thing swerved to the left, partly into Davidovich's driveway and mostly onto his front law. The vision that climbed out didn't look like any cop *I'd* ever seen.

Now the destroying-evidence point seemed *real* moot.

Chapter Fifty-seven

Jay Davidovich

A determined hum of tires on the street outside convinced me. Sounded like high school kids cruising around with a couple of beers in them and more to come. Flushing Halkani was the money play.

I was reaching for my phone to call nine-one-one when I heard metal scraping on metal near the lock of the front door. *FRONT door? What the hell? Had I figured this thing totally wrong—again?*

Things were about to start happening very fast. Don't know how I knew, I just knew. That little tingle you get from combat experience clicked on: hours of boredom were giving way to moments of terror *right now.*

Keeping an eye on the stairs, I got both hands back on my Colt, ready to swing the weapon toward the door. Didn't have to wait long. The door flew open like a special effect in a slasher flick. Rachel instantly stormed in, head on a swivel, face consumed with rage, and ranting in full castrating-Valkyrie mode.

"WHERE IS SHE? WHERE IS THAT BITCH? I'LL KILL HER!"

Providing a little bass-line to her aria was the *beep-beep-beep* announcing that the alarm would be sounding off soon unless someone punched in the stop-code. I viewed that as a second-tier priority.

"Any particular bitch, Rachel?" I tried to keep my voice calm, but the flight-or-fight juice pumping through me turned it into a bark.

She pivoted and ran toward me with her fists flailing.

"That *shiksa* bitch lawyer with the big tits that you were going to spend all weekend fucking in *my* bed while *your* baby and I cooled our heels in a Vegas hotel room waiting for you to show up—which you were never going to do, of course." As the *beep-beep-beeps* relentlessly continued, she landed a punch about as hard as a nana's spank on my left forearm; had to hurt her more than it did me. "Lucky I had a three-hour flight delay, so I spotted her arriving with someone—the pimp you're using, I suppose. I spent the night following them all over Alexandria, so *don't* tell me she's not here."

Another swing. I snap-blocked it, scraping my left forearm along my right on its way to collision with her arm. That gave my forearm enough extra speed and force to smart plenty when it parried her swing. She howled about what a brutal bastard bully I was as she grabbed her right arm in a convincing show of agony.

"You *hit* me!" Couldn't help admiring the indignation she put into that.

"Blocking doesn't count. Now shut the hell up."

The alarm ran out of patience. A full-throated ululation started ripping through the neighborhood. I'm not sure what Rachel said from that point. I couldn't really hold up my end of the conversation anymore. The glow at the bottom of the stairs disappeared. Company coming for sure.

Shifting the Colt to my left hand, I grabbed a fistful of dress and skin around Rachel's left hip and yanked her roughly to the floor. Our landline started ringing, presumably because the security company was calling to see if the alarm was real or accidental. I parked my right leg over both of Rachel's thighs to cut down on the kicking and thrashing. At the same time I planted my right hand on her face. It seemed like the most efficient way to communicate under the circumstances.

My eyes caught a glimpse of bulk and motion on the stairs. Halkani dove down the last four steps onto the living room floor and then rolled toward the dining room. Left-handed and fighting Rache's squirming, I had the sense to hold my fire. He'd rolled out of sight before I could get a bead on him. Hitting a moving target is one thing. Hitting a target you can't see anymore is a different matter.

A second later I spotted about three quarters of him pop out in a squat maybe fifteen feet away, swinging an Uzi toward me. I'd need at least six-tenths of a second to aim the Colt properly. I knew I didn't have it.

At that instant a voice screamed from near the front door.

"You're dead, you sonofabitch!"

Without an ounce of wasted motion but after an instant's indecision, Halkani stopped swinging the Uzi toward me and swiveled it in the direction of the voice instead. A six-shot burst erupted, followed instantaneously by an agonized scream. With the same stone cold efficiency the Uzi started swerving back in my direction. In one more second Halkani would hemstitch me like a butchered pig.

I'd needed six-tenths of a second and I'd gotten nine-tenths. I fired. Even in the mediocre light I thought I saw Halkani's deep black eyes widen in utter astonishment. The mangled Uzi clattered to the floor. He buried a bloody right hand shredded like tenderized round steak under his left forearm.

Sonofabitch. I shot the gun out of his hands! By accident, but I actually shot the gun out of his hands!

House alarm still shrieking. More noise from the door. Quick glance from the corner of my right eye. Jakubek on her knees now, checking Dany Nesselrode. Nesselrode who, armed with nothing more lethal than a mobile phone, had just spent his life to buy me one critical, unforgiving fraction of a second. A fraction that had saved my life. And Rachel's. And our child's. An act of supreme atonement for thinking he could use a bastard and then having the bastard use him.

No time right now for deep thoughts about that. Halkani knelt there with a kind of bored expression visible even through the pain radiating from his face. *Yeah, yeah, call the cops, get me to the hospital. Then we'll see.* I had no trouble sensing the pain radiating from his body as he tugged his right hand free and began to raise both arms above his head.

I shifted the Colt to my right hand. Leaving nothing to chance. I aimed the weapon just the way Sergeant Rutledge had taught me to in basic. I shot Hakani through the forehead. Not quite between the eyes, but close enough for government work. A heartbeat later I raised the gun up and to the right and fired into the molding on the wall side of the stairway.

Jakubek straightened up from her examination of Nesselrode. She looked at Halkani's lifeless body, then at the gouge in our molding, then at me.

"Warning shot?"

"Yep."

"Good one."

Chapter Fifty-eight

Cynthia Jakubek

Cops don't necessarily give calls from security companies top priority, so I called nine-one-one to hurry things along. Gunfire and two corpses got us to "Dispatching" in a hurry. Davidovich was tied up with whatshername, his wife, who looked like a candidate for an economy carton of Valium. Couldn't blame her. To tell the truth, I could've used a bourbon-and-sweet myself—hold the sweet.

A squad car reached us in three minutes flat. The first thing the well-trained cops did was make sure no one still breathing needed medical attention. Then one of them radioed in with whatever the code is for, "This is a huge deal." Not long after that the Davidovichs' first floor looked like the stateroom scene from *A Night at the Opera*: two detectives, two EMTs, two evidence specialists, and a crime-scene photographer. Looking around me I saw enough overtime to bump up Alexandria's property tax levy.

I told the detective who questioned me the absolute truth. Up to a point. Little vague about the *Eros Rising* scam, skipped the falling-out-among-thieves thing with Nesselrode, outlined the unpleasantness at St. Ben's, Rand's murder, and Nesselrode convincing me that if I didn't get him down here Davidovich would be next. Left out the envelope in Willy's Sable. Then we got to the end game.

"I heard the machine gun burst that killed Nesselrode. Then three handgun shots. One, followed by a pause of two or three seconds, then two more, one right after the other, just *bang-bang*, like that."

"So you're saying, what? A warning shot and then two shots in self-defense?"

"I'm just a lawyer, but that's the way I'd put it together."

"You're sure about the sequence? *Bang...bang-bang*?"

"Yes, I'd swear to it."

"You might get a chance to do that."

"At your service."

Not quite two hours after my call, they'd finally cleared everything out. Now I was *really* in the market for something alcoholic. At that point I'd have settled for Mogen David in a washed-out jam jar. Unfortunately, Davidovich *et ux.* were in the middle of a flesh-of-my-flesh-bone-of-my-bone thing. I sucked it up and headed out to the porch to give them as much privacy as you can have at a brightly lit crime scene that has attracted gawkers from every house on the block.

The last thing I saw before my exit was wifey on her knees, face in her hands, sobbing. Even on the porch, I couldn't help overhearing their dialogue.

"I almost killed us. All of us. I flew into a mindless, jealous rage just because I saw *her* at the airport, and I almost ruined everything."

"That's about the size of it, babe. Four alarm fuck-up, for sure."

"Is that you're idea of consoling me?"

"No, that's my idea of chewing you out. You know, Rache, next time you could just make a phone call. 'Judas Macabeus Davidovich, what's the deal between you and the hot lawyer from Pittsburgh? 'Cause you got some 'splainin' to do.' Something along those lines."

"You're right. You're right, you're right, you're right. I don't know why I do these things. I guess it's because I don't think I deserve you, and I can't believe you really love me."

"That's too high a bar, babe. No one could possibly deserve me. You can't beat yourself up over that."

"You're making fun of me to punish me by humiliating me, aren't you? Go ahead, I suppose I deserve it."

"Stand up, Rache."

"Remember, you never hit anyone you sleep with! Even me! That's what you said! Plus, I'm pregnant. Don't forget *that!*"

"I'm not going to hit you, Rache. The next time we're at your parents' I might suggest that your mom go old-school on you—but I won't do it."

"No, no, absolutely not! Mom hits *way* too hard!"

I *think* that was supposed to be a joke.

"Come here, babe...Look, I don't blame you for the jealous suspicion. She's not as beautiful as you are, but she's a dish for sure. And showing up at Reagan National coming into town at the same time you were there about to head out of town was a damn funny coincidence. So, suspicion, sure. But let's work on dialing back the psycho-bitch-from-Hell number. You know, count to ten or something first. And another thing: the next time you decide to hit someone, don't lead with your right."

Sobbing, muffled by what I assumed was a hug and mingled with laughter that sounded close to manic. With a little lust mixed in, triggered by the smell of cordite on Davidovich's hands? Not sure about that part. Interesting thought, though.

The next words I heard were the guy's, more tender than I would have imagined possible.

"My love for you is unconditional, Rache. I love you. Period. Can't help it. I just do. You don't have to worry about earning it or deserving it. It's just the way it is. What I can't understand with my head I have to understand with my heart."

More sobs after that, naturally, this time the cascading tears kind that sound like they're going to go on forever. On balance, I guess I'm glad I overheard it. Close question, but that's where I come down.

The Fourth Friday in August

The Fourth Friday in August

Chapter Fifty-nine

CYNTHIA JAKUBEK

So it's four months later. High summer. Sean and Abbey are within sight of their wedding date. Willy can talk in a reasonably normal tone of voice and has a hundred thousand on the ground floor of Project Woodshed. Shear Genius has a new counsel for distributor litigation. Clarence Washington's case is set for jury trial, and I intend to win it. I've hired a receptionist/secretary and moved out of the house I grew up in and into an apartment downtown. Phil has told me he'll become Catholic if I want him to. Or Wiccan. Theologically, he's pretty flexible.

Pitt MCM, believe it or not, has decided to go forward with the exchange program after all. In-*cred*-ible. Sign-off by the heirs, group hug, and the Rand murder has actually bumped up attendance from ghoulish curiosity-seekers. Transoxana will insure *Eros Rising* during the exchange. Davidovich has come to town to kick the tires and check the lug-nuts and do other routine loss prevention stuff.

Six of us—Sean, Abbey, Davidovich, Willy, Amber, and yours truly—are on our way to Sean's club for lunch. Willy is telling Davidovich what a great deal the Woodshed thing is, trying to talk him into dropping the insurance racket and buying a Woodshed franchise.

"Abbey came up with a great hook," he's saying. "Greatest hook for a retail start-up I've ever seen."

I have no idea what he's talking about, of course. Then at the end of the block, we turn up Fulton Avenue—and there it is, on a twenty-something dude who looks like he's taking Friday afternoon off. Black line-drawing of a Woodshed Street Wagon inside a stylized actual woodshed with peaked roof and rough-hewn sides and smoke coming out of its chimney. "WOOD-SHED" appears in simple print across the façade, just below the roof. A slogan snakes cross the bottom: "Fine Sandwiches and Wraps on the Go With Real Smoked Woodchip Flavor!"® in the lower right-hand corner identifies the images and slogans as Woodshed trademarks.

Fine, I guess, but it won't make anyone forget "Reach for a Lucky instead of a sweet."

Then the guy passes us and we get a look at Abbey's hook, on the tee-shirt's back. The street wagon drawing frames lettering that takes up most of the space:

"MY GIRLFRIEND TOOK ME TO
THE WOODSHED TODAY—
AND I *REALLY* DESERVED IT."

OoooKayy. *Fifty Shades of Black and White.* Or something. I'll never understand marketing. Good thing lawyers aren't allowed to do it. Except, you know, when we are. Is this a great country or what?

To receive a free catalog of Poisoned Pen Press titles, please provide your name and address through one of the following ways:

Phone: 1-800-421-3976
Facsimile: 1-480-949-1707
Email: info@poisonedpenpress.com
Website: www.poisonedpenpress.com

Poisoned Pen Press
6962 E. First Ave. Ste 103
Scottsdale, AZ 85251